praise

"A tightly plotted read with fascinating characters, *Bitter Like Orange Peel* compels readers to unravel the layers of intertwining stories until the shocking core is revealed."
TALLI ROLAND, BESTSELLING AUTHOR

"While the title of this book alludes to the fresh citrus, there's nothing sweet about this tale. At the story's heart is a rotten mix of lies, mistrust and lives half-lived. It's a very modern drama that reveals itself like a segmented orange, leaving behind the aftertaste of its zesty but bitter peel."
LILY MULHOLLAND, SHORT STORY WRITER

"*Bitter Like Orange Peel* IS rapid-fire story-telling through the eyes and mouths of multiple intersecting lives; it IS rough-edged dialogue and internal monologue; it IS soothed with narrative as smooth as poetry; it IS filled with perfect metaphors, uniquely-fitted and thought-provoking; and, it IS a work of art, as much poetry as personality mystery of the multiple characters. *Bitter Like Orange Peel* is NOT formulaic; it is NOT written from a single point-of-view; it is NOT predictable; and, there is NOT a single one-dimensional character in sight. ... It is a novel of lies and lies about lies abound. It is a novel complicated by those internal and external truths we all conceal from family, and ourselves. It is a novel about family strangers and strange family members. ... *Bitter Like Orange Peel* will not disappoint."
RICHARD HARTWELL, WRITER AND POET

"The author did an excellent job of keeping the reader on the edge of their seat, wondering what will happen next. It was hard to put this book down. I kept thinking about the characters and maybe was a little worried about them from time to time. If an author can evoke that sort of reaction from readers, they are a real talent. A very skillful author indeed."
JULIE WHITELEY, BOOK REVIEWER FOR *CLUEREVIEW*

about the author

Jessica Bell is an Australian award-winning author and poet, writing and publishing coach, and graphic designer who lives in Athens, Greece. In addition to her novels and poetry collections, and her best-selling *Writing in a Nutshell* series, she has published a variety of works online and in literary journals, including *Writer's Digest*.

Jessica is also the Co-Founder and Publisher of *Vine Leaves Press & Literary Journal*, a singer/songwriter/guitarist, a voice-over actor, and a freelance editor and writer for English Language Teaching publishers worldwide such as Macmillan Education and Education First.

Before she started writing she was just a young woman with a "useless" Bachelor of Arts degree and a waitressing job.

Visit Jessica's website: *jessicabellauthor.com*

Bitter Like Orange Peel
Copyright © 2016 Jessica Bell
All rights reserved.

Vine Leaves Press
Melbourne, Victoria, Australia

Second Edition
ISBN-13: 978-1-925417-48-7

First edition published by Vine Leaves Press Australia, 2013

Cover design by Jessica Bell
Interior design by Amie McCracken

National Library of Australia Cataloguing-in-Publication entry (pbk)
Creator: Bell, Jessica Carmen, author.
Title: Bitter like orange peel / Jessica Bell.
Edition: 2nd edition.
ISBN: 9781925417487 (paperback)
Subjects: Families--Fiction.
Absentee fathers--Fiction.
Fathers and daughters--Fiction.
Dewey Number: A823.4

bitter like orange peel

Jessica Bell

Vine Leaves Press
Melbourne, Vic, Australia

For Allison, my half sister whom I adore.

kit

His head is ripped off. In that photograph. Of *him*. Kit spots it buried among four years' worth of undergraduate essays—the photo she stole from her half sister, Ivy, and misplaced in an effort to keep safe.

She drags her bottom dresser drawer out too far. The stiff wood clunks as it slips out of its casing and hits the floor with a thud. Sitting cross-legged and naked on the hot, itchy carpet, she stares at the photograph. At five-year-old Ivy's carefree grin and trusting arms wrapped around her father's knees at the Melbourne zoo. A drop of sweat tickles Kit's crotch. She scratches herself and wipes her wet fingers on the carpet beside her thigh. Stares at her father's hand placed delicately on the top of Ivy's head, and Ivy's sideways and upward glance toward his nonexistent face. Kit touches the top of her own head, imagining what his touch may have felt like, what she would give to have been Ivy those twenty-five years ago, before she was even born.

She stands. Her knees crack. They've cracked ever since she fell off her bicycle when she was six and the rubber seat supposedly ruptured her hymen. It didn't hurt. *She rubs her left hand on her thigh to dislodge the tiny beige pebbles that have embedded themselves into her palm. Stupid new garden path.* She places the photo on her bedside table, propping it up against the wall behind her bedside lamp, where her four-year-old self drew a wobbly shape of a rainbow with blue biro on the cream parchment. It's still there.

Kit sighs, squints at Ivy's apparent joy in the photograph, and bites her thumbnail. It rips off too low and starts to bleed. She sucks it, then hooks it under the knuckle of her index finger to stop the flow. It stings like the time she accidentally lodged a sewing needle below the nail. She'd heard that the white crescents at the base of people's nails were actually full of air and wanted to see if she could pop one like a balloon and listen to the air wheeze through the hole.

There's no better time than now.

She scoops her university papers out of the drawer like an eagle catching prey, and with one swift movement drops her entire collection of archaeological lecture notes, research method essays, and Cypriot artefact analyses into the cardboard box on her bed. But the postgraduate application form she has to fill out and submit before the month is out, which is folded six times over and stuffed into the smallest pocket of her handbag, has a heart of its own. She whispers, "Not now. Not yet," to the rhythm of its beat, and zips her handbag shut.

In the staff room at Seattle's Ditsy Daisy's Café, Ivy is having a cigarette break when her mother, Eleanor, calls. With one glance at the caller ID, she switches her to voice mail. The last thing she needs right now is to be told she should quit smoking. Especially by someone who has the ability to scare the pants off an extinct ape with medical facts and statistics. Not to mention the fact that she was lectured enough about her smoking from her ex-husband, Amir. Enough to last her till she finds the missing link.

On Ivy's way out, her colleague, Raquel, gives her a snarly look as she returns to the floor. People are starting to walk out. She's been swamped with take-out coffees and unable to tend to seated customers. Ivy grabs her computerized notepad and approaches a middle-aged man with long grey hair in a ponytail, the only man alone in the whole café. He is wearing cowboy boots and has a briefcase under his chair.

Two things I never thought I'd see together.

"I'll have an Americano, please, ma'am. And don't put any sugar in it. Last time, the waitress put sugar in it." The man relieves a tickle in his nostril with his long pinky fingernail. He squeezes and rubs his nose several times during this request, interrupting his serious glare at Ivy with the occasional inspection of his fingertips.

What the hell am I doing working here?

"Of course, sir. I apologize for that, but it sounds very unusual because we never put sugar in the coffee ourselves. We leave that up to the customer for convenience." Ivy stands still, electronic pen to computerized notepad, fake smile on her face, trying not to look at the contents excavated from the man's nasal passage that he's rolling between his thumb and forefinger.

"Well, I know that. But I was just making sure you understood I don't want *you* to put any sugar in it, ma'am." He rubs his fingers on a napkin.

Ivy tries not to gag. "Okay. No problem at all. Americano with no sugar it is then."

"Thank you, ma'am. I'm so very grateful you find it no problem, seeing as you are the waitress and all. Oh! Ah, bring me a donut too."

Ivy smiles at his sarcasm and grits her teeth beneath her glossy lips. *Glad I risked being late this morning for a new lip gloss. Tangy, tasty. Complete shame I now associate it with snot.*

Ivy returns with his coffee and donut covered in icing sugar. She is about to serve another customer, when she hears him groan and click his fingers in the air.

"Ma'am. Can you please come here?" He pounds his fist on the table. Ivy rushes to him. "You goddamn waitresses don't give a good goddamn what customers want. All you girls care about is flirting with the pretty boys and touching up your makeup. You went ahead and put goddamn sugar in my coffee after I asked you specifically not to, didn't you? Where's your boss? I want to speak to your boss." He taps his heel. It's heavy, firm. No rhythm, no soul.

Flirting with the pretty boys? Touching up makeup? How dare you!

"I'm afraid he has just left, sir, but I assure you I did not put any sugar in your coffee. As I said earlier, we never put sugar in any of our customers' coffee."

"Well then, smarty-pants, can you explain why my coffee tastes so goddamn sweet?"

Ivy knows exactly why his coffee tastes sweet. But she

doesn't know if she has the balls to tell him. Perhaps she'll embarrass him. Or even worse, get spat in the face in front of an entire coffee shop of curious customers looking her way. It's happened before.

"Well, sir. I believe your coffee is sweet because—"

"Yes? Yes? Spit it out, doll." A chunk of chewed donut escapes onto his chin as he utters the word *spit*. Everyone is staring in their direction.

"Because you seem to be dipping your donut in your coffee, sir, and it's covered in icing sugar."

The entire coffee shop bursts into laughter and applauds. Ivy can't help but offer a victorious smile. He looks around, blushes a colour Ivy has never seen a man blush before, downs his coffee, throws a few coins on the table, and puts the remainder of his donut into his briefcase. It's full of sheet music, a harmonica, and a tambourine. *A struggling musician?* Now Ivy feels sorry for him. Well, sort of.

It's almost the end of Ivy's shift. Brian should be coming soon, just in time to ask her to sit and have a joe with him. Ivy wipes down the empty tables, enjoying the eye of the coffee-shop storm. It's the time of day when midday drinkers have finished drinking their coffees and the business people have almost completed their nine-to-five routines before strolling in to wind down.

Brian taps Ivy on the shoulder while she's wiping down the counter. She jumps.

"Oh, hi, Brian. How are you today?" Her feet melt into the linoleum floor as his musky aftershave overpowers the Ajax. His cologne is different every day. She wonders whether he's taking advantage of all the samples they've given out at Nordstrom recently. He looks her in the eyes as she admires his shiny black hair. But his hair isn't cut the way you'd expect an accountant to cut his hair. He looks more like a painter who's good at math.

"I'm great, thanks, Ivy. No need to ask how you are. You give me the same answer every day."

Ivy tries to butt in, but doesn't manage to.

"You do look extra beautiful today though. What's different?"

Ivy opens and closes her mouth, like the little boy watching Mary Poppins pull the lamp shade out of her bag, hoping to say something witty. *I must look like a complete idiot.* Ivy shuts her mouth and grins.

"Ah … new lip gloss, right? What's the flavour? Orange?" Brian puts his briefcase down and pushes it to the edge of the booth with the side of his foot.

How on earth did he know that?

He winks. "Don't look so amazed! I can see the tube through your apron pocket."

Phew! For a moment there I thought you might be gay. Ivy coughs up a convulsive laugh a bit like a backward gasp. *Now, not only do I look like a complete idiot but I sound like one too.* Brian still hasn't sat. He's grinning, hands hanging loosely in his tailored pants pockets, jingling keys around, rocking on the balls of his feet. Ivy's hand, the one that was wiping the counter, has gone rigid.

"Will it be the usual then, Brian?"

"That'd be great, Ivy. Thanks."

"Coming right up."

I'm so over having crushes. I can't deal with this so late in life. Twenty-one, twenty-two, even twenty-three is fine. Crushes can be handled. But a crush at thirty? Am I kidding myself? I should be happily married, knocked up, in love. I should have finished my PhD.

Ivy walks behind the counter toward the coffee machine. The bar woman, Raquel—well, girl, more like. You know, let's be PC here. The bar "chick" tilts her head, winks at her, then looks back down at the mocha latté she's making. *I could practically be her mother. Well, aunt—I should be winking at her.*

"Hot," Raquel says, licking her lips. "Been watching you two lately, you know. When are you, like, gonna go out on a date or whatever?"

"What do you know about going on dates? Mind your own business and make him a latté."

Ivy takes Brian his coffee and forces a smile. She doesn't want it to be forced, but for now it'll have to do.

"Here you go."

"Oh, thanks for the extra cookie." Brian salutes her.

"No worries."

"So how's your day been?" Brian looks up, sweetens and stirs his beverage like a robot.

"Um, you know, same old, same old. Well, maybe a little less than same old. Had a few unnecessary customers."

"Oh, right. What is it you call them again?"

"Waitress Warriors."

"That's right. Excellent." Brian chuckles.

"My shift is up. See you tomorrow?" Ivy nods and turns toward the staff room hoping to avoid an uncomfortable silence. But Brian stands and reaches out to her.

"Yeah, hopefully." The tips of his fingers brush against Ivy's hip. "Wait a minute. Why don't I buy you a coffee? You know I don't bite."

"Thanks, Brian, but I've had so much coffee today." *That sounded really rude. God, I didn't mean for that to sound rude.*

"Well, how about a drink? Later on? We can meet on Fifteenth Avenue somewhere."

"Sorry, but I really can't. I've got … well I've got other plans." *What's your problem? Get over Amir already and go out on a freaking date!*

"I see." Brian bites his bottom lip. "Okay, maybe some other time then?"

"Sure. Maybe some other time. Enjoy your coffee. I'm gonna go and grab my stuff." *God, Ivy! One day he's going to stop asking, and then it's going to be too late.*

At the back of the café, behind the staff room, is a little alley where all the kitchen staff from next door hang out and smoke joints. Whenever Ivy works the day shift, she can hear them carrying on from where the staff keep their coats and bags locked up, like the schoolboys did behind the shelter shed when she was a teen. The cooks who sit outside are used to Ivy's bag-and-coat collecting hours, and they sing to her through the back door.

"*Boom, boom, boom, let's go back to my room. We can do it all night ...*" They linger by the tiny window in their white linen uniforms, even when it's cold out. She doesn't understand how they have become accustomed to the weather. Ivy can barely handle the cold with her 1940s' maroon vintage coat.

On her way toward the exit, Ivy contemplates whether she should walk the Brian aisle or the stranger aisle. She decides to walk the Brian aisle. To challenge herself. Maybe she'll summon the nerve at the last minute to say she's up for a drink. But just as she's approaching Brian's booth, she trips over a customer's foot. She doesn't fall. It's worse than falling. Her drumsticks fall out of her bag and clatter on the floor.

"You're a drummer?" Brian's voice rises in pitch.

Ivy stands still and silent, as if she's been caught shoplifting, clutching her handbag to her chest in case more belongings decide to leap out.

Say something.

"No, I'm not. Well, yeah, sort of ... no, no, not really. It's not what I *do*. Well, it is what I *do*, but not what I *do* do, if you know what I mean. It's not my dream or anything, it's a hobby. It's not that I'm not passionate about music; I am. I don't want to do it professionally or anything. I don't want to be a professional waitress either, if that's what you're thinking. I don't want to be a waitress at all, actually, but no, I'm not a drummer and I'm not a waitress. They're things that I *do*, but not *do* do … if you get … what I mean." Ivy hangs her head and looks at her shoes, trying not to laugh at herself.

What is wrong with you?

Brian picks up the drumsticks and hands them to Ivy with a smirk. "Okay, so you're not a waitress, but you are, and you're not a drummer, but you are. That's … interesting … I must say. Are you sure you don't want to meet me for a drink later? It sounds like you need one, and I'd really like to find out what it is you *do* do." Brian touches Ivy's shoulder. She internally sighs.

"I will come for a drink one day, I promise. Just not today. As I said I have a, um, prior engagement."

"Do you mind me asking what this prior engagement is? I don't mean to pry. I'm interested in, you know. In you."

Ivy holds her drumsticks next to her face and smiles a big glossy orange smile.

"Oh. Band rehearsal?"

"Yep."

"Cool." Brian nods in approval.

"Yeah, it could be if I managed to stay in one band long enough." *Shoot! Now he's going to think I'm bad at making a commitment.* "That doesn't mean I can't. I just don't want to. There's usually some dickhead …" Ivy inspects Brian's eyes to see if he disapproves of bad language. He doesn't flinch. "Some dickhead who thinks he knows everything about music because he knows how to play solos on guitar. It's a pet peeve of mine." Ivy slouches.

Why do I keep joining bands? This is stupid.

Brian nods, inquisitively scrunching up his face. "Okay, well, I'll let you off then. See you tomorrow?"

"Yep. Tomorrow."

Ivy is just out the door, when her best buddy Gabriel comes running toward her in a fit of fake tears. Ivy met Gabriel at an archaeological exhibition of ancient Chinese art from Sichuan. He and his boyfriend have been living together for about as long as Ivy's been living in Seattle. Almost a year. But every now and then he likes to pretend that he's a single "chickee."

"Again?" Ivy whines.

"Oh, sweetcakes, I can't help it. I really can't help it. He called me a phony, and I just couldn't stand the sight of him any longer. Please tell me you don't have company this eve?" Gabe's expression looks as if he's had a face-lift and he's too scared to move.

"When do I ever have company?"

"Great. Can I?" He perks up and wipes away invisible tears.

"Of course you can."

"Great. I'll come with you now."

"I've got a rehearsal. You know where I keep the spare key. Just make your own way."

"Fantastic. I'll cook you dinner."

"Yeah, right."

"Well, okay, I'll pay for the pizza. Ooh!" Gabriel points in Brian's direction and whispers, "Who's that hunk-a-spunk? Is that … is that *the* guy?" Gabriel stands on his tiptoes and peers through the shop's front window.

Ivy grabs his upper arm and yanks him away. "Don't you dare."

"What? I won't say anything embarrassing."

"Gabe, please. I've already embarrassed myself enough today. Can you wait until we've at least been out on a date?"

"Okay, sweetcakes. But only because you're so very graciously hospitable."

On her way to band rehearsal, Ivy stops in front of Crossroads Trading Company, and spots a full-length, low-cut, slinky black dress in the window. It would hug her figure perfectly; her shoulder-length ash-blonde hair would brush against her collar bone and accentuate her hearty cleavage. She envisions herself wearing it at a congratulatory event for a unique archaeological find—making a speech, thanking her students for their assistance on the site … *Without my wonderful students I would never have had the opportunity to find this part of the skull of Sakyamuni, the founder of Buddhism, in east China's Jiangsu Province …*

Ivy grabs her drumsticks and stares at them as if they are about to lash out at her for not treating them with respect. They're tattered and splintery, in need of a good layer of StickShield. *Bugger it.* She throws them in the nearby trashcan instead. *I need to get myself together. Letting my anger out on a stranger's drum kit isn't helping.*

Ivy enters the store. *No. Don't look there. You can't afford them. Just the dress.* She finds her size and heads straight for the counter without trying it on.

A man and a teenage girl approach and wait behind her to purchase some kind of jingly accessories. They're talking about a winter ball. Laughing. Joking about how clumsy the girl's date is and that she's going to wish she never said yes, and that maybe she should drop him.

The man says, "Honey, give him a chance. Just make sure he doesn't drop *you* when you dance!"

"Very funny, Dad." The girl giggles. Without turning to stare at them, Ivy imagines the girl rolling her eyes and punching her dad in the shoulder.

Ivy remembers when she did her high school formal. All Eleanor contributed to the experience was a lecture about date rape and why not to get drunk, descriptively listing the effects alcohol has on the brain, and the statistics regarding catching an STD.

It's Ivy's turn, and she's about to put the dress on the counter, when her cell rings. It's Kit.

"Hello?"

"Hey, Ivy, it's me."

"Hey, I'm a bit busy right now, Kit. Can I call you back?"

"Wait. I've just one question."

"Hmm?" Ivy steps back and lets the father and daughter in front to pay first. They smile and nod a thank you. She smiles back.

"Interested in meeting our dad?" Kit asks.

Ivy swallows a breath, observing the father and daughter from behind as he rubs the upper part of the girl's back.

"You know where Dad *is*?"

"Nah. Wondering if you want to look for him. Together."

"Not really."

Ivy watches as the father reaches into his back pocket and pulls out his wallet. The girl doesn't want to let him pay. She says she's saved up her allowance, but the father insists. The girl giggles again, leans her head on his shoulder, and squeezes him around the waist with one arm.

"Why?" Kit whines, extending the word more than necessary.

"I gave up on him when he gave up on me," Ivy answers in a half-whisper.

The daughter pats her father's head like he's a pet dog while he hands over his credit card. She catches Ivy staring from the corner of her eye, turns to face her, and smiles kindly. *She's happy.* Ivy turns away, pretending she hadn't noticed the girl's attempt at eye contact.

"Can you help *me* then?"

"Kit. This isn't a good time." Ivy turns her back to the father and daughter.

"Please?"

"I don't want to," Ivy says a little too loudly, and shoppers turn their heads.

"Ivy. He mightn't be as bad as you think he is."

"Wait." Ivy puts her hand over the receiver and watches

the father and daughter leave. The girl has her arm linked with his and is bouncing while she walks, causing his body to move side to side involuntarily. He laughs and says something to her Ivy can't make out, and then kisses her on the temple.

"You there?" Kit shrieks.

Ivy briefly pulls the phone away from her ear. "Yeah, I'm here. No need to yell. My eardrums aren't instruments."

"Ivy, what if he had a reason to never see us again?"

"Like what? Honestly, when are you going to stop dreaming and screw your head on straight?"

"Ivy, just hear me out. Maybe he was a spy or something and was protecting us or—"

"God, get real."

The lady at the counter raises her eyebrows at Ivy, who is hovering in front of the cash register and preventing others from moving forward.

"Kit, I've really got to go."

"But haven't you ever wondered why our mums don't want to talk about him? Maybe they're both in on it. You know, I'm almost sure of it."

"In on what? What could they possibly be in on? He left them, remember?"

"Oh, please? Can't you humour me? I've just got this instinct."

Ivy huffs and mouths, "Sorry," to the lady behind the register and to the new people standing behind her in line. Still holding the phone to her ear, she puts the dress on the counter.

"Can you ask Eleanor if she knows anything? Please?"

Ivy grips the receiver tighter in frustration, thinking she is going to regret everything from here on in. "Fine. But she won't be happy."

"Eleanor's never happy."

Ivy laughs. "Yes, fine, I'll ask her. For you. But don't ask me for anything else." She hangs up and puts her cell into her coat pocket.

Ivy pays for her dress, gathers her bags, and makes her way out into the cold street. She looks up into the grey cloudy sky, and a couple of drops of rain land on her lips. She licks them. *Orange.* She shivers at the thought of digging up the rotten past.

kit

"Kit?" Ailish calls from the veranda. "Could you please fetch a large spoon for the sour cream on your way out?" *ABC News* is blaring in the background: "The annual Melbournian heat wave plagues homes once again. The bureau of meteorology declares it is Australia's hottest summer on record ..."

"And a ladle for the soup?"

"Yeah!" *Gazpacho is too bloody spicy. What's the point in making a* cold *spicy soup?* Kit leans against the kitchen sink, squinting at the sunlight creeping through the orange tree by the window. Overripe oranges are decaying on the concrete, and the acidic scent of trodden rind is wheedling its way through the cracks in the wooden frame. She thinks about her father rotting, staining with his bitter memory every footpath she is bound to tread, contaminating her mother's tongue with his tart taste at the mere mention of his name. But Kit wants to taste the fruit—a need that has been stalking her ever since Ivy moved away. She wants to find the real "him." She wants to know who he is below the rind.

Kit pulls out the drawer below the sink and sifts through the unorganized mass of cutlery for a tablespoon and ladle. She shoves the drawer back in with a little too much force and almost jams her already injured thumb.

On her way to the front door she grabs her olive-green sarong from the arm of the antique wood-framed sofa and secures it around the top of her breasts like one would a towel after a shower. It slips down after she takes a couple of steps forward. *Why did* Ivy *have to get the big ones?* Clasping the ends of the sarong together with one hand and holding the spoons in the other, she swings the fly-wire door open with her hip and walks out onto the veranda.

"So, what's next on the Kit front?" Ailish asks before shoving a proud forkful of home-grown rocket into her mouth. It's too much to swallow. Ailish coughs and splutters, signals Kit to pass a napkin by erratically waving her left hand in the air while securing the pins at the base of her French twist with her right.

"Whydya have to go and call me Kit? It sounds like kid

but worse. Kid with a Nazi accent." Kit passes Ailish a napkin and sits, scraping the cane chair against the decking as she pulls herself closer to the table. She wipes sweat upward from her brow and into her unbrushed auburn hair with both hands. Holding her hair away from her face, fingers woven into it like a comb, she blows upward to cool herself off.

Ailish pats her mouth dry with a napkin and clears her throat. "I think it's a very cute name."

"It's old-fashioned. I should be on a farm milking cows in Woolloomooloo."

"I've always liked your sense of humour." Ailish nods as if trying to nod the sarcasm into a truth. "Dry, witty. Sweetheart, I often think you take after Ivy's mother more than me." Ailish grasps the ladle in the oversized glass bowl and puts some gazpacho into Kit's dish, ignoring her groan. She gestures toward the sour cream with her chin and raises her brow. Kit nods.

"So?" Ailish wriggles in her seat as if Kit has the most exciting news to tell.

Kit glares. "What?"

Ailish narrows her eyes and picks between her front teeth while Kit tears off a chunk of bread from the unsliced loaf of homemade sourdough.

Ailish looks at her plate and frowns. "There is a knife there for a reason, Kit."

Kit shrugs.

"Never mind. So, are you going to tell me once and for all what you've decided to do?"

"I dunno. Should I know?"

"Well, yes, you're sort of supposed to be familiar with what you aspire to do before you select a field of study, not after. Perhaps you should look for some voluntary field work to prepare yourself for your postgraduate studies next year?"

"Who says I'm going to enrol? I never said I was going to enrol. Besides, I hate fieldwork."

"If you dislike fieldwork, what on earth made you opt to study archaeology?" Ailish's voice rises in tone, hinting at frustration, yet maintaining her sarcastic spark.

Kit ignores her pun. She knows her lack of acknowledgment will annoy her mother. "Ivy said I'd like it."

"If Ivy said you should jump off a bridge, would you?"

"Mum, that's a bit cliché, isn't it?"

"Well, sweetheart, like the talented Evelyn Waugh said, 'to be oversensitive about clichés is—'"

"'Like being oversensitive about table manners.' I know, I know. Anyway, Ivy said it was interesting." Kit rests her left elbow on the table and drops her head into her hand, letting it swing a little.

"I thought you were really taking pleasure in your studies, Kit. And surely you have a mind of your own? I remember when you announced what you had decided to study. It appeared to me that you had some sort of revelation! Why did you need to follow in Ivy's footsteps? Why ever did you not make a decision on your own?" Ailish flings her arms into the air as if conducting an orchestra. As her arms come down, she knocks her right hand on the edge of the table. And winces.

"Mum!" Kit lifts her head and screws up her nose.

"What? It's a valid question," Ailish mumbles, sucking on her knuckle.

Kit sighs with a compassionate smile, hoping it might warrant a little compassion in return. "Can we talk about something else?" She's tired of academic grandeur. She wants life, adventure.

And a reason.

"And what do you suggest we talk about, Kit? You don't talk to me unless I ask you questions. Heaven forbid you bring up a topic of conversation on your own accord." Ailish's upper lip becomes stiff—the only part of her face that seems to reflect the tone of her voice—and lifts her spoon to her mouth, taking extra care not to slurp.

Kit glares, with a hint of pity. "I hate getting my fingers dirty," she says, stuffing her mouth full of sour-cream-covered crust.

Ailish laughs. "Getting your fingers dirty?" She drops her spoon into her bowl. Pink flecks litter the pale wooden tabletop. Ailish doesn't notice.

"Mum. Stop it. I thought I'd like it, okay? I thought it would be fun. But now I don't. Comprendo?"

"No *comprendo*, sorry. You must have been vaguely interested in it to complete the degree. You never complained while you were studying or while you were out on practice digs, for that matter."

"I like the history stuff. I dig that." Kit manages a smirk, hoping the joke might ease the tension, the constant expectation that she should *be* someone.

Ailish smiles, tilting her head, and lets out a little scoff of apparent satisfaction.

"There you are. Kit in all her glory. Where've you been hiding?" Ailish winks, then wipes sweat from her brow with her napkin.

"In my air-conditioned room, away from the heat," Kit says, fanning herself with her hand.

"Can you please limit your use of the air conditioner? I despise paying through the nose for utilities when there are more natural methods of temperature control. Have a cold shower. Simple. Pleasurable. Cheap." Ailish nods, giving the suggestion of a physical full stop.

Kit, despite thinking she is too old to roll her eyes, rolls her eyes and tsks.

"So, why didn't you study history then?" Ailish asks after another spoonful of soup. She now notices the splashes and wipes them away with her bare hand. Her skin squeaks against the varnish.

"'Cause I didn't want to become a boring old professor who gets excited about reiterating historical facts to a bunch of lazy-arse students who are only studying history because they don't know what else to do with their lazy-arse lives." Kit smiles and shoves another piece of bread into her mouth, too large to chew, and spits half of it out into her soup bowl.

Ailish focuses on Kit's mouth movements. Her top lip twitches.

"What, Mum?"

"What do you mean 'what'?"

"Don't look at me like that."

"What am I looking at you like?"

"Like I'm the one with a lazy-arse life."

"You said it, not me."

"Mum! You're a literature professor, for God's sake. Quit the clichés already."

Ailish sips her herb water. "Anyway, what I'd actually intended that look to mean was that being a lecturer isn't like that at all. I essentially find it quite rewarding." Ailish blushes due to what Kit suspects to be a menopausal hot flush.

"Yeah, but you're different. You get to read new literature all the time and choose what to teach every year. You've also had your own stuff published. New stuff. Original stuff. As a history professor, what would you read? You can't get new history, can you? Can't go changing the past because you're bored of reading the same old story over and over again. Right?"

Ailish glares at Kit as if trying to find a way to debate the issue. But she clicks her tongue and says with a smirk, "I suppose that's correct."

"And that's why I chose to study archaeology. There's always the opportunity to find some *new, undiscovered* history."

"Wow. I'm impressed."

"You know, I was actually thinking of going overseas for a while, before I do any Postgradu—"

"Oh, speaking of overseas." Ailish feels her chin for that forever returning wiry hair. "I spoke to Eleanor the other day. She says Ivy is doing great. Have you been in touch with her lately?"

"Of course. I'm always in touch with her. You know that." Kit frowns. "That's where I was thinking of going, actually. Seattle—to stay with Ivy."

"Oh? When were you thinking? Have you spoken to her about it?"

"Dunno. I haven't asked her yet. But she should be cool with it."

"Well, please make sure she is *cool* with it before you make any imprudent decisions. I know what it's like to be unpredictably surprised. It's not very … nice."

Kit observes Ailish as she soaks up some soup with the inner crust of her bread and drops it into her mouth. It clicks on her teeth like wood against wood.

"Speaking of not very nice, I've been thinking." Kit puts down her spoon, leans back in her chair, and stretches her arms above her head before resting them in her lap.

"Hmm?' Ailish hums as she chews.

"Been thinking about tracking down Roger. I've decided I'd like to meet him. Once and for all." Kit feels her throat swell in anticipation.

Ailish stops chewing. "Oh, *him*. That's what's been occupying your mind lately." Ailish, despite losing a little colour in her face, shows no physical reaction. Kit wonders whether the bones in her face will one day turn brittle and break from lack of emotional expression.

"I know I asked you a long time ago if you knew where he was. But I was just wondering if you've heard anything since then."

"Sorry, Kit, I haven't."

Ailish continues to chew, then swallows and gulps down the remainder of her herbal water in one go. The sound of it gushing down her throat reminds Kit of the whitewater rafting documentary she recently watched. Ailish's eyes begin to water. She wipes her mouth with the back of her pale sun-spotted hand and narrows her eyes at the weeds to her left, which are invading her precious flower bed.

Kit anticipates a short outburst. Nothing loud or obnoxious, but one of angst riddled with years of practiced silence, moulded into polite dissatisfaction. An outburst as unexpected and potent as a skunk's defence system.

"Goodness, how did they grow back so—"

"Mum."

"What? Oh, um, no, sorry." Ailish's speech speeds up, as though speaking the words at a tolerable pace would mean she didn't care. "I have no idea where he is. You could ask Eleanor though. Or Ivy, I suppose. I'm sure Ivy would be interested in meeting her father properly too, yes?" Ailish fidgets in her seat, pretending to shoo away a fly, it seems, in order to avoid looking Kit in the eye. "I suppose if Eleanor knew his whereabouts, though, she would have already told her own daughter, don't you think? Hmm, I wouldn't be surprised if she's already asked Eleanor herself. But if that was the case, she would have probably said something to you already, yes?"

Kit grits her teeth at Ailish's phony charade of interest. "Could *you* ask Eleanor for me?"

Doesn't hurt to get two on the job, right?

"Oh, no, no, no, no. No. Sorry, no can do."

Ailish fills her side plate with more salad, maintaining a downward gaze. Kit wants to growl, to let her mother know how much she despises her pretence designed merely to keep the peace. She knows if she speaks up, Ailish will just leave the table and lock herself in her room until Kit goes to bed. So she doesn't growl. She gives her mother her wish: to have a lovely outdoor meal before the heat becomes unbearable.

In silence, Kit and Ailish eat, occasionally looking up from their bowls to flash each other insignificant smiles— smiles that embody the untold. As Ailish scrapes the last thick smears of gazpacho from her bowl with some crust, she looks over at their neighbour—a solidly built Hispanic student of hers called Sein, who's watering the garden. Ailish smiles as if composing herself for a lecture and clutches her empty water glass as if it were a hot mug of tea. Kit, however, would prefer not to make eye contact with the guy. Not now anyway.

"Mum, are you finished? I'll take your stuff inside."

"Hmm? Oh, yes. Thanks, sweetheart."

Kit puts the dishes in the sink, grabs a light beer from the fridge, and goes upstairs to her bedroom.

I've gotta move outta home. But what if Mum isn't strong enough for me to do that yet?

She turns on the stereo and sits on the edge of her bed. The corner of the cardboard box tickles her neck, and she elbows it out of the way.

Kit grabs her handbag off the floor from beside her bed and pulls out the postgraduate application form. She unfolds it, skims over its contents, then tears it into eight pieces and throws it into the cardboard box with the rest of her "garbage." She'd love to throw the box away, but she would never hear the end of it. *What's the freaking use of a collection of regurgitated information—regurgitated primarily to have a letter written on it with some useless connotation of intelligence? Nothing.*

She takes the photo from her bedside table and runs her finger around the edge of his legs. *My father's legs. Roger's legs. Dad's legs.* She tastes the different textures of the three possible names she could call him, rolling them around her tongue to see which attaches itself to the wall of her mouth first, like a fertilized egg to a uterus.

She folds the photo down the middle so that it creases Ivy's smile, then puts it into her handbag—into the smallest side pocket, to keep him close and safe like a Joey in a kangaroo's pouch. This is to remind her, every time she opens her bag, that the time has come to find his face.

It's eleven a.m., and she's lying naked on her bed. Staring at the half-sucked yellow Gummy Bears stuck to her ceiling, she realizes they've been there for years. Who knows how many. They look down on her like semi-lived mantras. *Gotta find Roger. Gotta find out what I'm made of.*

Last night Kit dreamed about meeting him. He wore a navy-blue suit, with hair smothered in Brylcreem and a face full of acne scars. He spoke in a Russian accent and had a square-shaped face. He told her stories about all the assassinations he'd been assigned, and she listened attentively, holding on to every word. She asked him to teach her his craft.

Ailish knocks on her bedroom door.

"Sweetheart, I think it may be time for you to rise and shine, hmm?"

"I'm busy."

"Doing?"

"Thinking."

"Kit, get up and eat some breakfast. I want to have a word before I leave for work."

Kit focuses on the sound of Ailish's clunky cork platforms clop on the wooden stairs. She runs her tongue across her furry teeth, gets up, and opens the blinds.

Sein, from next door, is entering the front yard through the squeaky white picket gate. *Crap.* Kit throws on a loose off-white cheesecloth dress, the only dress left on a coat hanger. She peers into the mirror just long enough to remove the smudged mascara from under her eyes with a lick of spit on her forefingers, then flips her head upside down to loosen a few knots from her hair.

She reaches the bottom of the stairs just in time to open the door for Sein. His hand is raised, about to knock.

"Oh, hey," he says, leaning heavily on one foot, a little too wide-eyed and gleeful for Kit's liking.

"Hey." Kit remains straightfaced, puts a hand on her hip. Her long auburn hair, hooked behind one ear, is hanging to one side over her pincushion left breast. After a moment, Sein swallows. Kit tilts her head, with a slight questioning shake.

"Hi. Is Ailish still here?"

Of course she is. "Don't think so. Why?"

Sein picks at a loose wire near the hinge of the fly-screen door frame. "Oh. Well, we, um, just arranged, last night over the fence, for her to give me a lift into Uni today. If she's already left, don't worry about it. I'll grab the bus." Sein turns to leave, smiling and nodding politely, but Kit grabs him by the elbow.

"Just teasing." Kit flicks her head toward the lounge. "Come in."

Sein laughs like his voice broke. "Oh, thanks."

"Go in. She must be in there somewhere," Kit says, waving her hand in the air, indicating Ailish's uncertain whereabouts.

Sein walks toward the open-plan kitchen-lounge area,

and Kit notices his bag has "I 'heart' Leila" written on the pocket in green glitter pen. *Bit old for that, isn't he?* The spine of a Mark Twain book is poking out of the half-closed zipper, but she can't see exactly which one, only that it's a Penguin Classic.

Ailish is washing a few remaining dishes, and a bowl of fruit salad is on the kitchen counter ready for Kit to eat.

Kit sits on a stool by the counter and spoons some pineapple into her mouth without looking into the bowl. "Thanks." Her eyes are on Sein, who is rearranging the fridge magnets.

"Oh, hi, Sein. I'm so sorry. I forgot you were coming with me today. If Kit hadn't taken so long getting out of bed I might have left without you. I suppose you can thank your lucky stars."

"Oh, don't worry. I would've grabbed the bus."

"What did you want to talk to me about, Mum?" Kit almost cuts Sein off, her eyes drilling into the back of his head.

Ailish dries her hands, and digs out a chunk of her own putty-textured moisturizer concoction from a little terra-cotta pot next to the sink with her middle finger. She rubs it into the tops of her hands while she speaks.

"There's a position available at the uni for an intern English tutor."

Kit opens her mouth to speak, but Ailish raises her right hand.

"And before you say a word, I'm well aware that you

haven't studied literature. But I can pull a few strings, and I'm positive you know more about literature than half the students attending my lectures." Ailish points her chin toward Sein, who is still messing about with the fridge magnets. He turns around and blushes.

"Oh, dear me, I'm terribly sorry, Sein, I didn't mean to insinuate that you were one of the incompetent ones, I just … oh, never mind. I apologize."

"'T'sall right." Sein zips open his bag to look for something. Kit can see the book now. It's *The Adventures of Tom Sawyer*. One of the texts Ailish is lecturing about today. Although classes have technically stopped for the year, Ailish is re-lecturing a few topics for students who were unable to attend the first time, to help them with their final assessment tasks. Kit doesn't answer. Ailish glares, clenching the back of her jaw and then sucking in her cheeks.

Sein zips his bag shut. Holding his forefinger in the air as if suddenly seized by a bright idea, he says, "The right word may be effective, but no word was ever as effective as a rightly-timed pause."

Oh no, not him too!

"Sein, if only Kit's pauses were so thoroughly thought through, then I might appreciate them as much as Mark Twain did."

Kit shoves her spoon into a big chunk of cantaloupe and takes a deep breath, trying not to snap at Ailish in front of Sein.

"Why would I want to be an intern tutor? I wouldn't get paid."

"I thought it might be interesting for you, regarding the teaching side of things. It might give you some insight as to whether you would like to pursue postgraduate studies in archaeology or not. If you don't like 'digging dirt,' you might as well use your knowledge to teach others. And this will most certainly give you those skills, Kit."

"But you know I want to ... you know." Kit scans Sein's face. "I've got other things I wanna do first."

"Well, start looking for him now, will you? Get it over and done with. You need to make a decision about your future. You're going to squander your life away like this." Ailish raises her voice just high enough for Kit to know she means business, but not aggressive enough to make Sein feel uncomfortable. "And, I'm afraid, I refuse to house and feed a degenerate. So get cracking before I find a reason to throw you out." Ailish blows a loose stand of hair out of her eyes. "In fact, now that I think of it, if you don't take this internship, or apply for a postgraduate position for next year, or find a decent job in which you're not degrading yourself to stacking supermarket shelves, you're out. So"— Ailish takes a deep breath—"what's it going to be?"

Sein shifts the weight from one foot to the other, screws up his face, and scratches his neck. He seems to have spotted something outside the kitchen window. Kit, focusing and unfocusing on a loose thread dangling from the hem of her dress, runs her fingers through her hair trying to untangle a few matted bits near the base of her neck.

"Got a lighter, Sein?" Kit asks. Sein blushes again. Only

Kit knows he smokes. He reaches inside the back pocket of his jeans and pulls out a black rubber-covered Zippo and hands it to her. He avoids looking at Ailish. Kit burns the thread loose and passes the lighter back. Ailish huffs, unties her apron, folds it animatedly, and hangs it over the rail on the oven door.

"Sein, I'll just fetch my belongings. You may wait by my car. I'll just be a minute."

"Sure. No problem," Sein replies with a keep-the-peace smile.

Ailish runs up the stairs, and the bathroom door shuts with an echoing bang. Sein and Kit look at each other, motionless and at ease for the first time since she pinched his bum in front of his dad and everyone pretended it never happened. Kit smiles an apology. Sein winks, moves toward her, squeezes her shoulder, briefly but with affection, then heads out to Ailish's car.

Kit watches glittery-green Leila follow Sein out the front door, and wonders whether she might have a competitor.

If only she knew how to skate, then maybe it wouldn't take her so long to get home. Trying not to slip on the wet roads is proving more difficult than she'd expected. Step, slide. Step, slide. Arms out to the side.

Ivy wonders if Gabriel has started a fire this time. Last

time, she found him curled up in her duvet on the couch, shivering and waiting for the broken central heating unit to warm up on its own. As if opening the front door was enough to trigger a switch. It was the first time he'd spent a winter night at her "humble abode," as Gabriel liked to say in his imitative Queen Elizabeth accent.

Drizzle turns to rain. A crack of thunder causes Ivy to lose balance, and her legs give way. Lying flat on her back, she's mesmerized by a sea of legs scattering around her. No one tries to help her up; they simply avoid stepping on her as if she's a deep muddy puddle. Just as she gets back on her feet, the rain comes down in paperweights. Running for shelter toward the nearest bus stop, she curses for forgetting her umbrella—again. Within moments, a torrent of water comes gushing along the ditch and rumbles below her feet in the drain. A minute ago the street was full of strolling nomads. Now it is empty. She's in a soundproof bubble. The rain becomes white noise, encompassing the world in a thick unwavering *whoosssssh*.

Ivy's eyes dart left and right trying to spot an indoor refuge. Every store and coffee shop along 15th is closed except for a tiny little bar where the world seems to have migrated. Creeping out of a very small window, into the blue moonlit street shrouded in rainfall, is an enticing yellow picture of soundless laughter. Ivy makes a run for it.

A bell chimes as she pushes open the heavy spring-hinged door. The white noise slowly dissipates, and soft jazz fades in as the door inches closed behind her, chiming again. Ivy scans the room for an empty seat. The place is furnished with dark mahogany-coloured leather booths. Ivy imagines the place full of women in the early 1950s with their stunningly defined hairdos, cigarette holders, and smoke rings floating from their cherry-red lips.

The wet customers have already received drinks. She expects to see a cascade of Chocolate Viennois or Irish coffees with temperatures like this, but instead, people are drinking whiskeys and vodkas on the rocks.

Is that a Sex on the Beach? Talk about cognitive therapy.

Ivy pulls off her coat and scratches her nose to relieve the tickling drops of water hanging from it. The patrons have already hung their coats and umbrellas on coat stands; they're overflowing, and she can't seem to fit hers on any of them.

She stops an approaching waiter dressed in a chic black-and-white uniform by gently touching his elbow. "Is there anywhere I can hang this so that it's near a heater to dry?"

The waiter nods and leads her to the other side of the bar. "I'll take that. You can collect it from over there." He points toward the staff room entrance, where a portable heater stands.

Inside, the bar is so much bigger than it looks from the outside.

Why didn't I look for a place like this to work in? Class, Ivy. What you need is class.

The waiter returns. "Would you like to sit at the bar, or would you prefer to wait for an available table?"

"The bar is fine, thanks." Ivy smiles, gathering her wet hair. She was hoping to tie it into a low knot, but she forgot it had just been cut. It hangs limp, the ends tickling her shoulders.

"Great. There's an empty stool right next to the gentleman in the dark-green shirt. Can I order you a drink?"

"Ah. Yeah." Ivy nods, squinting at the green-shirted gentleman's back. "Um … hot Brandy Alexander?"

"Certainly. Just take a seat, and I'll let the barman know."

Ivy walks toward the empty stool. It looks like Brian. It *is* Brian. *Shit. I look like shit. Shit!* She contemplates turning around and walking home in the rain, but he notices her too soon.

"Ivy, hey. What are you doing here?" He's clean-shaven. He wasn't in the coffee shop. Ivy scrutinizes his face. He has a small shaving scar on his chin.

"Got caught in the storm. Unprepared as usual," she says, pulling out the bar stool and almost tumbling over when she slips on the foot rail.

Brian smiles. "See, I knew there was a reason I shouldn't have gone straight home."

Straight home? But you shaved. Where did you shave?

Despite her curiosity, she can't help but feel flattered and smiles involuntarily in return, looking at her soggy shoes. She pushes her wet fringe from her forehead. Brian follows her movements with his eyes. Ivy remembers it's wet and how stupid it would look sticking up in the air. She flattens it back down and shakes her head a little so it doesn't look like her forehead has a slimy comb-over.

"No, no. Comfort beats looks any time," Brian says, gently pushing her fringe back up and caressing her scalp with his fingertips. His touch, although quite paternal, makes Ivy's stomach tighten. "There. That feels better, right?"

"Let's just avoid feeling self-conscious for today, hey?" Ivy pulls a scarf out of her bag and wraps it around her hair like a headband. Brian gazes into his lowball glass, at the ice cubes suspended in amber bubbles.

The corners of his mouth are fighting the urge to chuckle, and the bartender approaches with Ivy's drink.

"Here you go. Hot Brandy Alexander."

"Just a sec …" Ivy reaches her arm over the bar as if desperate for the guy not to leave.

"Is there a problem, ma'am?"

"Oh, no, no, of course not. It looks great. I was just wondering. Are there any jobs here at the moment?"

"Oh. I'm not quite sure. My manager is a bit tied up right now, but you could fill out an application form if you like."

"Okay. That'd be brill, thanks."

"I'll just get one for you." The bartender wipes his hand on a towel and disappears behind a door.

Brian frowns. "Who's going to serve me my afternoon coffee?"

"Are you serious? This place is so much nicer. You'll just have to come here."

"I'm just playing with you. Of course, I'll come here. I come here anyway. Some evenings. As you can probably already see." Brian laughs nervously.

They both look at the array of bottles behind the bar and take a sip of their drinks without toasting.

"Mmm, that's a good hot brandy."

Brian hums and nods, taking another sip. An ice cube touches his nose. "So, now that I've finally got you having a drink with me, why don't you tell me all about what it is you *do* do?"

Ivy snorts. "Well, I'm … well, I'm actually an archaeologist."

"What? You're kidding."

"Nope."

"What are you doing working in a café?"

"I needed a break. It was either this or finish my PhD."

"You can't practice archaeology without a PhD?"

"Well, yeah you can, but there are a lot more opportunities out there if you've got a PhD. Plus, I'd be able to apply for government grants and actually take charge of archaeological digs rather than assist someone else."

"So? What's stopping you from assisting someone else in the meantime? Why did you have to choose this?" Brian's voice raises a little and looks around the shop. "Surely one of your professors or someone could have scouted for some work experience for you, right?"

I like talking to you without an electronic notepad in my hand.

"Yeah, but …" Ivy smacks her lips.

"You don't look like the kind of person who would give up everything just to work in a café and play 'Hit Me with

Your Rhythm Stick.'" Brian smirks. "There must be some other reason. Or am I entirely off course?"

Ivy stirs her drink with her cocktail stick. She imagines bathing in it, immersed in a hot creamy bath. She rewinds her thoughts and plays them again with Brian in there too.

"Oh. I just crossed a line, didn't I? Sorry." Brian looks away. He pouts his bottom lip as he scratches his chin.

"No. No, not at all. I needed a break from the academic chaos. I've never taken time away from study since the day I started school. I needed to experience something new, something simple. I wouldn't have been able to convince myself to take a break at the end of the PhD, that's all." *Half-truth. That's not a crime, is it?*

Brian narrows his eyes and swishes the remainder of his drink around his mouth before swallowing it. Ivy still hasn't held Brian's gaze for more than a couple of seconds.

"Fair enough, I suppose."

"How about you? I mean, I know you're an accountant and work across the road from Ditsy Daisy's, but what do you do when you're not at work?"

"Drink Cutty Sark." He laughs and puts his empty glass on the counter.

"Really? You don't have any hobbies?"

"Promise you won't laugh?"

"Of course."

"I make candles."

"Candles? You mean *candle* candles? Real candles or wax sculptures?" *Please say wax sculptures.*

"Yeah, real candles. Scented, floating, tea light, votive, taper, pillar, gel. All sorts. And no, I'm not gay."

"Oh." Ivy laughs, "I didn't think that. Really."

"Uh-huh. I've come to learn what that expression means." Brian raises one eyebrow.

Ivy shakes her head and flicks her hand. "Just not something I expected. Yeah. Sounds really great. Do you sell 'em?"

"No. But my house is filled with them."

"Romantic type then?"

"You could say that." Brian puts his hand up to catch the bartender's attention, but the bartender doesn't see. "Enough about me. I want to know about you."

Damn. "Okay, what do you want to know?" Ivy silently cringes, wishing she had introduced a diversion to Brian's life story quicker enough.

"Well, so far I know you play drums, and that you like music, so what kind of music are you into?"

Phew. Avoided the family question. "Well, you know the band the New Pornographers?"

"Aren't they in town?"

"Yeah, they are. Would have loved to go and see them. Just can't afford a ticket." *I shouldn't have said that. Please don't get all charitable on me. If only you knew.*

"That's a shame. Maybe someone'll offer you a free one." Brian winks. The bartender finally responds to Brian's hovering arm. "Could I have another?" Brian lifts his glass.

"Certainly, sir."

"It's not often they tour, you know. It'd be a shame to not go," Brian says.

"Yeah, it would be a shame. My own choice though. My mother could have set me up with anything I needed if I'd wanted." *Shit. I did it again.*

"What do you mean?"

"Uh … long story."

"I've got time. And so do you by the looks of it. That rain isn't gonna give in a hurry."

Ivy's cell rings. "Sorry, Brian, just a sec. Gabe? You all right?"

"'Course, sweetcakes. I was ringing to see if you're all right. Did you get caught in the storm?"

"Yeah, I did, but I'm fine. I slipped and fell over though."

Brian pulls a curious face. Ivy smiles, rolls her eyes, and shakes her head in response.

"Oh, you poor darling."

"Pft. I got back on my feet eventually."

"Well, sweetcakes, now that you know how to literally get back on your feet, do you think you can attempt to do it emotionally too?"

"I bought a new dress and threw my drumsticks in the trash. That's a start, right?"

"Way to go, sistah. Let's celebrate."

"Well, I'm sitting in a little bar on Fifteenth at the moment."

"On your own? Oh, honey."

"No, I'm with Brian actually."

"Oh, sweetcakes, about time. You go, girl."

"Yeah, they've got nice hot Brandy Alexanders here. We should come together one night." The bartender brings Brian his drink.

"Oh, Ive. Don't be so shy. So what if he gets that you're talking about him. Get some balls, honey. Hey, you can have mine. I don't need 'em, and I don't wan' 'em."

Ivy's jaw tenses and becomes temporarily mute. *Why can't I just be myself?*

"Okay, sweetcakes. Never mind. When do you think you'll be coming home? Just so I know when to order the pizza."

Ivy can practically hear Gabe wink. The rain stops, and she cranes her neck to look out the window.

"Um, looks like I'll be on my way *now*."

Ivy steals a glance at Brian, who is looking into his glass. He brings it to his lips and swallows the whole thing down in one gulp. He pulls money out of his pocket, enough for both of their drinks, and slides the application form the bartender finally left on the bar toward Ivy.

"Sweetness," Gabriel sings. "What'll it be? Vegetarian with jalapeños and pineapple?"

"You got it."

Ivy flicks her cell closed. "Thanks for the drink, Brian. You didn't have to do that."

"I know. But it's my pleasure. I guess I'll see you tomorrow afternoon then?"

"Yep." Ivy collects her coat while Brian waits for her at

the entrance. He opens the door for her to exit first. Out on the street, he puts his hand out to shake, but Ivy, without hesitating, gives him a kiss on the cheek instead.

"Would you like to walk me home? I don't live too far from here," Brian asks with a smirk.

"I'd love to," Ivy says with a short laugh, elevating herself onto her tiptoes and back down again.

Brian almost puts his arm around Ivy's shoulder, but hesitates and puts his hand in his pocket instead.

When Ivy walks through her front door, the first thing she can smell is the fragrance of peach cleaning fluid. As she hangs her coat and bag in the tiny entrance hall, pizza aromas waft by. Gabriel has cleaned her house from top to bottom. The floorboards are glistening. He's even done her laundry and hung each item on the clothes horse in the lounge—not too close to the fire this time. Ivy stares at the amount of cotton panties compared to lacy thongs.

I'm getting old.

"Hey, sweetcakes. Welcome home." Gabriel appears in the lounge doorway, holding out a piece of pizza on a plate.

"Are you okay? What's going on?" Ivy looks around her.

"Just felt like cheering you up, girl."

"But I thought *you* were the one that needed cheering up. Didn't you have another fight with your boy?"

"Oh, don't worry about me. Gabe is peachy keen." Ivy is reminded of Riz from *Grease*.

"Why do you think I need cheering up? I've been fine. Haven't I?"

"You looked at yourself in the mirror lately?" Gabriel waves his hand over his face to indicate what Ivy should be looking at in the mirror. She thinks of the dancers in Madonna's "Vogue" video clip, and the chopsticks she used to bang to it, all over her bedroom furniture, when she was a kid. Sometimes Eleanor would interrupt and say something like, "I wish you'd practice using one of those chopsticks as a scalpel instead."

"What? What's wrong with my face?"

"You're a mess."

"Thanks a lot."

"Sweetcakes, you've had a long face since the day you said you were Amir-free. You looked better when you were heartbroken."

"I thought I said I never wanted to hear his name again."

"See, sweetcakes, that's just plain denial, and I'm sorry to say it, but that's following in your mother's footsteps whether you like it or not. And I've got news for you, honey, it makes no difference anyway. You've got Amir— see, I said his name, and I'll say it again: *Amir*. He's on your mind 24/7. You have to let him go, 'kay?"

Gabriel pulls Ivy out of the hall and sits her down on the couch in front of the fire, with a full glass of red wine and jumbo pizza. He picks up the glass and places it in her hand. Ivy succumbs to being handled like a puppet, almost expressionless, except for the fear she can feel glaze over her eyes at the thought of becoming like her mother.

"Well, don't just stare at me. Drink up. Wash that Amir right out of your hair, darling, once and for all." Gabriel swings his long bouncy curls around as if auditioning for a shampoo ad. "Enough's enough. You have to focus on Brian now. Move on. Eat, drink. Think about Brian. He's a spunk, and he loves your coffee better than Raquel's. Come on, sweetcakes—a little smile?" Gabriel imitates what he wishes to see on Ivy's face by moving the sides of his mouth upward with his fingers. Ivy reciprocates, holding the fake smile long enough to resemble a clay figurine.

"Gabe?" Ivy asks, breaking her statuesque pose.

"Yes, sweetcakes? I'm all ears."

Gabriel sits opposite Ivy in the armchair with his wine. He crosses his legs, lights a cigarette with a match, takes a drag, lights another one with his lit cigarette, hands it to Ivy, and swings his crossed leg backward and forward in nicotine-thrilled pleasure.

Ivy lifts her legs onto the couch to rest her feet. "Kit called me today and asked if I'd be interested in looking for Roger—can you believe it?"

Gabriel holds his breath and lets the smoke ooze from his nose. He leans slightly forward, elbow on knee, as if contemplating his response.

"Well, *I* think it'd be good for you." Gabriel's voice shifts a semitone lower than usual. "It might give you some closure. Some purpose."

"I've got purpose." Ivy flicks her head to the side to remove strands of hair stuck to her nose.

"Like what, exactly? You're the most-educated person I know, and you're a stinking waitress. You should be getting calluses on your hands, not the soles of your feet."

"She wants me to call my mother and ask if she has any leads."

"Are you listening to me?" Gabriel asks, exasperated.

Ivy puts a hand to her forehead. "I dread speaking to her about this. But I really think Kit should find out the truth. At least to finally realize he's not worth the trouble, you know?"

Gabriel downs his wine in one go. "Sweetcakes, I said you should do it. Who are you trying to convince here?"

"Actually, I think I'll give her a call now and get it over and done with."

Ivy picks up the cordless from the coffee table, pokes her tongue out at Gabriel, and goes into her bedroom closing the door behind her. She lies on her bed and counts the crystals hanging from the lace maroon light shade, holding the phone to her chest. *Twenty-seven. That's weird. Maybe one has fallen off.* She presses the green phone icon and puts the phone to her ear. *You've really got to get a new phone. This dial tone sounds like a nauseated robot.* She presses the speed dial with her thumb, a button she can now press without thinking about its position on the key pad or all the extra codes.

"Dr. Eleanor Manning."

"Hi. It's me."

"How are you? I tried to call you this afternoon."

"Good. You?"

"As good as can be. Emotionally drained."

I know.

This is more often than not the only insight Ivy gets into what life as a surgeon entails anymore. From the very day Ivy told Eleanor she wanted to be an archaeologist, she stopped telling her hospital stories. When Ivy was about ten, Eleanor took her into the operating room while performing heart surgery on a baby inside a mother's womb. It was the most horrific sight Ivy had ever seen. That's the day she also told Ivy she was named after *IV*, for intravenous. It means in the vein, and Eleanor insisted it represented Ivy flowing through her very blood. But the thought sickened Ivy, and she decided she never wanted to go into the hospital with Eleanor again.

"Any news?"

"No. Not really. You?"

"No. Not really."

"You know, Ivy, the point of making a phone call is having something to say." Eleanor laughs.

"I do have something to say. Something to ask, actually."

"Oh? You're not one for asking questions. I thought you knew everything already."

Silence. *That was uncalled for.*

"That was insensitive," Eleanor mumbles, apologetically. "What's on your mind?"

"Right." Ivy clears her throat. "Well, Kit asked me to ask you ... well, no, Kit asked me, and I agreed, thought it would be a good idea and all, you know, that maybe she could look for, well … *we* could look for … Dad?"

"*Him?*"

"Yes, him. Do I have another dad?"

"That wasn't a question, Ivy. That was stuttering rubbish."

"The question's coming." Ivy's stomach gurgles; her mouth goes dry.

"Okay then. Ask it."

Ivy counts the crystals on the light shade again. *How could there possibly be an odd number of crystals? I must keep missing one.*

"What are you doing? What's that jingling?"

"Do you think … you know, only if it's okay with you … if you feel okay about it, 'cause I really don't want to force you into giving me information that might make you feel sad, 'cause that's not my intention, you know …"

"Spit it out, Ivy. Just ask the question."

"Um …"

"Look. Ivy. I don't know why you've decided this all of a sudden. I persistently gave you the opportunity to see him when you were a teenager. And you consistently said you weren't interested. And now that I have no idea of his whereabouts, you want to see him again. Why?"

"For Kit. Look, I don't even know if I want to do this, but I think Kit—"

"Where'd Kit get this idea all of a sudden?"

"I don't know. We didn't have the chance to talk properly."

"I hope she's not nagging Ailish about this. That's the last thing she needs. Spare her the flashbacks. And the guilt. I hope you haven't told Kit any details about Ailish's relationship with him."

"Jesus. Why would I do that, Mum?"

"Well, let's try to keep it that way. It's too late in our lives to be dragging skeletons out of the closet. It's in the past. Let it stay that way. Ailish is more fragile than she lets on."

"Mum, I've never understood why you keep sticking up for Ailish all the time. Maybe you are right that Dad was going to leave you anyway, but maybe he wasn't—have you ever thought about that? And what about your hurt? Why do you keep talking about Ailish's pain and never your own? I mean, I love Ailish and Kit—don't get me wrong. But Christ, Mum, what about yourself? What about how it makes *you* feel? Why do you keep pretending it never happened?"

Ivy bites her bottom lip at the realization that she just blurted out years of confrontational thoughts to a woman she's spent her life being afraid of. *Why the sudden confidence?* She pinches the bridge of her nose and tightly closes her eyes, wondering whether the silence on the other end of the phone means Eleanor is concocting an intelligent, hurtful response.

Eleanor clears her throat. "And what do you call running away to the other side of the world and living a hopeless, financially unstable life after divorcing Amir, hmm?"

Ivy's limbs stiffen; the crystals stop jingling. She hangs up and cups a hand over her mouth to stunt a frustrated scream. She counts the crystals on the lamp shade again, holding the handset above her shoulder. *I was right the first time. There are twenty-seven. Oh my God, I just hung up on my mother.*

Gabriel calls out from the lounge. "Sweetcakes? You better come and eat before I eat everything myself."

Ivy walks back in. There is only a quarter of the pizza left and half a bottle of wine. "Oh, and you just got a text."

Ivy runs into the lounge and flips open her cell.

I'm sorry. Tell Kit 2 go 2 the university Ailish works @, & speak 2 the dean. He used 2 b his best mate in those days. They were in the Army together. Maybe he knows something. Just please, do me a favour, and don't involve me in this any further. Eleanor.

The Army? Maybe Kit's idea that … Ugh. No, Ivy. Don't be so ridiculous.

kit

On a whim to get her hair trimmed and straightened, Kit is at the hairdresser's, when she gets a text message from Ivy.

Go 2 C the dean @ A's Uni. Was Dad's pal.

"Not hurtin' ya, am I, Kit?" Eydie says, sliding a hot comb through Kit's hair. Eydie is not only her regular hair rescuer but an accustomed victim of Kit's eruptive rants. Of course, Kit doesn't really care what her hair looks like, but she likes the attention, to feel pampered sometimes. And for some reason, getting her hair done by Eydie helps her to relax, to feel like she's a *girly* girl, even though she doesn't want to be perceived as one.

"Nope," Kit says, smiling at Eydie in the mirror. *Pathetic excuse of a smile, that is*, she thinks, catching a glimpse of herself. It looks as if she's cut it out of a magazine and pasted it onto her own face. Bleak, washed out.

Eydie nods, smiling in return, her short emo red hair falling over her eyes. She flicks her head to move it off her face and winks at Kit through the mirror. She seems happy working on Kit's hair. Kit notices fogginess in her eyes. Her smile doesn't show anywhere on her angled face but her mouth.

"Who's the message from? You've gone all sulky." Eydie frowns and tilts her head to the side.

Kit laughs. Limp. "I decided I wanted to find my father and, well, to cut a long story short, had no idea where to start looking until just this minute."

"Oh, cool. What's with the long face then? Shouldn'tcha be happy?" Eydie asks, bunching a mass of hair to the top of Kit's head and clipping it down.

"I suppose. But it kind of just dawned on me what I'm doing. I mean, what if I'm not cut out for what I might find?"

"Yeah. I know whatcha mean. Me dad dis'ppeared when I was a kid too. He's been sending me letters 'n' puttin' cash into some kinda fund for me, all me life, but I just found out 'bout it not long ago. Me mum's been using the bloody dough to pay for grog, I'm sure of it, and hidin' the letters in her dresser. I found 'em when I was scrounging for a ciggy."

"What? You're kidding?" Kit turns around in her seat to face Eydie, her eyes ablaze.

"Nup." Eydie nudges Kit's shoulder to turn around and face the mirror. Kit obliges.

"My God. And I thought *I* was hard done by."

"Yeah, nah. But what really pisses me off is that me mum spends so much bloody money on grog that she can't pay the rent no more. I had no freakin' idea she was wasting more money than what she got from the dole. And I quit bloody school 'n came to work at this joint, so that we could pay the bleedin' rent."

"Oh my God, Eydie. How have you never told me this before?" Kit moves a little closer to the mirror as though Eydie's reflection were real.

"Well, who am I to ruin your girly hairdressin' experience? Anyway, I can't afford to lose control. I gotta eat. What's that saying thingy you once said to me? If ya c'n walk on water, or something, ya no better off than a … somethingerather in a puddle?"

"A twig floating on a puddle. Arabian proverb." Kit wonders what the relevance is, but thinks better of asking.

"Yeah. That. Man, I wish I was smart like you."

"You are smart. Just in a different way," Kit replies. But Eydie hardly acknowledges it. "Not many people would remember stuff like that, you know."

Eydie nods. Squints. Drags the hot comb carefully through another mass of waves.

"I hope you had a good go at your mother about it," Kit says.

"Nup. Can't be stuffed." Eydie screws up her nose.

"Why?"

"She's always so bloody off her face she wouldn't half understand what I was talkin' 'bout anyway."

"Eydie, you have to do something. You could use that money for something worthwhile. Can't you just send a letter back to your dad and tell him what's going on?"

"Nup."

"Why?"

"He stopped sendin' the letters. And the phone number for the address I found don't exist no more."

"Well, just … just physically go to the address."

"Can't."

"Why not?"

Kit can see Eydie's eyes go wet in the mirror.

"Just like ya said—what if I'm not cut out for it?" Eydie wipes a knuckle under her right eye. "Anyway, hair's done; you can geddup."

Kit stands, unties her smock, and brushes runaway hairs off her top. She hugs Eydie, making comforting noises while rubbing her on her upper back.

Eydie pulls away prematurely and says, "Aw, don't worry 'bout me. I'm used to this shit." She winks, sniffs back some tears, and blows on Kit's neck and around her ears to loosen the odd fleck stuck to her skin.

"Well, you've got my number if you need anything, right?" Kit asks. *I might have more in common with you than I thought.*

"Yep. Ta."

Eydie goes to the cash register, prints off a receipt, and holds out her hand for Kit to pay up.

"That'll be twenny bucks."

Kit pulls a twenty out of her olive-green corduroy bag and hands it to Eydie. The photograph of her father has replaced the beat of her postgraduate application form. *Doof, doof. Doof, doof.*

Dad, I'm coming.

"Ta," Eydie says as Kit puts the twenty-dollar note into her hand. "So, what's the lead?"

"Hmm?" Kit asks, wondering how to pull her knickers out of her bum without anyone seeing her do it through the shop window.

"To findjya dad?"

"Oh. Right. The dean of the uni where my mum works was apparently a friend of his. Got no idea how I'm gonna go about speaking to him, though, without pestering my mum." *But I have the right to pester her about this. Don't I? She's the one who's kept all this info a secret. What am I so afraid of? What's the worst she can do?*

"Why dontcha do that intern tutor thingy you were talkin' 'bout before? Then you'll be there all the time and you can speak to 'im yourself."

"Hey. That's not a bad idea, actually." *Why didn't I think of that?*

"Just make sure you fill me in on the goss." Eydie winks.

On Kit's way out, she makes the shape of a phone with her hand and holds it to her ear. She knows Eydie won't call. She never does. But this time things seem different.

eydie

Eydie nods and dismisses Kit with a flick of her hand. Her hot-pink acrylic nails collide and click. She goes out back for a cigarette.

What fuckin' life is this? Tears stream down her cheeks.

She gazes at the rows and rows of hair dye. The layer upon layer of shelves containing a chemical substance that, according to statistics, sends many hairdressers into the loony bin. So she's heard, anyway. Eydie wonders if there's any way she could use them to end her life. *Like gassing myself in a car? Is it possible to poison myself in a salon? On my lunch break, maybe.*

The counter bell chimes. Someone's feet shuffle, stumble. She can hear the visitor fall onto the orange vinyl couch. A magazine crinkles. The customer sat on it. Eydie left it there by accident earlier. *Damn.* She quickly dries her eyes with the tea towel lying by the kettle and walks back out.

Her next client is flicking through the crinkled *Elle* magazine. The client looks up. Her eyes are bloodshot. More burst capillaries seem to have appeared around her nose.

"Luv, ya stink like smoke," the client croaks.

"You stink like vodka," Eydie replies, straight-faced, repulsed. Sad.

"Where's ya boss?"

"Day off."

"I told ya I wanted ya boss to cut me hair, luv."

The client puts *Elle* on the empty seat beside her. She looks up at Eydie, who stands rock solid, hands on hips, staring at the floor.

"Well, stiff shit," Eydie replies. 'You're stuck with me. Here. Put this on." *You freakin' reek!*

Eydie hands her a black smock. She doesn't help her put it on and watches the client's awkward attempt at tying a bow behind her neck. She stumbles getting into her seat.

Eydie sprays conditioner mist and runs her fingers through the client's course bleach-blonde curls. They make eye contact in the mirror.

"Well, get on with it," the client snaps. "I haven't got all bleedin' afternoon, luv."

"Can't the bottle wait for half a freakin' hour, Ma?"

"Don't use that fuckin' tone with me, missy."

Eydie takes a deep breath and begins to snip off some split ends, but puts the scissors down again—far from reach. She walks over to the door and turns the sign around from "bring your bootie in" to "shake your bootie out."

"Ma?"

"What the bleedin' Joe is it, luv?"

"We need to talk. Right now."

#

By the time she wakes, Gabriel has left. She's lying on her stomach, cheek squashed against her cell phone from when she disabled the alarm in a sleepy daze. *Over half an hour ago. Fuck.* On the bedside table is a plate of blueberry pancakes, Gabriel's specialty, and a little note that reads: "True blue, baby, I love you."

Ivy sits up and winces at the snow piled up outside her bedroom window. The house is still warm from last night, but she shivers at the thought of going outside.

I never knew Dad was in the Army. Why didn't Mum ever tell me? What if Kit's right? What if he didn't want *to leave Mum and me? What if the Army was a disguise for something more serious? What if they threatened to do something to us if he didn't obey? Maybe that's why he left without saying goodbye. Maybe …*

Ivy shakes her head and whacks her forehead four times with her right palm. "IV. Stop. It."

She gets out of bed and her cell beeps. *Bloody hell, Kit. What now?* But it's Brian.

Can't stop thinking about u. What time do u start work? Let's meet earlier?

Ivy looks at herself sideways in the mirror, pulling her stomach in and out. She pulls her hair into a ponytail, then lets it loose. *Fuck it. Let the customers complain.* She looks at her jeans, sports bra, and pastel pink mohair sweater hanging over the chair by the wall. She has worn those four days in a row. Yesterday Raquel looked her up and down and pretended she hadn't noticed. She said, "Luurve that sweater. Have I seen that before?"

Ivy glared. Raquel didn't look her in the eye for the rest of the shift.

Ivy grabs the jeans and sweater and puts them in the laundry basket. She pulls on a pair of black tights, picks up the sports bra, swings it around her torso, fastens one hook, then takes it off again and throws that in the basket too. She puts on a padded push-up bra instead, slips on a grey woollen knee-length dress, and some black baby-doll flats. She looks at herself in the mirror again. She stares for a few minutes, seeing through her reflection, then sits on the edge of her bed and hangs her head in her lap. *I suppose I had better put some makeup on. Gabe, I'm trying. Can you at least give me credit for that?*

Ivy takes the plate of pancakes into the kitchen and contemplates throwing them in the trash, but covers the plate in plastic wrap and leaves it in the fridge instead. She thinks about the plastic wrap prank she played on Amir. She'd covered the toilet bowl with it one morning, and he got a nasty surprise during his morning pee. She laughs at the thought, but the back of her throat constricts trying to hold back tears. She picks up her cell and writes a message: *Can't come in early. Just got up & now late.*

ailish

It's almost eleven at night before Ailish hears Kit shuffle out of her bedroom. From the couch in the lounge, she lifts an arm in the air, and claps her fingers in her palm to acknowledge Kit when she enters.

"You want some OJ?" Kit calls from the kitchen. Ailish can hear a knife slicing through the oranges she just picked off the tree.

"No thanks, sweetheart, I just brushed my teeth. Will you come and join me? There's an amazing documentary on ABC about Gustave Flaubert."

"Yeah, okay . Coming."

Kit sits on the couch chewing a chocolate-coated teddy bear biscuit. She mumbles, "He's the one who wrote *Salammbô*, isn't he?"

"Yes. Yes, he is." Ailish turns her whole body to look Kit in the eye. Her pose acquires finesse. An elitist air of power. Most of all, pride. "How are you familiar with *Salammbô*? I've only ever taught *Madam Bovary* in my course."

"At one of my lectures about nineteenth-century France." Kit scrunches up her nose and bends her fingers into a quote. "'It was criticized for its encrustations of archaeological detail,'" Kit says in a deep posh British accent.

"Oh yes. They just mentioned that. Gee, you honestly surprise me sometimes, Kit. Where do you hide all of this knowledge?"

Ailish stares at Kit for a few seconds, lips pursed, trying to differentiate between feelings of delight and frustration, as Kit shrugs and downs her juice. She wants to ask her about the tutor position, but is hesitant to break Kit's apparent (and rare) tolerance of her in fear of ruining a perfectly pleasant midnight hour of quality time.

Ailish sniffs and pulls pins from her hair. She holds her thighs together and rests the pins in her lap. As the pins come out, one by one, her long locks of grey-streaked chestnut hair fall over her false left breast. It's been almost three years since she'd beaten breast cancer, but she still can't get used to the lack of feeling there. She wonders whether this is why Kit has hung around so long. *Is she afraid to leave me alone?*

"You should wear your hair out more often, Mum. It suits you." Kit places her empty glass on the coffee table, beside the Indian art coaster.

"Oh. Thank you. That was much unexpected." *And now a compliment. Should I be suspect?* Ailish puts Kit's glass on the coaster, trying not to make a deal of it.

Kit smiles as if to say, "You're welcome," and gets comfortable in the corner of the couch with her legs stretched out.

"Mum?"

"Hmm?" Ailish hums, trying to decipher Kit's expression and listen to the documentary at the same time.

"I've been thinking ..."

"Hmm?" This time a little lower in tone. *Yes. It looks like I should be suspect.*

"I guess I'll take you up on your offer."

Or not. "Oh, that's wonderful, sweetheart."

Ailish, confused by Kit's sudden obedience, turns to look at the TV again, just while she ponders what the sugar is going on. She's frightened of Kit seeing her face. Ailish knows that if one tiny ill expression escapes, the whole world will certainly discern what she is thinking and feeling. Well, that's what Roger told her when she had to learn to mask her thoughts and feelings for fear of being caught in their act.

"'Oh, that's wonderful?'" Kit laughs.

"Well, what do you want me to do, Kit? Pat you on the back? You're old enough to make your own decisions," Ailish snaps, head turned, still staring at the screen, hoping to make it clear she is no longer obligated to live at home, without saying it outright.

"No. I just thought—"

"Thought what, darling?"

"Ugh. Doesn't matter."

"So you're not going to go overseas then?" *How did my daughter become so scatterbrained?*

"I guess not."

"You guess not, or you are not? The last thing I want is for you to establish yourself at Uni and then abruptly depart." Ailish tries to keep a straight face, but underneath her calm display she kicks herself for disturbing the peace with her transparent tone.

"I won't leave, Mum. Chill."

Chill. Chill? Why ever does she speak like that? Why is she constantly fighting against her educated nature?

They sit in silence. Ailish pretends to watch the documentary, but all she can think about is Roger. Kit's desire to look for him has dredged up those sickening feelings again—feelings of guilt for keeping her long-lasting relationship with him a secret, and that "event" she keeps trying to persuade herself never happened. She wonders if she should confess it to Kit, but she's afraid she'll ask Ivy about it, and Ivy will ask Eleanor, and then Eleanor's trust—not to mention Kit's and Ivy's—will be destroyed. Despite wanting her daughter to be happy, she prays Kit won't find any clues to Roger's whereabouts. Because if Kit does find out where he is, she'll sooner or later find out the other secret too. The secret she's kept from everyone. The secret she's afraid will banish her from Kit's heart forever.

Ailish runs her tongue over her front teeth and sighs. The sigh that involuntarily slips out when she wants Kit's attention. She wonders if Kit has noticed this and just not mentioned it. She can feel Kit sneaking glances at her, like electrical currents.

"What's wrong?" Kit asks as she smells under her left arm.

"Nothing. It's good deodorant, isn't it?"

"Yep. Will you make me some more?"

That's a first. "Sure."

"Cool."

"Well, I'm off to bed," Ailish says, desperate to relax her face. "Don't forget to turn off all the lights before you go to bed."

Kit nods, rolling her eyes and squeezing an infected mosquito bite on her inner thigh. Ailish wants to tell her to leave it alone, but she bites her tongue.

Ailish gathers her hairpins and goes to her bedroom. She closes the door behind her and quietly turns the key. She doesn't usually lock her door, for fear of a bush fire scare. But tonight she's afraid Kit will walk in on her, despite not having done so since she turned thirteen.

She grabs a footstool and places it in front of her closet so she can reach the highest cupboard. From the top shelf she pulls out an old 1970s' Australian-made Ugg boot shoebox, filled with letters and loose photos, tinged orangey-brown over time.

She steps down, with perfect balance, conscious of the strength in her thighs and proud of herself for being so fit in her late forties. She empties the box onto her bed and finds what she is looking for: a photo of her and Roger smiling happily for the camera. Roger's sister, Constance, took the shot.

Before Ailish got pregnant with Kit, she and Constance had been really close. Together they'd plotted how Roger would finally leave Eleanor. Constance never liked Eleanor. Thought she was cold and clinical. Eleanor didn't like Constance either, and always found excuses to keep Ivy away from Roger's family.

Ailish kept in contact with Constance for a little while after Kit was born and Roger disappeared, but soon lost touch after developing a close bond with Eleanor and Ivy.

When Kit was four, Ailish received a letter from Constance, saying that Roger had returned, remarried, and had another daughter, and to call if she wanted to introduce Kit to him and meet her baby sister. She regrets visiting Roger and Beth that day more than any other in her life. And from that day forward, never contacted any of them again.

Ailish finds and opens the letter she received twenty-one years ago. She stares at the phone number scribbled at the bottom. She lifts the receiver of the phone by her bed and slowly dials the number, taking even breaths, in and out, to maintain her calm. She brings the phone to her ear. It only rings once before a young lady answers.

"Yeah?"

Ailish opens her mouth to speak, but nothing comes out. Her ears grow hot and her mouth turns dry. She lifts her hand to her mouth as though she has just said something offensive and wishes to apologize.

"Hello? Hello? Ma, if you're drunk 'n' been picked up by the coppers again, you can stay there the bloody night, I freakin' mean it this time, orright? Hello?"

Without a word, Ailish hangs up the phone, taking care not to make any noise.

ivy

On her way to work, Ivy watches happy huddled-together couples stroll through the gently falling snow, arms linked, hands held, heads leaning on shoulders. Her sixth sense and cerebral cortex are negotiating the possibilities a relationship with Brian could bring. Perhaps they are meant for each other. Why else would they have met, and be constantly drawn together? But that's how she'd felt about Amir too.

Now there's another factor to take into consideration. Roger. Memories of her father are activating her hate circuit, which in turn reminds her of Gabriel's constant pressure to speak to a therapist.

Paying ridiculous amounts of money to be told she needs to forgive her father in order to accept the men in her life is useless. She knows this. The thing is, though, she doesn't want to forgive him. She doesn't ever want to forgive him. Nor does she ever want to see him again. But deep down there is a little voice that keeps probing at Ivy's soft spot—a spot she never had the nerve to ask Eleanor the medical term for. It nudges at her, mimicking her heartbeat.

As she enters Ditsy Daisy's, the first person she sees is Gabriel, sitting in his usual position in the far right corner by the window.

"Hey."

"Hey, sweetcakes. Sit." Gabriel gestures with an upturned hand for Ivy to take the seat opposite. "How much time do you have?"

"Um, 'bout twenty *minuten*."

"Das ist gut," Gabriel replies dragging out the last word and wobbling his head side to side.

"Thanks for the pancakes."

"My pleasurooni." Gabriel takes a sip of his cappuccino and swallows it with an expression of disgust.

"What's wrong?"

"It's cold."

"Well, how long have you been sitting here letting it get cold?"

Gabriel looks out the window with an expression of deep thought. "About half an hour."

Ivy laughs. "Why don't you try drinking your coffee when it's given to you, for a change?"

"Because it's usually too hot."

"Gabe."

"What?"

"You're a case."

"Looked in the mirror lately?"

Ivy ignores him. Gabe looks out the window again and grins. "Lover boy's here." He winks.

"What? Shit. I told him I was running late and couldn't meet. Cover for me—I'm going out back."

Gabriel grabs Ivy's elbow as she stands. "Too late. He's spotted you."

Ivy mouths, "Fuck."

As Brian struts down the aisle, Gabriel whispers, "Say it was an emergency," and assumes an expression of anxiety, hanging his head in his hands.

Brian approaches with hesitant steps. "Ivy, I thought—"

Ivy holds her finger to her lips and flicks her head in

Gabriel's direction. Brian looks at Gabriel and frowns. He mouths, "Is he okay?" Ivy shakes her head, gets out of her seat, and pulls Brian aside so that Gabriel can't hear. Supposedly.

"He's having boyfriend troubles."

"Oh. But—"

Ivy bites her thumbnail, head down, glancing upward.

"—didn't he stay at your place last night?"

Ivy stiffens from the inside out. *Shit, shit, shit.* "Um, yeah, but, he, er … he went home this morning and"—Ivy raises the level of her voice a little—"and the bastard moved half his stuff out of their house."

"That's terrible," Brian whispers.

"Yeah, I think I should stay with him before I start my shift. Sorry, for, um—"

"Oh, no, no, I understand. Don't worry. I'll just be over there, okay?" Brian points to an empty table next to an elderly couple who are sitting arm in arm, reading from the same newspaper. Ivy becomes momentarily entranced by their glowing content.

"Sure. I'll come over when I start my shift."

"Great." Brian kisses Ivy on the cheek, as if a habitual act, and walks away too fast to notice Ivy blush. Ivy sits back down with Gabriel, and he lifts his head a little, making sure Brian can't see him before opening his mouth.

"Well, that was a memorable way to meet someone for the first time. Thanks a lot, Ive," Gabriel hisses.

"I'm sorry. But it was your idea, and you were *brill.*" Ivy touches Gabriel's hand. "Thanks."

"Yeah. You owe me big-time, sweetcakes. Anyway, what's your problem?"

"I just couldn't do it."

"Do what?"

"Have coffee with him this morning."

"Ivy!"

"Shh, Gabe."

"Honey, if you ain't gonna get yourself back on your feet, then I'm not gonna waste my time saving your sorry ass." Gabriel shakes a finger at Ivy's nose.

Ivy clenches her teeth and pouts her lips. "I'd better go out back."

"Yeah. You do that. And while you're at it, start to picture yourself, seventy years old, living in Eleanor's hospital-white overly-disinfected house, alone and miserable, with an unwanted mental list of existing operating tools and medical jargon to show for your life."

Ivy screws up her nose and punches at the air in Gabriel's direction. Gabriel shrugs and begins to flick through a *National Geographic*.

In the staff room, Ivy guzzles a 50 ml bottle of water without coming up for air before laying herself bare in the coffee jungle. Raquel has just signed in too and is already inundated with takeaway orders. Once again, the floor has been neglected due to Ivy's delay in clocking in on time.

"Wow. And here comes the queen," Raquel says as she froths milk and avoids eye contact as usual.

"Sorry. I'll get straight onto the floor."

Raquel pauses, looks up, and smiles with shock. "Cool. Thanks."

Ivy realizes she's been a little disrespectful of Raquel's coffee-making skills. She wonders what it's like to actually enjoy making coffee, to take pride in something so simple, like Raquel does. To not long for excellence, or the need to succeed in something unique. Ivy has tried to experience it here in Seattle, but it's not working. She's not living up to the notion that a simple life is a better life. She needs something bigger, despite not being entirely convinced she feels that way.

While Ivy scans the tables to see which ones need clearing, the elderly couple next to Brian signal for her attention.

"Good morning, what can I get you?" she asks the couple. Ivy can sense Brian staring at her, masking his action by typing on his laptop, but she can't find the nerve to turn around and see for sure. She scratches her left brow, at the little bump that remains under her skin from the eyebrow ring that lasted less than a week, attempting to hide her uncontrollable embarrassed smirk. She turns a couple of degrees to the right so she can't see him.

"Could you bring me another cappuccino, dear?" the man asks in a kind British accent, pushing his reading glasses up his nose.

"Certainly, sir. Can I bring you anything, ma'am?"

"Oh no, dear. I'm still sipping on my tea. But"—the lady lowers her voice into an almost whisper and leans forward—"I think the lad on your left might, dear." She winks and slips back into her previous position.

Ivy nods, trying not to smile, but she can't hold it in any longer when the man turns to Brian and says, "She is quite a splendid specimen of a woman, if I might say so myself."

Brian looks up, turning quite red. "Thanks for pointing that out. I'm not sure I would have found the courage to say that myself." Brian chuckles in an oddly feminine way. The man and woman nod in approval.

Ivy slides her feet to Brian's table. "Okay, Brian. What can I getcha?" Ivy asks, looking at Brian's laptop.

"A proper date?"

The couple next to them pretend to ignore their conversation, but they are both smiling in what seems to be quiet satisfaction.

Ivy looks up from the keypad. "A proper date? What's a *proper* date?"

Brian closes his laptop, puts it in his briefcase, takes his time gathering his belongings, and throws a couple of dollars on the table. He hadn't even ordered anything. He stands as close to Ivy as possible without being threatening or indecent. Close enough for his briefcase to brush against her dress and send shivers down her legs and into her toes. He pulls a slip of paper out of his back pocket. As he slides the slip of paper into Ivy's apron pouch, his hand hovers directly above her crotch. She holds her breath and his glare for just a moment, before he removes his hand, smirks, and walks casually out of the café.

"I'll be waiting," Brian says, right before the door swings shut behind him.

Ivy's skin tingles with lust and fear as she watches Brian walk across the street through the front shop window and enter the high-rise building on the other side. He doesn't even look back to see her reaction. Ivy envisions a victorious smile on his face.

"Well, dear. What is it?" the lady asks, pouring the last little drop of tea into her cup.

"Um, I, er …" Ivy puts her computerized notepad down on the table where Brian had been sitting, pulls out the piece of paper, and reads it out loud. "The Moore. 7:30 p.m. Tonight."

"What's the Moore, dear?" the lady asks.

"It's a live music venue."

"Ah. Isn't that lovely, dear? He's taking you to see a concert," the man says, pulling his specs down his nose a little to gaze over them.

Ivy folds the piece of paper and puts it back into her apron. Her lips curl up at the edges, but it's not really a smile. *Is it?*

"Ivy," Raquel calls. "Can you deal with table seven? *Please.*"

Ivy's head fills with guilt. If guilt could be heard, it would sound like hail. She's supposed to be supervising Raquel, not the other way around.

kit

It's been quite a few years since Kit has stepped foot into Ailish's office. Not because she hasn't been invited, but because the smell of the wall-to-wall shelves of books prods at her subconscious, *You should have studied literature. You should have studied literature.* A voice she's been trying to ignore.

Ailish's feelings and responses after reading these books are pressed firmly into the pages like dried flowers. The smell triggers some of Kit's fondest memories, hours tucked safely behind many a hardback on the beanbag in the corner while Ailish prepared lectures at her desk, looking up every now and again with a proud smile. Before she started high school, she was convinced she would one day become a famous writer, but then puberty took over, and literature became a nuisance and a bore. She needed something more hands-on, adventurous, but in the end archaeology didn't turn out to be much like *Indiana Jones and the Last Crusade*. She persisted with it though, and now it seems too late to turn back.

"So now what?" Kit asks as she sits in the seat where Ailish's students are often interrogated as to why they've failed to hand in their assignments. "Who's gonna be my superior?"

"Er … you're looking at her, sweetie."

"Excuse me?" *Oh shit.*

"I'm your superior. You are going to be my shadow."

"Mum, you've got to be kidding me."

"Do I look like I'm kidding you?" Ailish puts her hands on her hips, smiling as if she's just succeeded in executing the world's best con.

Kit nurses her forehead and stumbles and falls into the twenty-year-old beanbag. "I think I'm going to faint."

"Kit, stop overreacting. I'll assign you to other lecturers as well. Don't be so histrionic."

"I thought I was going to be completely assigned to another lecturer." Kit flings her arms out to the side and waves them about as if she were a washed-up fish.

"May I ask what is so bad about being assigned to me?"

"Because I've been your shadow for, like, my whole life."

Ailish sifts through some papers on her desk, reading glasses perched on the end of her nose. With a forced smile, she extracts what she is looking for.

"Here it is. Fill out this form. Sign it, so I can take it to the dean's office for him to approve.

The dean! "Oh, okay, cool." Kit jumps to her feet with a little too much enthusiasm, holding out her hand for Ailish to pass her the form.

"That was a mighty quick change of tune." Ailish takes off her glasses and lets them dangle from her neck, but her head is slightly bowed, eyes peering upward as if her glasses are still on her nose.

"I'm just being cooperative. Don't get your knickers in a twist," Kit replies, snatching the document from Ailish's hand. "Got a pen?"

"Yes." There is a pen in a holder on Ailish's desk that is clearly within Kit's reach, but Ailish obliges and hands her one anyway. Kit signs her name on the dotted line without reading a word.

"Okay. It's signed. Where's the dean's office?" Kit asks, holding the form to her chest.

"Oh, don't worry, sweetie, I'll take it." Ailish holds out her stiff hand to retrieve the document.

"No, I'll …" Kit's voice is a little desperate. She realizes so, and brings her volume down a notch. "*I'll* take it. Anyway, I'd like to meet him."

"What's the hurry? You'll meet him eventually." Ailish breaks eye contact and turns her computer on. For a split second, Kit is stricken with panic, triggered by guilt. Has Ailish caught on to her agenda? Unlikely. Especially since she doesn't even know if Ailish is aware that the dean and Roger were friends.

"Um, yeah, but I just want to show my appreciation for the opportunity, that's all." *Please don't have a red face. Please don't have a red face.*

Ailish stands up straight, squints, puts her glasses back on and her hands on her hips. Kit gulps down a build-up of saliva.

"I don't think it's a good idea. Not yet. Go get a cup of coffee or something. What is it that you young folks drink nowadays? Frappélatte?" Ailish shakes her head as if fending off an insect. "I'll have your schedule finalized by the time you get back."

Kit wonders when Ailish is going to stop treating her like she's twelve and holds back a frown.

ailish

Ailish shoos Kit away and wonders when Kit is going to grow up—a speculation that requires too much of her attention at this stage of Kit's life. When Kit enroled in the archaeology course, Ailish thought she had finally taken control, finally assessed future possibilities and made a life-changing choice on her own, until she discovered Ivy had influenced her decision. *The last thing I desire is to throw her out, but how else am I going to get the message across?*

"Mum, seriously, I think I can handle it. Where's the dude's office?" Kit asks, putting her hands on her hips, then instantly returning them to her side.

Ailish huffs. "Well, for future reference, it's left out of my door. At the end of the corridor is a flight of stairs. His office is the last door at the end of the corridor on the right on the next floor. The plaque reads 'Dr. Harold Whittaker.' And please, *please,* if you happen to cross paths, address him with some articulacy, will you? The last thing I need right now is for Harold to think I've hired an incompetent intern. He graciously agreed to overlook the fact that you are my daughter and hire you on the basis of your credentials and 'apparent' academic skills. Your grades are startlingly high, Kit. Why on earth you choose to pretend you're so dense is beyond me." Ailish protrudes her bottom lip and blows upward to remove a loose stand of hair tickling her nose. "Anyway, please don't disappoint me. And do not call him dude."

"Chill, Mum. All's cool."

"Kit!" Ailish raises her eyebrows. *Gosh!*

Kit laughs. "The more articulate one is, the more dangerous words become."

Ailish tsks. "Okay, know-it-all, who did you just quote?"

"May Sarton."

Ailish licks her lips. "Who was she?"

"A poet?"

"And?

"A novelist?"

"And a memoirist. What was the main theme in her works?"

"Lesbianism."

"Where was she from?"

"America."

"Okay, fine." Ailish scratches her brow and cringes. "You can take Harold the form."

"Wicked."

Ugh.

As Kit exits, Ailish walks over to the window. The window she has spent many a contemplative moment at, searching her soul, Roger's soul. Their souls. She remembers the day Roger kissed her for the first time. Right here. By this window. Looking out over acres and acres of green—green that has now been replaced with the new Genetic Research Wing—commenting in imitative Danish accents about the black swan sitting at the edge of the duck pond below. Roger was Hans Christian Anderson, and Ailish his muse.

kit

Kit reaches Dr. Harold Whittaker's office. His door is open a tad, and she can hear him muttering to himself. She looks through the gap to spy before interrupting him and having to go in. He's distributing sheets of paper evenly across his desk, click-clicking a pen on his teeth. He slips and grunts, dropping the pen on the desk. He gets up to inspect his injured gum in the brass-framed mirror on the wall. Hanging next to the mirror are army medals and photos of soldiers in military uniform.

Oh my God. I knew it!

Kit's palms clam up. When Harold sits back down behind his desk, she taps on the door. If she knocked it properly, it might deafen her with its certainty.

"Enter." Harold has a London accent, his voice low and precise, like that of James Mason. Kit pushes the door open, and it brushes against a pile of papers a meter high by the door.

"Hello, Dr. Whittaker?"

"Indeed. That *is* what it reads on the door, is it not?"

Great. I've already made myself look stupid.

Harold looks at Kit over his thick brown-rimmed spectacles, his frown causing a vast array of wrinkles in his forehead. He rests his elbows on the arms of his chair and his wrists on the edge of his desk, holding someone's postgraduate application form in one hand and his pen in the other. He looks like Gregory Peck, from *To Kill a Mockingbird* gone *Crocodile Hunter*.

"Um, sorry to bother you, but I'm Kit." Expecting him to recognize her name, she pauses. Harold clears his throat, still glaring at her over his specs, waiting for her to continue. "Er, right. Ailish Healy sent me to give you my details. I'm the new intern for the English department."

"Oh. Kit." Harold stands and walks to the front of his desk, holding out his hand for her to shake. Kit wipes her palm on the back of her loose olive-green dress before shaking it, hoping the move was sleek enough to not be noticed. "Yes, your mother had nothing but praise to preach about you. I hope you can *up* the department's reputation with your innovative and unique opinions about literature, just like she said you would?" Harold winks and scratches behind his ear.

"Of course. I wouldn't let her down. Or the department, for that matter."

"Marvellous to hear it. Would you like to take a seat?" Harold gestures toward the dark-brown vintage lounge chair that looks like it might weigh as much as an elephant. No beanbags in here. Kit takes a seat and pulls the form out of her bag. She hands it to Harold, and he looks it over briefly before filing it away at the bottom of his filing cabinet, the only relatively modern contraption, aside from the computer, in his office.

"Rightio, Kit. I don't think there is much to say at this moment, but welcome aboard, and we hope your experience here next semester is a pleasant one, and knowledge learned plentiful," Harold recites with a nod.

"Thank you, Doctor." Kit smiles, hoping the twitch of her top lip isn't obvious.

"I hope Ailish has explained you will not be required to be here until the new semester begins next year? I suggest you use this limbo period, as I like to call it, to become familiar with the material you'll be scheduled to teach. I will also provide you with a key card for the department's entrance so you can take advantage of the facilities anytime you wish, which will also serve as an ID to get in and out of the security gates before and after hours. And please, do call me 'sir.' 'Doctor' is rather impersonal, don't you think?"

"Yes. Okay . Thank you, sir." Kit hesitates to get out of her seat, not quite certain if it's her cue to leave.

Just ask him, for God's sake. What have you got to lose?

"My pleasure. I'm sure we'll meet again soon." Harold stands and holds out his hand, towering above her. For a moment Kit looks upward, feeling insignificant. Not an unusual feeling, seeing as she has a mother like Ailish to constantly compare herself to. Kit shakes his hand, stands, and hangs her bag over her shoulder so the handle crosses her chest.

"Thank you, sir. It was a pleasure to meet you."

"Likewise."

Last chance, till who knows when. Do it. Kit opens the door to leave. *No! Just do it!*

"Um, I'm sorry," Kit says, spinning around on her heel. "I don't mean to hold you up, but I have a quick question."

"Of course. If I can be of any assistance to my staff, I'm always available."

Kit flicks her hair behind her shoulders and adjusts the position of her bag. "Well, it's not literature-related, but you wouldn't happen to know how my mother can contact Roger Price, would you?"

"Ah." Harold pauses for a moment to stare at the floor. "Yes, I think I still have his number somewhere. Ailish desires to contact him? May I ask what initiated such a decision?" Harold's demanding posture weakens, and his shoulders slouch. The confidence and certainty in his voice depletes, assuming a more casual and concerned manner.

"I'm not sure. She wouldn't say." Kit clenches the handle of her bag, praying this doesn't get out of hand.

"Hmm, doesn't that make you just a little curious? Surely, you'd … oh, I'm terribly sorry—this is none of my business. One moment while I have a look in my address book."

Phew! "Thank you." Kit loosens her grip and hangs her arms by her sides. She lingers by the door, biting the dry skin from her bottom lip and searching for someone who might resemble Roger in the photographs on the wall by the mirror. But she can't see the soldiers' faces. If only she could take a closer look to see if he were in there some-where. Not that she'd recognize him, but perhaps she might experience some sort of instinctual connection. Maybe if she shuffles a little closer …

"Here it is." Kit is startled by Harold's uncharacteristic and enthusiastic tone. "I'm afraid I don't have any direct contact with Roger anymore. Though, I do hold very fond memories of our time together in the Army. I do, however, have his sister's contact details. Surely she will be able to steer Ailish in the required direction. Let me jot the number down for you. Here you are—Ms. Constance Price."

With Constance's phone number throbbing beside the photograph in her handbag, Kit makes her way back to Ailish's office. She walks quickly, glancing backward every few steps, as if Harold might be about to chase her down the corridor to retrieve the number, realizing she lied.

Kit has never lied to anyone before, let alone a superior she is supposed to respect and one she has just met—not to mention one who is offering her an opportunity to learn for free. Of course, she's kept secrets. But that's not techni-cally lying if you haven't been asked, right? The realization that she has just betrayed her own mother hits her in the chest and burns, as if she has swallowed a chilli whole, and it's lodged itself in her airway.

Innovative and unique opinions? Does she really think that about me, or is it just a ploy to get my foot in the door? Fuck.

Ailish's office door is completely shut, and for the first time Kit looks at the plaque with Ailish's name on it. It's not like all the others, though. It's curled up at the edges, and yellow like aged sticky tape. Kit picks the right edge with her index finger, and it peels away with ease. She reveals the letters *I-C-E* before the sticker begins to tear and she thinks better of continuing. She pushes it back down with her thumb. She remains in this position, with her thumb holding the corner of the sticker firmly down, frozen, as name possibilities sift through her mind. *I-C-E? … Price! What the …? This was Dad's office?* Kit clenches her fists and opens the door so hard that it ricochets off the wall.

"How could you lie to me, Mum?" Kit screams. "I've never lied to you. Ever."

ailish

Ailish is finishing up with Kit's schedule, when her door bursts open and a picture frame drops from the wall. *I knew I hadn't nailed that up properly.* Her daughter's face is flushed, and tears anticipate escape. She blurts out something desperate, almost incomprehensible, except for "How could you …?"

"How could I what, sweetheart?" Ailish puts her glasses on her head in order to secure some loose strands of hair hanging in her face.

"Lie to me!" Kit's hands are on her hips and her frown more vivid than Ailish has ever seen. *What on earth did Harold say to her? What could he possibly …?*

"Honey, lower your voice. What has got into you? What are you talking about?"

"That's Dad's name on the plaque underneath yours, isn't it? Isn't it?" Kit yells, throwing her bag to the floor. "How could you say to me all these years that you don't know where to start looking?"

Ailish brings her hands to her face and cups them around her mouth and nose, focusing on her feet, her big black ugly toenail hiding underneath five layers of matt apricot enamel. She releases her hands from her face and looks up, takes a deep breath, and stares at the skirting boards, not wanting Kit to see the shame flicker through her eyes. *Damn it, Ailish! Me and my stupid need to preserve his presence.* She bites her lip, about to respond, but Kit interrupts.

"Why didn't you ever tell me he worked here with you? You could have easily found out how to find Roger all these years. Couldn't you? You just didn't want—"

"Kit. Stop yelling and sit down for Pete's sake, and let me explain." Ailish guides Kit toward the beanbag, knowing she feels secure there, her right hand gently on her upper back. She shuts the office door, pushes off her beige leather sandals from her heels, and sits down beside her on the carpet, crossing her legs yoga style.

"Kit, we didn't work together. I was his student."

"His what? What do you mean?" Kit asks, holding onto Ailish's gaze. Ailish can feel Kit's stare search for truth. Through her reflection in Kit's hazel eyes, Ailish can see, for the first time, what she has been running from all these years: the fear of not being loved; of breaking through the self-built glass wall and being judged, not only for what people can see, but for her past; for the secrets she's hidden and almost convinced herself weren't real.

"I thought you said you had only known him long enough to get pregnant with me?" A tear lingers at the corner of Kit's left eye.

"I know. I know I said that. Kit, I …" Ailish clutches at the roots of her hair with her elbows resting on her knees. She lets her hair down and runs her fingers through it, without taking the usual care to loosen the pins one by one. A few fly across the room. "This is very hard to say," she mumbles behind the mop of hair hanging over her face. Kit isn't moving or saying a word, but Ailish can hear her swallow sorrow in her extended breaths.

"Mum, please. Just tell me. I won't be angry. I promise. I just want to find him. Get to know him before … Well, Mum, what can possibly be wrong with wanting to know my father?"

"Get to know him before what, Kit? Getting acquainted with Roger is not going to define who you are. You don't need your father to shine. You already shine. You are already *you*." Ailish pushes Kit's hair behind her ears and rests her hands on her cheeks. "You haven't recognized your own potential yet."

Kit flicks Ailish's hands from her face with a swift shift of her head.

"You're right," Ailish says. "You deserve to find your

father. And I can completely understand why. But you have to understand that this is difficult for me because I ... well, the affair between Roger and me lasted for ... a very long time. We were both very secretive about it because I was his student. And he was married."

"To Eleanor." Kit's frown grows deeper.

Ailish nods toward the floor, focusing on the cracks in her heels.

"Does Eleanor know it lasted so long?"

Ailish shakes her head, pressing her lips together. "Not that I know of."

Please don't cry. Please don't cry in front of Kit.

"Does Ivy know anything?"

"No one knows, Kit. I know it was thoughtless of me to keep this from you. I do know that, but ..." Ailish takes Kit's hands in hers and rests them in Kit's lap, leaning forward enough to feel her breath brush across her face. "I was afraid of ruining my friendship with Eleanor. She helped me through my pregnancy with you. She helped her husband's lover, for goodness' sake. Darling, Eleanor did a very selfless thing, and as a result we became great friends. I just couldn't tell her, not after all she'd done. And then, of course, if I had, what would have become of you and Ivy? You may never have had the opportunity to grow up together. To be sisters. I made the decision I thought was best at the time, for you, for all of us."

Ailish pauses, sensing Kit's reluctance to keep holding hands. She releases her grip and strokes Kit's face before folding her arms below her breasts. "I haven't been able to summon the nerve to tell you. I apologize, Kit. I truly do. Please. Can you forgive me?"

Kit still hasn't broken her stare. Ailish attempts to hug her, but Kit stiffens in her embrace.

"Is there anything else I should know?" Kit asks, her tone bringing on the winter solstice.

Yes. "No. No, of course not."

"So you seriously have no idea how to get hold of Roger?"

"No. I don't."

Kit looks out the window, her eyes becoming a pale green from the reflection of the eucalyptus trees outside. She stands up to leave, but Ailish grabs her hand and pulls her back down.

"Please, don't tell Ivy about this. Please."

Kit's eyelids drop.

"Please?"

"I won't."

"Thank you."

"Yeah. Whatever."

Kit is halfway out the door, when Ailish asks, "Are we okay? You and I, are we okay?" Kit nods, vacancy oozing from the sadness in her eyes, and closes the door behind her.

Ailish falls face-first into the beanbag, drawing and releasing a manic breath as if she has been underwater for the last ten minutes. Kit's scent is bleached into the fabric, Ailish's breath and tears doing nothing to rid the years and years of her daughter's smell encompassing her face. *You should have told her about the other sister. You should have told her. It was your chance. Oh my God. You stupid, stupid woman.*

Ailish punches the beanbag with both her fists, one on each side of her head, and screams into it, muffling the sound, stretching her mouth as wide as it can go so that her lips sting, the pain not even whispering the punishment she thinks she deserves.

Gabriel and Ivy empty Ivy's wardrobe onto the bed. Ivy stares at her clothes, shivering in her underwear. *Maybe I can just say I'm coming down with something. Got a high temperature, maybe. It's not a good idea to be going out in this weather, right? Especially if I have a fever.* Gabriel squints at Ivy, hands on his hips, weight on one foot, head tilted to the side, and taps his toes.

"I'm not going," Ivy shakes her head and rubs her goose-pimpled arms.

"You can't stand him up," Gabriel squeals as if his entire clothing collection is about to be thrown out into the muddy street. "Sweetcakes!" Gabriel quickly alters his tone after seeing her more-adamant-to-not-go expression.

"Why not? It's been done to *me* before." Ivy shrugs. "And I got over it."

"Are you trying to frustrate the bejesus outta me on purpose, or are you trying to frustrate the bejesus outta me on purpose? I mean, just let me know, you know, so I can figure out how to proceed here," Gabriel says, moving his head side to side like a Motown soul sister.

Ivy pushes her clothes to the right side of her bed and gets under the covers to warm herself up. Gabriel sits next to her on the edge and rubs her legs from above the duvet as if trying to comfort a child.

"Okay, Ive, you are so not thinking straight. I think we have to do something to get you in the mood. Brian's a spunk on a stick. You're mad to even contemplate standing him up."

"Can you keep telling me that?" Ivy asks, frowning at her own ridiculousness. Gabriel strokes Ivy's hair. "Have I got a fever? It'd be great if I had a fever," she says, ignoring her conscience.

"Ive. Listen to yourself. You're wishing yourself to be sick. And for what? So you can avoid going to see what is probably the best thing that has happened to you in, like, a really long time?"

"I'm an idiot, aren't I?"

"Yeah, sweetcakes, you're an idiot. And I'm confused. You seemed so ready to jump back into life the other day. You threw your drumsticks away and even bought a revealing dress. When was the last time you showed off your flawless skin? See, that was a step forward. And I was so rooting for you. Come on." Gabriel pats Ivy's legs. "Tell me why you went and bought that black dress. There must have been a reason."

Ivy leans her head back. It makes contact with the wall. She closes her eyes and thinks back to her vision of archaeological genius standing outside the department store. The dress made the idea all the more realistic. It gave her an air of confidence she hasn't felt since before the divorce. If only the positivity didn't come in such erratic waves.

"I had a revelation."

"What kind of revelation?"

"That I need to forget Amir and get my confidence back." Ivy squeezes her fingers on her left hand until her knuckles dig into each other and throb.

"Only your confidence?"

"No. Motivation to succeed, I suppose." Ivy swallows a build-up of saliva and gets a flashback of making love to Amir in the back of the laboratory at Uni, surrounded by ancient Chinese shellfish fossils. She sinks further down into her bed until she's lying flat on her back.

"Well, here's your chance. Use Brian to get over Amir, and the rest will follow. When you feel good about yourself, you'll want to succeed."

"I just need a push." Ivy turns the corners of her mouth down in a playful frown to mask the real pain.

"Okay. Where are your New Pornographers CDs?"

"Don't bother." Ivy groans, lifting herself up on her elbows. "That won't help."

"Why not?"

"Because I associate them all with Amir. He's the one who introduced me to them."

"Well, sweetcakes, this is *the* perfect time to start associating them with Brian." Gabriel narrows his eyes. He means business. He stands and puts his hands on his hips.

"Yeah, okay." Ivy rolls onto her side and pushes herself into a sitting position on the edge of the bed. Her hair hangs over her face in a matted mess. She flicks her hand toward her bookshelf. "They're in alphabetical order. You'll find them."

"Sweetcakes, can you get out of bed and choose something to wear already?"

"Hello? I'm sitting up."

Gabriel shakes his head, huffs, and mumbles something under his breath, picks up a pair of funky purple corduroy trousers with silver stripes down the vertical seams and a tightly knitted silver sweater, and shoves them into Ivy's chest.

"Here. Wear these."

"Aren't I a bit old for these?" Ivy holds the trousers in front of her face.

"You're never too old for anything, sweetcakes. Just get up and put them on before I punch your nose in."

Crikey. I'm not suicidal or anything.

Ivy runs her fingers through her hair and edges out a few knots. She puts the clothes on, cringing as if being forced to wear an ugly bridesmaid's dress.

Gabriel goes to the bookshelf and scans the CDs from

top to bottom. Not only are they in alphabetical order, but all the ones beginning with vowels are grouped together at the top and the consonants grouped below.

"Hey. I've never noticed this before. What's with the organization?" Gabriel swings his torso around to offer a questioning glare. One side of his face is contorted so much that his cheek is touching his bottom eyelid.

"Oh. Well, can you remember that little singsongy clay-mation cartoon on TV? The one that goes 'a-eee-iii-a, e, i, o, u'?"

"Er, no." Gabriel scoffs as if some food has gone down the wrong hole.

"Must have been an Australian thing."

"That still doesn't explain the grouping."

"I like being reminded of the song. That's all." Ivy thinks about Roger singing and dancing to it with her in front of the TV and hums the tune in her head. Eleanor had been making a cake and whistled as she whisked. The only memory of Eleanor she has that doesn't involve medi-speak.

"Anyway," Gabriel looks at Ivy as though she has completely lost it. "Which album do you want?"

"You choose," Ivy mumbles, head trapped inside the neck of her silver sweater.

"Okay. *Twin Cinema* it is then. What's your favourite song?"

"I don't care."

Gabriel shrugs and puts the disc in the CD player as Ivy goes into the bathroom to put on makeup and fix her hair. "The Bleeding Heart Show" begins to play.

"This is a bit depressing, isn't it?" Gabriel calls with a shrill.

"Just wait. It livens up," Ivy calls back, shocked by the thickness of her voice bouncing off the tiled walls. *Geez, wouldn't want to have a band rehearsal in here.* She sings to herself in the mirror while applying mascara. As the notes exit her mouth, doors to feelings that have been long awaiting revival open. She hasn't listened to any music for months, aside from coffee shop crap, and has completely forgotten how light it makes her feel.

I leapt across three or four beds into your arms
Where I had hidden myself somewhere in your charm

When the middle-eight begins, Ivy jumps out of the bathroom, legs spread wide for balance, mimes playing the building drum rolls, and jumps up and down to the beat. She hits the air, the walls, the couch, and the TV with her invisible drumsticks. Gabriel joins in with the jumping, adds a little air guitar, and sings the *oohs*. They bounce into every room as if trying to find the one that best amplifies their imaginary instruments. A familiar chord pattern reminds her of what was playing at Ditsy Daisy's in the afternoon. She thinks of Brian slipping the piece of paper into her apron and the tingling sensation following it. She closes her eyes and imagines Brian's hand slipping down the front of her pants. Ivy's breath pauses at the thought.

Oh my God. She flicks her eyes open and looks at the zebra clock on the wall of the lounge.

"Turn it off," Ivy yells above the music.

Gabriel flicks his right hand by his ear in question.

"I'm gonna be late."

Ivy pokes the first pair of earrings she finds on her dresser into her ears, grabs her bag and coat, and bolts out the door without her keys.

Ivy and Brian stand outside the Moore after the New Pornographers concert. They head toward Waterfront Park to escape the entwined roar of excited chatter stifling their shy voices. During the ten-minute walk toward the sea they are silent, separated by an arm's length. All that can be heard are their footsteps, the collision of clothing, distant sirens, car horns, and ebbing voices. Brian's aftershave is so strong, Ivy imagines herself hooked under his arm, breathing him in until he disappears; a quick high before telling him she can't do this and is sorry for leading him on.

I don't know what I want.

They reach the violent, obsessive, and thunderous sea. Snow covers a few burned-out spherical lampposts on the pier by the high curved railings. Apparently it's the first time it's snowed in Seattle for years.

"I've got a surprise for you," Brian says after a few moments of admiring the city skyline and the West Seattle Bridge in the darkness.

Ivy mouths, "Who me?" playfully tilting her head. Flakes of snow fall down the back of her neck, chilling her.

She expects him to pull a gift out of his inside coat pocket, but instead he says, "The Seattle Asian Art Museum is looking for a new exhibits developer. You interested?"

Ivy's eyes widen, and she laughs involuntarily. "You're kidding? Of course I'm interested. Do you have contacts there?" Ivy tucks her gloves into her sleeves.

"My brother is an anthropologist. He's their development specialist. He said they were planning to advertise next week, but if you wanted to go in for an interview before week's end, he'd be happy to put you in touch with the deputy director. I put in a good word." Brian smiles, oozing with proud satisfaction.

"Oh my God, Brian!" Ivy bounces on the balls of her feet, crunching the snow beneath them. "You actually asked your brother if there was anything going? Why would you do that for me?"

"Just wanted to help you out. You look so miserable at the café. Anyway, it was good timing, wasn't it?" Brian says, and breathes into his bare hands.

"I don't know what to say." Ivy takes his hands and rubs them between hers without realizing she's actually making physical contact. She jogs on the spot, half to keep warm and half at the prospect of a new job.

It's just what I need.

"'Thank you,' will do," Brian says, not making any move to retrieve his hands from Ivy's.

Ivy tilts her head. "How am I going to repay you for this?"

"Don't be ridiculous. You don't owe me anything."

Ivy gives him a peck on the cheek, places Brian's hands on his chest, and looks out to the sea. The wind blows strands of loose hair behind her shoulders.

"Well, there is something that I'd like," Brian says, putting his arm around Ivy's shoulders and pulling her close to his side.

Ivy's body goes limp, giving in to his touch despite every inner voice yelling at her to pull back. She watches condensed water vapour swim through his mouth as he speaks.

"Anything. What is it?" Ivy says, her voice hovering through the fog, feeling as though she's been possessed by another woman.

"For you to come home with me tonight?"

Ivy stiffens. Brian turns her around and kisses her forehead. Ivy shivers and looks up at him with raised eyebrows.

All this because he wants sex? Seriously?

"I'd just like you to come see where I live," Brian continues. "No naughty stuff, I promise. Unless of course"—he winks and lifts Ivy's chin—"you'd like some."

Normally Ivy would consider these as off signs, and run. But there's something different about this man she can't put her finger on. The inner voices are yelling even louder now, but she chooses to ignore them. There's a reason they have been brought together. She knows it.

"Hug me?" Ivy asks, shivering a little more on purpose.

"Sorry?"

"Can you hug me?"

Brian shrugs a *yes* and opens his coat. Ivy leans into him, and he wraps his coat and arms around her. He squeezes her tight enough for their chests to press together. She doesn't want to get warm. She wants time to think, to get a sense of who Brian is beneath his agreeable and almost "too Mr. Nice Guy" exterior.

Ivy puts her ear to Brian's chest and his heart beat slows. It *slows*. Perhaps she relaxes him? Perhaps he needs her as much as she needs him?

Just go. You've got nothing to lose.

Ivy lifts her head so her nose is touching Brian's chin. "I'd love to come home with you," she whispers. She kisses him, shallowly slipping in her tongue.

I can't believe I'm doing this.

Oh.

Soft lips.

Brian pulls back. His eyes widen, and a huge grin transforms his face from attractive to … *oh-so-yummy.*

Ivy returns the smile as she cups his cold face in her hands.

"Come on," Brian says with a flick of his head. "Let's hail a cab."

brian

Brian opens the door to his small yet cosy open-plan studio apartment, hoping Ivy doesn't freak out over the number of candles scattered all over the joint.

"Wow, this is colourful." Ivy takes her hat and gloves off, and puts them into her coat pockets. Brian chuckles, picking up a pair of elephant-decorated boxers and a mouldy coffee mug from the floor by his bed. Ivy slides to the stereo and CD collection. "Where are your New Pornographers CDs?" she asks. "I need some more beats."

"I don't have any," Brian utters quickly while contemplating where to put the mug. In the sink? He throws it in the trash. He rolls his boxers into a ball and shoots them into the hamper by his bed like a basketball into a net.

"What?" Ivy shrieks, dropping her jaw.

"I just remembered seeing an ad for the concert in *Seattle Sound* when you mentioned them the other night."

"That's cheeky."

I know. "No. Just clever." *Just do it. She wants you. You know it.*

Ivy turns around shaking her head and mumbles something to herself as she inspects the shelf of CDs. Brian wipes his sweaty hands on his thighs and approaches Ivy from behind. He wraps his arms around her, trapping her arms against her body. Ivy loosens in his embrace. *Just. Do. It.* He slips his right hand beneath her sweater and rests his hand on her smooth, flat stomach. The tips of his fingers tease the opening of her pants. Erect and aroused, he bites her ear. Hesitation in Ivy's slight gasp indicates it might have hurt, but doesn't want it to seem so.

"Don't you want any beats?" Ivy asks, bordering breathlessness.

"*You* are my beat," Brian replies, twisting Ivy around to face him and thrusting his tongue into her mouth with a groan. Her tongue is hot and thick and soft like a rose petal. He imagines his penis inside her mouth and groans again.

Ivy undoes Brian's belt buckle with one hand and reaches urgently into his pants, moving his erection so that it pokes through his zipper. They scratch tenderly yet urgently at each other until they are naked and spread out on his bed. Brian presses his groin into Ivy's crotch without slipping himself inside, teasing, licking and nibbling at her nipples. As Brian penetrates her, she moans in what seems like relief. He loses himself in her smell, her soft, sweet jasmine perfume corrupting all rationale. He wants to tell her how much he is in love with her right this very second, but he can't. *I won't.* He couldn't. *I love you.* Could he?

Ivy's cell rings. *Don't answer it. Don't answer it.* Ivy ignores it. It rings out. But it starts again. She fumbles blindly in her bag on the ground by the bed and pulls it out, glancing briefly at the screen with one open eye while gently biting Brian's tongue.

"It's my mother," she pants and slips out from beneath him. "I have to get it." She stands. "Just gimme a minute."

Brian admires her slender and indulgent figure, her ivory skin, her succulent curves. The slight curl at the ends of her wispy locks caress her shoulders as she walks into his bathroom. Brian turns onto his back and massages his erection so it doesn't turn limp. Ivy's voice rises.

"I haven't said anything to Ailish. What are you talking about? Well, just go and visit her if she doesn't pick up the phone. Why do you always have to accuse me? No, wait. Don't hang—"

The flick of Ivy's phone closing infiltrates the frosted glass door. She exits the bathroom flinging her head back and mouths something Brian can't make out. Ivy throws her cell back into her bag and climbs on top of Brian. She inserts him, moves up and down like a robot, directing her stare at the headboard instead of his face, distant, emotionless. Brian stares at the blankness, aroused by Ivy's rapid, powerful pounding as he gets closer and closer to ejaculating. But he is emotionally lost, stranded, confused, afraid to ask her to stop, afraid to wish her to continue. *I want more.* But not like this. *Keep going. Don't stop.* Together, they come, allowing only the slightest of sound to part their lips.

Ivy falls limp on top of Brian's body, her face nuzzled in his neck. "I'm sorry," she mumbles. Her breath is hot against his skin. Brian runs his fingers through her hair, wondering what the hell just happened.

"Sure. It doesn't matter," he replies, wishing he had the nerve to say it did.

kit

As Kit tries to open the jammed front gate to her yard, she spots Sein, sitting on his porch step, cigarette hanging from the corner of his mouth, legs spread, elbows on knees, watching her with a distant gaze. He snaps out of his trance and bolts to the dividing fence. He flings his whole body over at once, balancing himself with one hand.

"Just needs a little nudge, that's all." Sein opens the gate from the inside. He smiles, standing in Kit's path, white teeth glowing in the twilight.

"Yeah. Thanks. Do you mind?" Kit clenches her jaw, narrows her eyes. She wishes the crickets would shut the hell up and Sein would piss off. She's had enough crap to deal with and wants to be left alone. On the other hand, if Sein could finally summon the balls to initiate it, she wouldn't object to a good mind-numbing fuck to forget about her family.

Sein steps aside, barely, and Kit squeezes through the gate, banging her upper arm against his chest by accident. His thin white over-worn T-shirt is damp with odourless sweat. The scent is almost pathetic. But attractive nonetheless. She can't deny that.

Sein is still holding the gate open and staring at her when Kit unlocks the front door.

"Well, you wanna come in or are you just gonna stand there like a bloody guard dog?"

"Yeah, I'll come in." Sein shakes his head. He closes the gate and leaps over a flower bed to get to the door, instead of following the gravel path.

Inside, Kit throws her bag on the couch, slams her keys on the kitchen counter, and gazes out the window at the setting sun. An orange drops to the ground before her eyes. *One by one they're going to rot, until there's nothing left but empty branches and dry leaves. If Mum thinks I'm gonna pick and save all those oranges myself, then she can bloody think twice.*

Ailish still hasn't come home. Kit hopes she doesn't. She hopes she spends one of those sleepless nights in her office assessing monotonous essays, and beats herself up over her pathetic lies.

After all I've done for you, you fuck.

I love you.

"What's wrong?" Sein asks, sitting on the stool by the kitchen counter. Close, but not too close. Kit switches her attention from the orange tree to Sein's face. "Have you been at Uni the *whole* day?" Sein cranes his neck forward in disbelief.

"No. I went to see a friend at work."

"Who?"

"And why is that any of your fucking business?" Kit opens the fridge and pulls out a small bottle of water.

"Sorry." Sein raises his eyebrows sarcastically. He grabs an orange from the fruit bowl and begins to peel it.

"Her name's Eydie. Happy?" Kit downs half the bottle of water in one go, and Sein continues to peel the orange, dropping the skin on the counter. Kit looks at the peel, and then at Sein, wondering if he is just going to leave it there and expect her to clean it up. His lazy expression briefly reminds her of Ivy's ex-husband, Amir, a man she would prefer not to associate with Sein, the one and only guy she has ever been attracted to, but too proud to admit. What a cliché. Falling for the boy next door.

"Did you and your mum have a fight again or something?" Sein focuses on his orange.

Kit tries to catch her breath from gulping down the water. "Why haven't you ever tried to kiss me all these years?"

Sein, having begun to chew a slice of orange, laughs with a hoarse throat and a little waver. He splutters juice on the counter. Quickly chewing what he has left in his mouth, with an expression of disbelief, he swallows, and rests the remainder of the fruit on the peeled skin.

"You're kidding, right? Why have you been so mean to me all these years?"

"I haven't been mean to you."

"Yeah, you have."

"Okay, maybe I have. A bit. But don't you men find that appealing?"

Sein guffaws. "Not where I come from."

Kit puts the half-empty bottle of water back in the fridge, shrugs, and walks out of the room toward the stairs.

"What did I say?" Sein asks, defensiveness gurgling in his throat. "Where are you going?"

"My room," Kit calls, already halfway up the stairs.

She lies on her bed and stares at the ceiling. Kit hears the front door slam shut. The windows rattle. She can hear Sein kick the gravel. And then a rock. She gets up and opens her window, sticks her head through it, and calls out for him to wait. Sein turns around, looks up toward Kit, and lifts his arms in question. They fall back down, slapping on his faded ripped jeans.

"Why? You're just going to push me away again. You wanna know why I've never tried to kiss you? Because you're cold, cruel, and you don't give a shit about anyone but yourself. Why would I want to kiss a girl like that? A girl that has no …"

Stunned, Kit closes the window to shut out his voice, and turns her back to it.

A wave of overwhelming despair flushes through her, head to toe. Years of frustration and pressure to keep her emotions under control during Ailish's ordeal with cancer and then uncertain remission come gushing out in thick silent tears, causing her body to quake and drop to the floor. "I hate you, Mum! I *fucking* hate you!" she screams toward the ceiling.

Kit can hear Sein re-enter the house and come running up the stairs. Kit pounces to lock her bedroom door, ashamed at herself and what she has become. *You're an adult, for God's sake.* She sits on the floor in front of her door, holding her knees to her chest. Sein pounds at it, twists the handle up and down.

"Leave me alone," Kit cries. "I'm not worth it. Really."

"Kit, I'm sorry. Can you please let me in?" Sein's voice is calm, smooth, sympathetic.

Kit monitors the gap under the door, where she can see the white soles of Sein's sneakers. They disappear. She panics that she has driven him away for good, and unlocks it, opens it. Sein is halfway down the stairs, looking up, with one hand holding on to the railing. He walks to the top again and stands in the doorway, smiling the peace-maker smile—the only thing that has stopped Sein and Kit from hating each other all these years. Even as small children they'd fought like brother and sister.

Sein leans his shoulder against the door frame and crosses one leg over the other. Kit looks at the floor and steps aside to let Sein come in, but he doesn't. Instead he takes Kit's hands and lifts them up against his own; he is her reflection. He slips his fingers in between hers and pulls her close, then wraps her arms around his neck. Body heat penetrates their clothes, begging to be let loose, pleading to be given the freedom to roam each other's naked skin, naked hearts, naked souls, without the need to have sex.

"I've wanted to kiss you ever since I saw one in the movies," Sein whispers, his lips almost touching hers. "Can I kiss you now?"

Kit nods and softens in Sein's warmth.

ailish

A sharp beam of sunlight wakes her. Her teeth are furry and eyes swollen from an unbearable night of incessant crying. Her underarms are sweaty and in need of a shave. She sits up in the beanbag that cradled her through the night, wishing she could just disappear into it, like Alice in Wonderland down the rabbit hole.

She stands and straightens out her skirt, fingers spread, and gathers her hair into a twist. Holding it together with one hand, she collects her hairpins off the floor, one by one, and secures her hair with them. It's just like riding a bike.

From her desk drawer, she pulls out what she likes to call her bible—Marilynn Robinson's *Housekeeping*—which she's read cover to cover so many times she has lost count. Roger gave it to her as a gift for being the only student to get a perfect score on a thesis, hers being: "Broken Eyes and Buoyant Hair: An Exploration of Gwen Harwood's Pseudonymous Poetry." She holds *Housekeeping* to her nose, breathing it in as if its smell might soothe sorrow.

She opens it to a random page and reads the very first sentence her eyes land on: *And she would feel that sharp loneliness she had felt every long evening since she was a child. It was the kind of loneliness that made clocks seem slow and loud and made voices sound like voices across water.*

Tears stream down her cheeks and stain the porous page with nostalgia for those precious moments she'd had with Roger. She flips to the back inside cover, where Roger has written: *I salute you. Forever yours.*

Interrupted by a knock at her door, she closes the book and places it back in her drawer. After using her thumb knuckles to quickly wipe away her tears, she rubs below her eyes to remove the possibility of smudged mascara.

"Come in," she says in as bright a tone as possible.

Harold enters.

"I'm sorry to disturb you, Ailish. It actually hadn't occurred to me that you might be in this early. I was about to slip this under your door." Harold hands Ailish an envelope. She nods a thank you and places it on the already-built-up pile of mail.

"May I ask if everything is all right?"

"Of course. Why would you think otherwise?"

Do I really look that dreadful?

Harold puts his hands in his pockets and smiles like a psychiatrist. "No particular reason. But you would let me know if there was anything the matter, would you not?"

"Of course." Ailish puts on her happy face, switches on her computer, and pretends to search for something in her handbag as if she has just arrived.

"Would you like me to fetch you a coffee?" Harold asks, rapping the door with his pen.

"That would be delightful. Thank you." Ailish puts on her glasses.

"Black, yes?"

"Yes, thanks. And in my—"

"*Live Love Write* mug. Yes, I'm familiar with that mug." Harold taps the side of his nose as he exits her office and closes the door gently behind him.

Ailish spots Harold's handwriting on the front of the envelope and realizes it's not regular mail. She opens it. It reads:

Allie,

I'm terribly sorry you felt the need to send your daughter to fetch a number for Roger. There's no need to be ashamed of wanting to speak to him again. It has been a very long time. Perhaps he has changed? Please do know that I am always available to confide in if the desire should arise.

Harry

The room caves in on Ailish's head. She empties the contents of her wastepaper basket onto the floor, and scrambles on all fours for the scrunched-up paper bag from yesterday's lunch. She flattens it out, sits up straight, her feet under her behind, and places the paper bag over her mouth and nose. Holding the sides firmly to her cheeks, she breathes in, vacuuming all the air out of the paper bag and into her chest.

In.

Out.

In.

Out.

Dizziness takes hold, her stomach a hurricane. She bends over to vomit on the carpet, but all that escapes is air and spit—spit slippery with fear—fear that she will soon be left with nothing. Nothing and no one.

Nothing.

No one.

kit

It's almost dark outside, and the crickets are making a racket. Sein has been lying naked on Kit's bed all day, listening to her go on and on about calling Constance without the slightest hint of being bored. He's eaten all the icy poles. Maybe that's a sign. He even made some juice from the oranges he picked. He drank most of it, but that's beside the point.

A breeze has picked up, and Kit stands by the open window to take advantage of the cool air. "I'm gonna call Constance today."

"Are you sure you're ready to do that?" Sein lifts his arms above his head and rests his head on his hands. If there wasn't any railing at the bottom of the bed, his feet would be hanging off the edge.

"Yeah. Why wouldn't I be?" Kit gathers her hair and twists it to one side.

Sein shrugs. "Okay. You want me to leave?"

"Nah. Why?" Kit turns around to face him. She fiddles with the elastic of her sports bra and glances down at her breasts to make sure they're straight. Not that they could really de-align themselves too much.

"Thought you might want some privacy. That's all." Sein scratches the edge of his groin.

"Never had any all my life; why would I need it now?"

Sein levers himself into a sitting position and crosses his

legs. "Aw, don't be so hard on your mum. She's a real nice lady." His limp scrotum hangs like melted fudge on Kit's blue cotton bedspread.

Kit scoffs. "I don't think you have a right to say that. You have no idea what I've been through." She hands Sein his boxers, which are flung over the bottom left bedpost.

Sein puts them on. "Ah, come on. She's helped me out so much at Uni. You do know she even tutors me privately for no cost, 'cause she knows my dad can't afford it. Right?"

Kit shakes her head, biting her bottom lip.

"Well, I think that gives me the right to say your mother's a champ." Sein punches emphasis into the mattress with a closed fist and a grin so wide Kit can feel her own lips sting.

You're too young for me.

An internal smile creeps up on Kit like a sun shower. She grabs her handbag and sits next to Sein on her bed with a bounce. "You wanna see a picture of my father?"

"Sure."

She pulls out the photograph and hands it to Sein with a sigh. She rubs her face with both hands as if to wipe away need.

"Why'd you rip out his face?"

"I didn't. At first I thought Ivy had done it, but she said Eleanor did it."

"There aren't any other photos?"

"Nope. Ivy said Eleanor burned them all, and she only found this one because it had accidentally dropped from the box while Eleanor was moving it to the fireplace."

"Why did Eleanor rip out his face if she had planned to burn them?"

"I dunno. Therapy?"

Kit stands on the bed and jumps on it like it's a trampoline, hoping she can free her mind, travel back to when she was a kid and didn't care about anything but cooking up a storm with mud and food dye. Sein holds onto the bedposts to stop himself from bouncing off.

"Kit!" A bedspring pings.

"What? Who cares? I'll get a new bed when I move out."

"No. I don't mean that," Sein shouts, and points to the window. "Ailish has just driven up."

"Crap." Kit gets down and throws on the dress that is lying on the floor beside her bed. "Come on. Get dressed, damn it."

ailish

She turns off the ignition and rests her arms and head on the steering wheel, trying to come to terms with what she may be confronted with inside the house. She has to be strong. She has to summon the power she feels when she quotes someone else's prose, to transfer that control of memory into the muscle of self-worth. Yes, she has made mistakes. And she should use the regret to fuel forgiveness, and hope that the idea rubs off on her daughter too. She can do it. She knows she can.

When she enters the house, Kit and Sein are eating Chinese crackers at the kitchen counter. Kit's hair resembles a bird's nest, and Sein appears to have been roughed up by the mafia. They both look up at her, chewing. They mumble "hi" in unison. Ailish smiles in return, conscious of every minuscule crease in her skin as her lips part and teeth are exposed. She holds the smile a little too long. The front of her gums go dry.

Ailish opens the fridge. "Looks like we need to go to the supermarket." She wipes her brow, her own touch echoing through her body. She can feel Kit scrutinizing her as she massages the back of her neck with her right hand. *Just tell her and finish this mess. You'll get through it just like everything else in your life. Foolishly. But you'll cope. She'll cope.*

Ailish closes the fridge door and turns around. She catches Kit whispering something to Sein and licking the inside of his ear. *When did this happen?* Ailish clears her throat. She would do anything right now to run away like a rebellious adolescent and guzzle down a Slurpee from 7-Eleven. *Yes, even a grown woman like me has a hankering for some frozen consumerist cordial on occasion,* she says to herself to justify her craving.

"Um, Sein, would you mind going home, so I can have a private word with my daughter?" Ailish's pulse flits in her eardrums, teasing balance. The hum of the refrigerator is the only thing keeping her from slipping into another time zone. Kit stops chewing and glares at her.

"Sure. No worries." Sein scoops up a handful of crackers

and signals something to Kit with his hands. Kit nods and winks, her face turning a baby shade of pale. The fly wire springs closed.

"Oh, Mum, I'm *so* sorry. I knew it as soon as I had done it that it was a rotten thing to do. Fuck, I'm really sorry, but you kinda gave me no choice. You know? What else was I supposed to do? Am I fired? Has Harold completely lost respect for me now? Shit, I'm sorry. Are you in trouble with him?" Kit blurts out with chewed-up crackers still in her mouth, her shoulders receding with apparent regret.

Ailish takes a deep breath. A gulp of air that only a few moments ago was ripe with Kit and Sein's newfound lust. Something she wishes she could let Kit devour without family troubles getting in the way. But if she doesn't say something now, things are only going to get worse, and then she might be forced to expose everything.

"Kit. Calm down. Harold hasn't the slightest idea that I didn't send you. You can still intern for us." Ailish leans against the sink by the window, one leg crossed over the other and her arms folded rigidly. "That is, if, after what I'm about to say, you still wish to."

Kit drops the crackers back into the bowl that she's been cradling in her palm. "What's wrong?"

Ailish looks at her feet again. She slouches, too lazy to support her own body weight, laden with regret. She's been doing it a lot lately. And it's something she always told Kit off for. *"Stand up straight; don't slouch. Show the world you are confident and able."* Ailish looks up and clenches her teeth. Their collision echoes in her ears. "There's something you must know. Something I've neglected to tell you."

Kit draws her chin to her chest and swallows. "Okay. What is it?" Her tone is blunt and cold.

The air softens around Ailish's body, as if the cosmos is making room for truth. She can sense a horrible reaction on Kit's part, but it'll be worth it, and she'll be freer. One less thing cluttering her conscience. More room for love and acceptance.

"I'm not sure Constance will know how you can get in touch with Roger, but she might know how to get in touch with someone else. And I think you should hear who that someone else is from me first."

Kit's eyes glaze over as she nods a slow, hesitant acknowledgement. "Okay."

Ailish brings a hand to her forehead and closes her eyes, as if soothing the sound of anxiety and hiding from the preoperational disappointment on her daughter's face might soften the blow.

"You have another half sister." Ailish lowers her hand. The air thickens again as if tampering with the earth's gravitational pull. She opens her eyes. Kit is gone. The rattle of the fly wire slamming shut resonates as Ailish spends the next half hour analyzing the orange tree outside the kitchen window. It's stripped bare of all its fruit. Lifeless. A frail barren trunk with nothing left to offer—not even a remnant of its skin on the ground to flaunt what it used to be proud of.

kit

Sein is sitting at the front gate on the concrete slab Ailish likes to call a step when Kit bursts out the front door. He stands, runs his fingers through his hair, and jiggles his legs as Kit runs up the path. Invisible tears mute her. She can't hear a thing except a buzzing rage, rampant with vehemence behind her brow and between her ears. It siphons through her limbs, right to the very tips of her fingernails. It pleads for her to punch something. Anything. She swings her fist at Sein, lost and confused at where to direct this overwhelming energy. He catches her punch midway in an open hand.

"Are you freakin' crazy?" he yelps as Kit drills her violent thoughts into Sein's eyes. Kit pulls her arm away from Sein's sturdy grip and kicks the fence, over and over in the same spot, until she cracks a picket.

"What's going on? What's got into you?"

Kit stops kicking and crouches to catch her breath. Her fragmented wheeze runs deeper than her lungs; it runs into bones and pokes little holes in them, deeming her skeleton brittle. She wants to collapse and break and go to sleep and forget she ever started this shit—anything to stop finding out about the hidden truths her mother seems to have boxed up and try to forget herself. How could her mother have lied to her for so many years? To the only person who has stood by her side through everything. Through her cancer and her suicide threats and her pleas to never let her wind up abandoned and alone.

Kit gives in to her body weight and drops backward onto the lawn, fanning her arms and legs. She spreads her fingers so the blades of velvety grass sweep between them. The ground smells like burning rain. *If only I could always feel this. Release.*

Sein kneels by her head. He doesn't touch her, but she can feel his leg brush against her shoulder.

Kit lifts her head, balancing herself on her elbows, cheeks flushed. "I have to call Constance. Can I come over to use yours?"

Sein hums an affirmative response. "But what's going on with Ailish?"

"Nothing. Don't worry about her." Kit gets up and brushes off her bum as if nothing has happened.

Sein sneaks Kit up to his room, trying not to wake his dad, who has flaked out on the sofa. Kit can't help but notice the bottle of scotch sitting on the coffee table. Her eyes flit to it and away again.

"It's not what it looks like," Sein whispers as they tiptoe up the stairs.

Kit nods. Jittering remnants of anger still prickle her skin. She just wants to get on the phone and get her sister's number from Constance. She needs to find Roger, and then everything will fall into place.

Then I'll know what to do.

Sein opens the door to his bedroom and gestures for Kit

to enter first. She sits on his bed, which is covered in coffee-brown sheets with green stitching around the edges. His room is empty. Just a bed, a wardrobe, a desk full of uni stuff, and thick black drapes. No old toys, posters, electronic gadgets. Nothing. No boyishness. Not a hint.

"Anyway," Sein says, "just so you don't get the wrong impression, Mum gave that bottle to him just before she died."

"Hmm?" Kit looks up from scratching her infected mosquito bite.

Sein shakes his head and chuckles with unease. "The bottle of scotch."

"Oh."

"He hasn't even opened it. He just stares at it all night."

"Oh. You want to talk about it?"

Sein shrugs and sits next to Kit on his bed. He slips his hands between his knees and sighs into a slouch. Kit hesitates to rub his back. She decides not to touch him at all.

"She died when I was two. Dad won't tell me how. I used to get pissed off that he'd never give me any answers, but then I realized he wanted me to remember her in good way, so I just let it alone."

Sein puts an arm around Kit and pulls her close. She shuffles over a little, lies on her side, and rests her head in Sein's lap. He bends over and kisses her cheek. "I don't bother trying to know anymore. I'm happy with the flashes of her face I get now and again. The problem is, though, I don't know if they're just memories of photos I've seen or if they're real. But I suppose that doesn't matter now."

"Doesn't it make you mad he won't tell you?" Kit half-whispers into Sein's knee. She turns around so her head is facing upward. "It'd make me mad."

"There's no point. What's done is done. It's not going to stop me from loving him. And he does his best, you know? He does what he thinks is right. And that's really all he can do. And that's all we can really ask for, isn't it? For them to do their best?"

Kit smiles with closed lips, suddenly realizing what he's getting at. She sits up. Blood rushes from her face, and she feels a little dizzy. Sein blinks, takes her cheeks in his hands, and gives her a peck on the nose. "Anyway, the phone's on my desk. Dial your heart out."

"Sein. I'm sorry, but I think I should go back home."

"Did I say something wrong?"

Kit looks into her lap and swallows a lump of guilt. "I think you know very well that you haven't." Kit wraps her arms around Sein and whispers "thank you" in his ear.

In bed, she stares into Brian's eyes as if behind one-sided glass, unsure of what neurological action is taking place behind them. One of Brian's hands rests below Ivy's head, tangled in a sweaty mess of hair. The room fills with the first inkling of morning light, and a neutral silence that masks Ivy's deeper thoughts. Thoughts that go beyond the temptation to make love to Brian for a third time, beyond the desire to surrender and allow herself to fall in love again.

Sitting restless in the corner of her mind—as she examines the rippled brown rims around Brian's irises—is the unwanted written connection she has with her father, a connection she wishes she could forget by just tearing the letter into pieces and burying deep below the earth.

She hasn't told anyone about this letter, having hid it in her wardrobe, in a box she keeps trying to ignore. Its contents have haunted her ever since she received it at eighteen. But what has haunted her most is knowing that acknowledging this letter could give her the life she has always dreamed of, a kind of closure, and freedom to discover the world, to learn how it evolved. To become that successful archaeologist she has always dreamed of being. But there is no way she can accept the cash. No. Way. It wouldn't be right. It would be a declaration of forgiveness. And that is out of the question.

Ivy rolls onto her back, and Brian rests his right hand on her stomach.

"Can you call in sick today?" he asks, circling Ivy's belly button with his middle finger. "I don't have to go into the office if I don't want to."

Ivy turns her head to face him. "You know I'd love to, but I can't afford to miss a day of work."

"Aw, come on. You're going to get that awesome job at the museum." Brian winks. Ivy smiles and looks at the ceiling.

"I can take you in and introduce you today or tomorrow

if you like. You never know—they might interview you right then and there."

Ivy laughs under her breath and lets out a little groan. She inches closer to Brian and kisses the tip of his nose.

"Yeah, why not? Screw the café."

Brian makes a gurgling noise as if trying to imitate Cat Woman and runs his tongue between Ivy's lips. Her body dissolves into his cream cotton sheets as he kisses up and down her arm like Gomez would do to Morticia.

"Coffee? About time I served you, right?" Brian leaps out of bed and wraps himself in his red-and-brown striped robe. Ivy nods, pulling the duvet up to her chin and spreading her body across the mattress.

Brian spoons coffee into the percolator. "What was that all about? With your mother? Last night? What is she accusing you of?"

Ivy was wondering when that might come up. She shouldn't have answered the phone. Period. But she did, and she shouldn't have expected anything less of Eleanor than to annihilate the first night she's been able to let go in ages.

"Long story. Seriously, don't worry about it."

"I am worrying about it. You became really, I don't know … absent. I have to say it was the, er, strangest sex I've ever had. I felt like the woman." Ivy scoffs as Brian switches the percolator on and crosses his arms in front of his chest with a shrug. "I'm sorry if that sounded sexist, but you get what I mean, don't you?"

Ivy takes a deep breath and lets the air gradually escape over her protruding bottom lip. Is she ready for this? Is she ready to let him in, to involve him? Her real life? Her past? What if everything comes crashing down right when she needs him the most? Will he remain by her side even after he discovers her unhealed emotional wounds?

"Anyway, we've got all day. Whenever you're ready," Brian says above the crackle and drip of the brewing coffee.

"No, it's okay." Ivy takes one last courageous breath. "No, wait—gimme a cigarette. I can't do this without a cigarette. You mind?" She flicks her fingers in the direction of the kitchen counter, where she dropped her handbag last night.

Brian shakes his head and probes Ivy's bag for the packet of Marlboro Lights and her Zippo. He throws them on the bed along with a small white dish for an ashtray. Ivy lights one, and breathes in virtual relief.

"Right." Ivy pats the bed for him to come back in. "Where would you like me to start? When my father left me to be raised by a depressed paediatric surgeon, and the woman he had an affair with, or when I filed for divorce after discovering my husband tried to have it on with my sister?"

kit

"Why couldn't you tell me when I was a kid?" Kit leans against the door frame and crosses her arms.

Ailish rests her hands on the edge of the kitchen sink. Lights off. Moonlight hushed. Smoke wafts from between two trembling fingers, toward the ceiling—a muted tornado of memories. Her mouth opens and closes, as if resisting the urge to spit the first response that comes to mind.

Resentment constricts Kit's throat. She swallows. It echoes in her ears. "Mum. I know you're hurting." Kit's voice wavers. "I'm sorry I got upset. But I'm hurting too."

"There are no oranges left on the tree." Ailish speaks like a ventriloquist. She takes a drag from her thick loosely-hand-rolled cigarette, and stares at the backyard.

"Sein picked them," Kit says. "They were getting too ripe."

"Oh." Ailish briefly turns her head to acknowledge Kit's presence. The corner of her mouth twitches. A one-quarter smile. Her head surrounded by a halo of moonlight, her face invisible when she turns around. "You want some?" Ailish asks, with a hint of shame in her voice. She holds the cigarette out in front of her, its burning orange tip a contrast against her dark silhouette. It dims as the clock ticks—a sewing needle tapping eggshell.

Tick. Tick. Tick.

"What is it?" Kit asks. Moonlight caresses her face as she walks closer to Ailish. She squints as it passes over her like headlights through bedroom blinds. As Ailish looks at her feet, light shines through her eyelashes. Remnants of tears are caught in them like drops of water in a web, creating prisms of light resembling flecks of silver glitter.

Ailish shifts the weight from her left foot to her right. "Weed," she replies with a heave of satisfying disgust. She exhales the smoke. Her eyes shift intermittently over Kit's face, as if gauging a reaction.

Kit leans against the kitchen counter half a meter away from Ailish and cracks her knuckles behind her back. She shakes her head, wants to cry, but her tears won't obey. They're trapped behind her nose like globules of phlegm. Ailish takes another drag. She exhales toward the ceiling. Thick breaths. Bitter secrets.

Kit slides against the edge of the counter toward Ailish. Closer. Closer. Until their thighs touch. Upper hands touch. They look at each other. Kit takes the spliff from Ailish's hand. Ailish lets her. She watches as Kit extinguishes it under the tap.

Kit kisses Ailish's cheek, hugs her, and gently rests her head on her shoulder. Ailish responds with a tight embrace instead of the usual loose gesture of affection she habitually yet reluctantly displays. She responds with warmth, with regret, a plea for forgiveness.

"Do you want me to fix you a cup of tea, Mum?" Kit whispers into her ear.

I love you. I wish I could say how much without you clamming up. Would you still do that? Would you believe me if I said I still loved you?

Ailish nods, her cheek brushing against Kit's hair, and sniffs, "Yes."

Ailish and Kit sip their tea on the veranda.

"'If you reveal your secrets to the wind, you should not blame the wind for revealing them to the trees.' Kahlil Gibran," Ailish says, as a breeze blows through the spotted gum tree on the roadside. The crisp, firm eucalyptus leaves collide tenderly, like rice shifting in a plastic jar.

"Hmm." Kit nods, wishing Ailish would just use her own words for once. Kit glances at the tree blowing in the wind too. Appreciation hits her like a falling twig. *How does she keep all that knowledge so accessible? Ready, waiting to be plucked from her mind the instant some sort of logical association presents itself?*

Ailish places her tea by the front right leg of her chair. Kit wonders why she doesn't use the table.

"Mum, how do you do that?"

"Do what?"

"Remember all those quotes at the very right moment?"

Ailish frowns and looks across the street.

"I don't know. How do you do it?"

"Me? I don't do it."

"Most of the time you are finishing them off for me. Aren't you?"

"Yeah, but, that's because I've heard you say them over and over."

"Well, it's the same thing then. Isn't it? I learn them. I recall them. Just like you."

Ailish tilts her head back and looks into the sky. It's the first summer night that isn't heavy with humid, suffocating clouds. "Kit. Look at all those stars."

Kit focuses on an ant navigating the edge of the table. Ailish brings her gaze back down to earth and puts her forefinger in front of the ant, cutting off its path. It climbs onto her finger. She lifts it to her nose to take a closer look, and then lowers it onto a lavender stalk.

Kit looks up, surprised to be able to see the teapot shape in the stars again for the first time in years. Or perhaps it's just been years since Kit looked up. Kit swallows, feeling guilty for dragging Ailish through this obsession of hers and not realizing how much it would affect the people she loves. The least she could have done is reassure Ailish that she wasn't out to hurt her. Why did it not even occur to her to ask Ailish why she is so afraid? Now she's not even sure she wants this. What if her instincts are right? Maybe he doesn't want to be found and that's why Ailish has been so secretive? What if she has put her mother in danger? *Maybe I should stop this.*

ailish

"It's a sign." Ailish rests her head on the back of the chair, searching for identifiable patterns in the stars and wondering why it's taken her so long to reach this point of utter clarity.

"What do you mean?" Kit's nostrils flare.

"Well, maybe the sky has opened up … for us. Maybe it's time to …" *Why didn't I ever think of this before?* "Darling. I think I might have your sister's number."

"Mum. Seriously, we don't have to do this now. I don't even know if I can anymore."

"It's okay. We might as well do this together. I think we *should* do this together." The surface of Ailish's skin tingles with anticipation.

"Together?"

"Yes."

Then I can control the information that gets to you.
I can make sure you never find out the whole truth.
I can make sure you won't get hurt.

"Wow."

"No need to say anything," Ailish says. "This is long overdue. It's the least I can do for keeping your father from you all these years."

"You know, I can stop this whole thing. I should have waited until you were ready." Kit crosses her arms.

Am I doing the right thing? Yes. You are protecting your child. Your only child.

"Don't be ridiculous. I would never have been ready if you hadn't pushed me, and you should find your father. He's your father. Don't you want to know the other half that made you *you*? I certainly would if I were you. And I have been so naïve in hoping you wouldn't. I've long known this day was coming, but I denied it. I haven't allowed myself to prepare for how it might make me feel."

"Well," Kit whispers with a hint of hesitation and a compassion Ailish hasn't sensed since she was diagnosed with cancer. "How *does* it make you feel?"

Ailish looks at the slight wave and rich auburn colour of Kit's hair and wants to bury her face in it, breathe in the scent of her daughter's innocence.

You're so beautiful. I'm so proud of you.

She thinks of yet another Mark Twain quote, and it summarizes the way she feels to a T: "*It is a time when one's spirit is subdued and sad, one knows not why; when the past seems a storm-swept desolation, life a vanity and a burden, and the future but a way to death.*" She is tempted to say it, but her shoulders drop with a sigh, and she lets it float away with Kahlil Gibran's breeze.

"Well." Ailish sighs. "I feel s*ad*. I don't know how else to describe it. I know that sounds silly coming from me. But the truth is, there aren't really any words to describe how I feel. My mind is so cluttered with other people's perceptions, I can't seem to measure my own anymore." Ailish crosses her arms and pushes her fists into her armpits with a forced shiver. "You know, I've tried to forget Roger your whole life. I miss him. I've always missed him. I don't think I've ever stopped loving him either. Bringing him back into my life is like putting salt on an open wound. He was the only man I'd ever loved, and if I could take him back, I would do so in a heartbeat. But I can't have that. Not anymore." Ailish pauses, picks up her tea from the ground, and screws up her mouth. "So, let's get him back for you. I think that's the next best thing."

Ailish catches a tear escaping from the corner of her eye with a knuckle, turns her head, stands, and goes inside. She returns to the veranda with a ripped corner of a newspaper and hands it to Kit.

"I think this is your sister's number, but you might still want to call Constance to confirm it."

But Kit doesn't take it. She looks up, her face reflecting a fear she is hiding from herself, a fear Ailish understands too well—the fear of getting to know someone new, when all you really want is your old life back, and the people you used to love back in it.

"Darling, would you like me to call for you?"

"Oh my God, would you really? I don't think I have the nerve." Kit stares at the piece of paper in Ailish's hand as if it's a weapon.

"Sure. First thing in the morning, then. Okay?"

Ailish is about to sit back down, when Kit grabs her hand.

"I love you, Mum." Kit brings Ailish's hand to her cheek and hugs her around the waist. Ailish strokes her hair and brings her long thick auburn locks to her nose, and breathes in the unconditional love.

"I love you too, Kit."

And now I can keep you safe.

eleanor

At the very back of Eleanor's garage, behind her mint '72 plum Valiant Charger, she dusts off a tiny cardboard box, full of memories she had intended to burn, but when the time came couldn't bear to destroy. They are photographs of Roger which she thought Ivy might one day want to see. She thought, as Ivy grew up, she might learn to forgive him, even though there is nothing really to forgive.

Roger loved Ivy. He'd sent her gifts and money, and little poems on the backs of postcards from all the different places of the world he'd visited—about the children he had saved and given an education, about how he wished she would come and share his unique experiences together. And Eleanor had condoned it, encouraged it, even. She was even willing to pull Ivy out of school to spend time with him, to learn more about the world—*his* world.

When Ivy decided she'd like to become an archaeologist, Eleanor had assumed she'd finally given in, that she was trying to find some sort of connection to her father, and an excuse to travel. But despite the promising signs, Ivy kept saying no to seeing him again.

Where did all Ivy's bitterness come from? Didn't Eleanor try? Didn't she conceal it well enough? What did Ivy see? Her sobbing in the bath at night? Did Ivy recognize the put-on brave face while tucking her into bed?

"I hate him, Mum. I hate what he did to us," Ivy would say.

"Just because he left, doesn't mean he doesn't love you," Eleanor would reply, over and over, stroking her hair, trying to make her believe everything was fine without him, that they had a good life and should no longer feel sad.

"Yeah, but he left because he doesn't love you, and that's a good enough reason for me not to love him."

Eleanor couldn't argue with that. And although she felt guilty about it, she was honoured that her daughter loved her so much to voluntarily sacrifice her father for it. So, as a way to respect her daughter's feelings, from the moment she'd uttered those words, she stopped hassling her to see him.

But now she regrets it. Because now he's in no shape to start afresh.

She should have kept pushing. She should have forced Ivy to visit him before it was too late. To see for herself, that deep down he is a good man. A loving and generous man. Despite his inability to commit, despite his adulterous nature, he would have done anything in his power to be a good father, even if it meant being one from a distance. But she can't encourage Ivy to see him now. Not after what has happened to him. It wouldn't be fair.

Eleanor returns the box of photos to the shelf without opening it and decides to take a drive. She listens to Gold FM all the way to Sorrento, priding herself for being able to refurbish a car like a man, a passion she has kept secret all these years, a symbolism of independence from her life-sucking profession. The only one who ever knew she fixed cars was Roger. She never even told Ivy in fear of tarnishing the discipline she spent so long trying to establish with her. Disclosing this would make her seem human, vulnerable, *likeable*. Ivy didn't need a friend. She needed a mother. A provider. A rock.

In Sorrento, Eleanor sits on the end of the pier, where it all began—when she was a first-year intern, newly married and in love. She watches seagulls glide and squawk above the sea surface, hunting for fish, and wishes she too could have lived the simple life. Be a hunter and gatherer. But she's too old to change her habits now. In another life perhaps, a life she isn't supposed to believe in, being a woman of science and all.

But lately the certainties of science aren't enough to cure her woes. Cutting into a mother's womb and fixing embryonic deformities doesn't give her the thrill it used to. Now she has an overwhelming desire to find something spiritual to believe in. Perhaps having a little faith in the unknown might give her some hope, some happiness in this life. Perhaps she could then figure out where it all went wrong, and make it all right again.

Ivy and Brian stand outside the Seattle Asian Art Museum in Volunteer Park. Ivy is smoking to kill her nerves. Brian stands in front of her with one side of his coat open to block people's view of the forbidden cigarette. After every drag Ivy waves her free hand about trying to direct the smoke away from her clothes. The last thing she needs is to reek like smoke when she walks into the interview. The whole situation reminds her of high school when she'd hide behind the canteen, snagging cigs off boys in return for flashing her boobs.

"Calm down. They already know you're brilliant." Brian smirks, closing his coat and rubbing Ivy's upper back.

"Hey. Keep it open. I'm not finished." Ivy takes such a heavy drag that she can hear the crackle of the tobacco as it burns. "And how is that exactly? That they know I'm brilliant, I mean." Ivy accidentally blows smoke into Brian's face. He cringes, but hardly moves. In an attempt to waft the lingering smoke away from his face, she blows more directly into it, "Sorry. Sorry!"

"They've got your résumé."

"What? How?"

"I bumped into Gabriel the other day outside the café, and he dropped it off to me at my office." Brian's expression turns from cheeky to triumphant. A bit like when he announced he wasn't really a fan of the New Pornographers.

What a cheek.

"How? Oh, he's still got my keys." Ivy play-punches Brian on shoulder. "Brian!"

"What? I thought you'd be happy." He laughs, rubbing his shoulder.

"I am, but, you know."

"No, I don't know. What?"

"Well, I feel like I'm going to get the job because I'm your friend, instead of for my expertise." Ivy tugs on a hair that's tickling her nose, and pulls it out. "Shit. Is that grey?" she asks, mortified, holding it up to Brian's face.

Brian squints. "No, it's blonde. I'm just your friend?" Brian puts his hands into his pockets and gazes at the museum entrance.

"No." Ivy butts her cigarette out on the ground and hides it with her left foot. "I didn't mean that. You know what I mean."

Brian jogs on the spot and pokes his chin toward Ivy's left foot. "You really should put that in the trash."

Ignoring the comment, she nudges Brian's chin to look her in the eyes. She kisses him, lightly brushing her tongue against his lips. She slips her arms into his coat and around his waist, pulling him close so her body touches his. Brian goes a little limp and wavers as if losing balance.

"You're not just a friend, okay? You're more than a friend," Ivy whispers, and bites Brian's earlobe.

Brian nods as if to say he's heard it all before. Ivy pulls back and looks him up and down, wondering why he has become so sulky. All she wants right now is to snuggle up in bed with him and make him warm, to show him he is a lot more than a friend. But is he? Has she started pretending again, or does she really feel something for him? The main thing now is to get this job. Regain a sense of purpose, of power, and then she can figure out her feelings. She's too far in. Once that act of good will is taken advantage of, there's no turning back, is there? She's got to follow through, otherwise what will she look like? Horrible and selfish don't even begin to describe her.

"You should go in." Brian cups Ivy's cheek with his right

hand, and brushes fly-away remnants of ash from below her eye with his thumb. The fingers of his left hand comb through her hair at the base of her neck. She leans into them and closes her eyes.

"I should?"

Brian lowers his arms. Cold air washes his warmth from Ivy's cheek. He taps his boutique watch. "It's time."

"It is?" Ivy folds her arms below her breasts and props herself up on her tiptoes, taking a look at the watch without really looking at the time.

"You're stalling."

"I know."

Brian hugs her, locking her arms vertically by her side. It's like stepping into a warm house after being caught in the wintry rain. Ivy shuts her eyes and remembers how Roger used to hug her like that, wrapping her in his firm hold, as if packing her away for safekeeping. The last time Roger hugged her, he'd said, "I have to leave for a while, but I'll be back soon. You'll wish my return every night before you sleep, won't you? For me?"

For years she recited what she thought was a "prayer" for him to come home. Then one day, without realizing it, she stopped, void of transition. Roger's face had become a mere skin-coloured blur with an indistinct male body attached to it. The body of this *thing* eventually disappeared too, until all that Ivy knew anymore was that he existed, having no trace of emotion with which to track him down.

Thank God for boys and cigs.

"I should go in," Ivy says, psychologically removing herself from reverie.

brian

Ivy squishes Brian's cheeks between her icy-cold hands, forcing his mouth into a fish pout.

His wife does that.

It makes him feel like a little boy.

He doesn't like it.

Brian removes her hands and brings them to his mouth. They smell like lavender. He blows into the kitten-like softness with his warm breath. Ivy closes her eyes and smiles.

I want to be your moisturizer.

"Thanks for doing this for me, *more than friend*." Ivy winks. She climbs the short flight of steps between the stone camel statues guarding the entrance, blows him a kiss, and disappears through the sky-high art-deco doors.

I love you. I have to slow down.

As Ivy wanders by the exhibit of Japanese woodblock prints, intricate snuff bottles, and jade sculptures, she realizes she should have spent a little time browsing the museum before attending the interview. *Why did I waste my time smoking a*

cigarette? You moron! You don't even know what this museum contains.

In a panic, she speed-walks past every exhibit, trying to memorize the displays, just in case she is asked, "And why do you believe you would be an asset to this museum?" *They always ask that question. Why didn't you prepare yourself? See, that's what happens when you get involved with men. You lose your freakin' good sense.*

As she walks, she takes mental notes of everything her eyes can grasp in her manic speed. *Dynasties: Majiayao, Han, Tang, Song, Yuan, Ming, Qing, Kangxi; Watercolours: Cherry Blossoms, Chickadees, Wild Peach Blossoms, by Nihonga artists: Hobun, Hosen, Shiho; New Artist: Zhang Xiaogang … goddesses, Yaksi figures, tribhanga curve, Guanyin, Dehua ware. Okay. My God, I'm so late.*

She approaches the door to the director's office, a little out of breath, her confidence slipping through her toes and into the solid marble floor, never to be retrieved. She raises her hand to knock on his door with one knuckle, but hesitates. Taking off her coat, and straightening out her navy-blue tailored dress, she chants to herself: *You can do this. You can do this. You were the highest achiever in your class. You have what it takes. You have what it takes. Don't let your fear get in the way. Don't be scared, Ivy.*

Interrupted by a tap on her shoulder, she swings around. The *swoosh* of her slippery-soled black pumps on the marble echoes through the corridor. Behind her is a man wearing jeans, a white shirt, and a white tie loosened under his collar with black Chinese writing on the end of it: 無畏. *No fear. Oh my God. If that isn't a sign, I don't know what is.*

"Hello. You must be Ivy. I'm the director. Call me Ron. Have you been waiting here long? Sorry to keep you waiting. I was in dire need of a coffee." Ron flicks his head toward the door. "Come in." He opens his office door and gestures for Ivy to enter. Her jaw drops when she sees the walls covered in enlarged copies of the paintings from the watercolour exhibit.

"Thank you. Wow." Ivy looks around the room. "Hobun, Hosen, Shiho," Ivy says softly, just in case her short-term memory has failed her.

"Yes. Indeed. Great wallpaper, isn't it? I had it made personally. Please, take a seat." Ron sits on the corner of his desk, crosses his legs like a cabaret singer on a piano, and points Ivy to the seat in front of him.

Oh yeah, I know you. You're the type that needs to tower over people to feel in control. Huh. Typical. Just what I need.

"Thanks," Ivy chirps, her mind transiently sucked dry of social and/or professional conversational skills. Blonde moment. They're becoming more frequent. She cringes at herself.

"So, are you familiar with the Nihonga artists?" Ron asks, tilting his head.

"Not in great detail. I like bone and pottery." *I like bone and pottery? Have you lost it? What about, "My expertise revolves around bone and pottery." Socks up, Ivy.*

"Oh yes?" Ron smirks and pushes a pile of papers further from his butt.

Don't think your intimidation is going to work on me. I'll pull myself together in a minute, and I'll knock your socks off. Just give me half a sec while I reallocate my brain.

Ron uncrosses his legs. "Well, we have plenty of pottery on display, but our museum is certainly lacking bone exhibits. Could you elaborate on what bone *art*efacts you are the most interested in?" He laughs like computer-generated American sitcom laughter, air-quoting *art* in *artefacts*, and swings his legs under his desk like a restless child.

Ivy takes an internal breath of courage. "Two years ago I worked with a team of archaeologists in New Delhi, where I assisted in carbon-dating the oracle bone characters found in Qishan County in the Shaanxi province of China," Ivy recites. *Ha! Bet you're speechless now, buddy.* "We dis—"

"Hmm, interesting," Ron says, wide-eyed, wriggling his butt side to side. Ivy doesn't quite know what to make of this guy. "Yes, sorry, please, continue."

Strangely enthused by Ron's interest, Ivy brightens her tone. "Well, we discovered they actually dated back to the Western Zhou dynasty."

"From 1046 to 256 BC?" Ron leans forward as if being enlightened by a secret conspiracy theory.

"Yes! Which of course shed significant new light on the number of such existing inscriptions. It was a remarkable discovery, and I'm certain I'd be able to get in touch with the leader of the team I worked with to negotiate something for the museum. I'm sure we'd be able to get hold of some tortoise-shell inscriptions too. Would you be interested in those?"

"Oh definitely. Ivy, this sounds fascinating."

"Thank you."

"Well, let's talk about your résumé. I recall it saying something about you having deferred from continuing your PhD, is that correct?"

"Yes."

"May I ask why?"

"Well …" *Don't mention the divorce. Don't mention the depression. Don't mention that your husband harassed your sister and you flipped out. And don't mention that you miss your father but are too stubborn to admit it. And don't mention that you resent your mother for never keeping your love for him alive. And don't mention you had promised to eternally hate men until you fell in love with Brian. And don't mention … no, I think you can mention that.*

"While I was assisting in New Delhi, I caught malaria and needed to be hospitalized. My professor suggested I take time off and come back when I was completely healthy again. When I recovered, I realized I really needed the time off, so thought I'd try something different and move overseas. I can always continue my PhD a little further down the line. And there's nothing more educational than experiencing a new culture, I find." Ivy flicks her fringe out of her face and offers a pursed-lipped smile.

"Interesting. Well, how much longer are you intending to live in Seattle?"

"I have no intention of leaving in the near future. In fact, I was thinking of picking up my PhD again here."

"Do you have a green card?" Ron bounces off the desk and sits in his regular position. In his chair.

"Well, my father was born here, so I have automatic permission to stay."

"Ah, excellent. Then there should be no problem obtaining a long-term working visa then?"

Ivy shakes her head, displaying her straight white teeth. She thinks about the day she visited Roger's childhood home and watched a happy nuclear family exit the front door and drive off in their four-wheeler.

brian

"I got the job. I got the job!" Ivy shrieks as she half runs, half skips toward Brian who is sitting on the park bench hoping for good news. He's never seen her smile so hard. Well, maybe once, the first time he saw her at the café. He was distracted by her impish beauty and accidentally spilled his steaming hot coffee all over his groin after bumping into someone's table.

Brian stands and walks toward her, stretching his arms out to catch her and break her speed. She runs into him so hard that he has to lift her off the ground and spin her around to avoid falling flat on his back.

As Ivy laughs, cute wrinkles frame her eyes. He wants to kiss them. He wants to kiss every wrinkle on her body. The ones on her neck when she looks down, the ones at the corners of her mouth when she smiles, the ones on her belly when she's sitting cross-legged on his bed. But what he wants to kiss the most is the little lonely dimple hiding away in her left cheek that likes to fleetingly emerge when he least expects it. It's like trying to catch a firefly; as soon as you spot it, it disappears again.

"That's excellent. When do you start?"

"In three weeks," Ivy squeals, bringing her hands to her mouth to dampen the uncharacteristic shrill. Ivy takes Brian's hands and leads him to a nearby park bench. "I think I need a cigarette to celebrate." She reaches into her handbag for the packet, but Brian rests his hand on hers to stop her.

"How about we forget the cigarette and just grab some lunch at an Irish pub? I've got a hankering for fish 'n' chips."

"Can you smoke in there?"

Brian laughs with a pitying frown. "I don't think so." *I hope not.*

"Bugger." Ivy drops her hands into her lap, bites her glossy lip, and looks over at a couple walking hand in hand into the museum.

Brian stares at Ivy's profile. Her absent gaze emits a mist of ethereal thought across her face. Brian wonders whether he should tell her how much he hates smoking and that he's never dated a smoker before, or that he has decided it no longer bothers him. *Does it?* He also wonders if now would be the right time to tell her he loves her.

"Ivy, I ..."

Ivy turns to face him with a smile that seems now to have landed on earth.

"I know this is incredibly soon, but ..."

"Yes!" Ivy hugs Brian so tight he almost loses his breath. He clutches at her elbows and levers her into clear view.

Uh-oh. "'Yes' what?"

"Let's move in together." Ivy brings her knuckles to her chin, her shoulders to her ears, and grins.

"Oh!" Brian's arms go limp while trying to maintain ambiguous surprise.

"Well, that *was* what you were going to say, wasn't it?" Ivy manages an expression fit for a pantomime.

"Yes." Brian hesitates. "Yes, it was." *Can I take this back?*

"Great," Ivy says, pulling her cigarettes out of her handbag and lights one with a certainty so intense Brian is afraid to rectify the situation. She takes Brian's right arm and puts it around her shoulder, leaning into him and shutting her eyes with the grin of a plastic clown. Smoke wafts from her fingers directly into his face. He looks at her—an injured little sparrow in need of some warmth and food. A fragile, sensitive soul, who needs to be taken care of, yet is too proud to admit it. She is all he has ever wanted.

Or is she not?

eydie

A bottle of Smirnoff lies on the floor, open, pleading for her mother, Beth, to wake up and take down its remaining drops with her morning cigarette. Beth's skeletal feeble limbs are splayed in all directions, similar to the dead, bruised victims Eydie's seen on Crime TV.

Their suburban house is small—slightly bigger than a caravan—but at least it doesn't have wheels. At least this means they're not quite "trailer trash."

Eydie passes Beth to go into the kitchenette, making as much noise as possible. Frankly, she couldn't give a damn if she woke Beth up; she'd probably take that last sip of vodka and pass out again anyway.

Beth is wheezing a little, so she's still alive … so far. Eydie wonders if she'll ever have to face the inevitable time when "passed out" evolves to "deceased." If she wishes for that day to come a lot sooner than fate has planned, what will follow? Devastation, or devastating relief? And if the latter, will guilt wheedle its way into every passing thought? Into her meals, dress, makeup, false nails?

Escaping is not easy. Escaping has just as many unattractive consequences as staying with this antediluvian witch. This mother. This bitch. Who has kept a lifetime of funds a secret from her in order to feed her own bottle-raising addiction. An addiction Eydie attempted to cure, by dropping out of high school and using her own meagre hairdressing salary to pay for counselling. But the money didn't only go toward that. It went toward the booze Beth would smuggle into her bag on the way, and devour quickly before returning home.

A glob of drool vibrates in the corner of Beth's mouth

with every breath of air that struggles through her sticky cracked lips. Strands of stiff bleach-blonde hair, clumped together and matted below her ear, look petrified with dried saliva. Her fingers twitch. She has two black nails from when she jammed them in the hinge of the alcohol cabinet door. She groans. One eye opens. Eydie stares right at it—a vibrant crystal blue bordered with a yellowy blood-shot white.

Ugh. You make me fuckin' sick.

Beth's eye closes, and she sits up, blindly reaching toward the coffee table for her pack of 50s. It's empty. She scrunches the packet and throws it across the room. It lands between an urn and an empty bottle of gin on the mantle.

"Luv, get me a packet of cigs from the servo, will ya?" Beth croaks, her eyes still closed. She opens and closes her mouth in an attempt to rehydrate it, and clicks her tongue, as if tasting something foul—most likely the roof of her mouth. One of her cheeks is creased and streaked with red lines that look like giant broken corpuscles, temporarily marking her with pathetic addiction and a plea for concern—that is, until the marks fade and Beth's blatant midday drunkenness reminds Eydie that sympathy claimed its freedom long ago, descending down their street in triumph.

Beth pushes hair out of her face, trapping her fingers in the soggy matted clump near the base of her neck. She stands, almost losing balance, and shuffles into the kitchen. She pulls a sharp knife out of the drawer. Eydie doesn't flinch, secretly hoping Beth will drive it through her stomach, but then instantly retracts the thought.

Beth grabs the clump of hair in her fist and saws it off with the knife. The hair crunches along the blade, as if it were alive, crying for help. She stares out the window, leaves the mass of hair on the bench, and puts the knife back in the drawer.

As if remembering Eydie is in the room, Beth yells, "Luv, I aksed ya a fuckin' question. Are you and ya chubby arse gonna get me those cigs or do I 'ave to go out on the fuckin' street and strain me poor old legs?" She stumbles back to the couch. Eydie focuses on Beth's dirty cracked heels as her sweat humidifies the air around her.

Eydie slaps two slices of white Tip Top bread on the cutting board and spreads them with salted margarine, promising herself that she'll cut out all dairy products and carbohydrates tomorrow.

"There's a spare pack on ya dresser, Ma." She shoves a whole slice into her mouth, chewing aggressively. Filling her mouth with an edible cushion is the only way to save herself from saying something she'll regret and enduring Beth's blistering slap.

"Well, get it for me, will ya, luv?" Beth lies back down on the couch, closes her eyes, and nurses her head. She rubs her temples, swallows saliva, coughs it back up, swishes it around her mouth, and washes it down with the dregs of vodka from the bottle on the floor.

The phone rings when Eydie is about to fetch Beth's cigarettes.

"Jesus, pick up the fuckin' phone and tell 'em it's too bloody early in the fuckin' morning. Tell 'em I'm not 'ere."

Eydie mutters under her breath, "You're never bloody 'ere," and answers it. "Yeah?" she snaps, expecting a tele-marketing rep to be on the other end.

"Oh, er, hello, I was wondering if I can speak to Eydie."

"Sorry, but we're not in-ter-res-ted in your products." Eydie looks at Beth, who has already gotten up to raid the alcohol cabinet for a fresh bottle of booze. She's just about to slam down the phone, when the voice on the other end cries out.

"No, no, I'm not selling. My name's Ailish Healy. I got your number from Roger Price's sister—your *father's* sister."

"Oh …" Eydie looks at Beth again. Beth pours herself a glass of scotch, trembling, spilling it all over the cabinet. Eydie turns her back to her and looks out the window at the deflated children's floating-aid duck in the middle of the lawn, faded almost white from years in the sun. "Can ya hold on a min? I wanna switch to the cordless," Eydie whispers and hangs up.

"Who wassit?" Beth grunts.

"Telemarketer." Eydie glances at her feet. "I'm gonna get your cigs." She goes into her bedroom, picks up the cord-less phone, and sits on the edge of her bed as if for some reason her two feet need to be securely and firmly placed on the floor to prevent an accidental fall.

She brings the cordless phone to her ear. "You know my father?" Her heart beats like a cog train gaining speed. This could be her way out. Out of this hellhole. Out of this pathetic attempt of living. Away from the fear of waking up to a dead body on the couch. A chance to be selfish, for once—once in this useless life.

"Well …" Ailish gives a nervous and small cough. Eydie can hear her hand cover the receiver on the other end. "I'm sorry, this is difficult, awkward, sorry … I, er, well, my daughter is your half sister. Your father is her father too, and I was wondering if you'd like to meet us?"

Eydie, dying to speak, to cry out in excitement, stares at the wall, muted by future possibilities sifting through her mind at rapid speed.

Sisters. Friends. Family.

Ailish clears her throat again. "I hate to ask you this out of the blue, but I was hoping you might know where I can get in touch with Roger too … Hello? Are you still there?"

"So you're my aunt?"

"Well, no. Stepmother, perhaps."

"Oh!" Eydie drops the receiver into her lap, relief flushing through her body, tingling through her fingers, to the tip of her nose.

I'm not alone. I'm not alone anymore.

She hears Ailish's distant voice—"Hello? Hello?"— between her knees, and in a panic takes hold of the receiver again and presses it firmly to her ear as if a gentle touch might let Ailish slip away.

"I'm sorry," Ailish says. "This must have come as a shock. And I'm being selfish asking you for your father's details right off the bat. Would you, perhaps, like me to leave you with our phone number and maybe you can call back once the information has sunk in?"

"No! I mean, no, please don't go. When can I meet you?" Eydie speaks slowly. Taking care to pronounce her words properly.

"Oh, thank goodness. What a relief. I thought this news might have shaken you. Shall we come over to your place today or tomorrow afternoon? After school perhaps? When do you get home from school?"

"Um, no, I think it'd be better if I come over to you guys. I'll come over after work. What's ya, um … your address?"

Ailish gives her an address, and a time is set for the following afternoon. Eydie can't believe it. Another family. She can have a new family!

Oh my god oh my god oh my god.

Eydie hangs up and looks at herself in the mirror. She smiles at herself, examines her features. Her dark red hair that curls up at the edges after a shower; her hazel eyes that sometimes look green under the apple tree; her crooked yet strangely button-like nose and chubby cheeks; her thick bottom lip, and the way her top lip curls up a little in the centre as if preparing for a kiss. *I wonder if we look similar. I wonder if she likes getting her nails done like me. We can get our nails done together. Like … sisters.* She plays with the word *sisters* on her tongue. It feels good—like sucking on hard candy.

Eydie runs into Beth's bedroom and rummages through her dresser drawers—the place she found the letters from her father. The place that eased her guilty thoughts of wishing Beth was dead. Where she **discovered Beth had** been accepting money from Roger **for years without** uttering a word about it and spending it on booze. The place that is now … empty.

The letters are gone.

Strobe lights inject Ivy with an energy she hasn't felt since Uni. Heavy disco beats thump through her feet, sending electric currents via the bar stool, through to her calves and thighs. She clenches her butt trying to tame a twinge of orgasmic energy between her legs triggered by the vibrations and thoughts of Brian. *Or Amir?*

She has a sudden hankering for a snort of speed. She scans the raving crowd for a drug dealer. *They all look too young.* She downs the rest of her margarita and licks the entire rim of her glass free of salt.

"Sweetcakes, seriously now. Isn't it kinda soon?" Gabriel asks, finishing his question with a wink toward the bartender as he signals for him to bring two more margaritas.

"Gabe, Brian's been eyeing me for almost a year. How is it too soon?" The edges of Ivy's mouth twitch, as if hesitant to reveal her first-ever crush on a good-for-nothing teenage delinquent. She's dying to embellish this high, this buzz, with some drugs.

When did I become so proper? When did I stop flashing my tits for a joke?

She grabs the arm of a young man, a spitting image of Ringo Star with a bounce in his step. She looks him up and down, at his clothes for the hidden bulge. *Nope.*

"Hey, lady, you wanna take a breath of fresh air?" Ringo runs his tongue along his front teeth and winks. Ivy is certain she's seen this guy in a toothpaste commercial.

"No thanks, bud. Thought you were someone else."

Ringo shrugs and walks away with a minuscule limp. Gabriel squints at Ivy as if he has no idea what's got into her.

"Okay … but have *you* been eyeing him for a year?" he asks, clicking his tongue.

Ivy tsks. "What's the problem? You've been encouraging me to date him for ages, and now you have a problem with me taking the next step? We're just moving in together. What's the big deal?"

It hits Ivy that perhaps this is a big deal. Perhaps it is too soon.

He wasn't going to ask me to move in with him, was he? What was he going to ask me? Why didn't I let him finish?

She doesn't even want this. Not really. She just wants life to be easy again. And Brian is easy. Who needs love anyway? It's so overrated.

Ivy looks at Gabriel and his long, thin face, wordlessly beseeching him to approve.

If you weren't gay, I'd so want to snog those thick lips of yours right now.

Gabe responds with a look of concern, lips pressed together in a sympathetic smile.

"The big deal is, sweetcakes, a few days ago you were so depressed that you could hardly get dressed to see a band play that you apparently adore, and now all of a sudden, you're head over heels, you've got a new job, you're thinking of finishing your PhD, and you're moving in with a guy you practically just met. Not only this, but why on earth would Brian want to move so fast? He's a *man*, darling."

"And he's good for me." *Right?* "You said so yourself. Why can't you be happy for me?"

"I am happy. I'm just saying, keep a cushion under your belt, you know? This all seems way too good to be true. I mean, Jesus, I hope for your sake it is, but—"

"But what?" *Please say you're just jealous. That you want some Brian cock for yourself.*

Gabe removes a strand of hair stuck to his sweaty top lip.

"Gabe, I fell fast. I know that. But life's too short. It really is. And he loves me. He's already given me the world by encouraging me to go back to Uni, *and* by helping me get that job. He's more than I could ever dream of. Why would he do all of that for me if he didn't want to be with me?"

"Ive …"

The bartender brings them their fresh margaritas, and Gabriel breaks into a full-fledged smile. He stares into the glass as if about to jump into it, and pouts his lips.

"All right. Screw logic. Just dive right in, baby!" Gabriel raises his glass. "To you and Brian."

"To me and Brian." Ivy and Gabriel clink glasses a little too hard, and frozen margarita spills down both their arms and into their crotches. In a fit of laughter, they put their glasses down and pat themselves dry with serviettes the bartender brings. To Gabriel, it seems, spilling the margarita was the simple result of getting too enthusiastic. But to Ivy, behind the laughter, it's the initiation of a bad omen. It has begun to nibble. At her bones. Like a microscopic germ contaminating an archaeological find to the point where it becomes unidentifiable. A lifeless shell of what once was. Something's not right and she knows it. But will she ever admit it to herself?

Seven margaritas each later, and a snort of coke from Ringo—who returned realizing what the whole exchange between him and Ivy was about—Gabriel and Ivy dance, Patsy and Edina style, to Pet Shop Boy's *Absolutely Fabulous* theme song.

Ivy (Patsy): Dull, soulless dance music.

Gabriel (Edina): Bip bip bip, bop bop bop.

Ivy (Patsy): Dull, soulless dance music.

Gabriel (Edina): Ride on time, ride on time. Techno, techno, bloody techno, darling!

Gabriel is about to go to the bar to get them both two more drinks, when he asks in an Edina accent, "Is Champas all right for you, darling?" with a wink and butt wiggle.

"La Croix, sweetie, La Croix." Ivy shakes her head and holds up her fingers to form a cross. She shuffles off the dance floor behind Gabriel and throws herself onto a stool, grabbing the edge of the bar to prevent an embarrassing fall.

"Whoa, little too much to drink, darling?" Gabriel asks,

appearing completely sober. Ivy looks up at his wavering foggy face and at the tri-image of the large TV screen of the Pet Shop Boys' *Absolutely Fabulous* video clip overhead. Her body convulses forward, and she cups a hand to her mouth, stunting a vomit warning in its tracks. "Darling, I think we'd better get you home."

Ivy nods, managing to keep the spew at bay. Gabriel grabs Ivy's bag and helps her to stand.

"Can you walk?"

"Mmm … yep." Ivy stands, holds her head high, straightens her silver spandex boob tube above her beasts, and pretends to be fine. At least until they get out of the claustrophobic atmosphere to where she can take a nice deep breath of oxygen.

Out on the street, waiting for a cab, the cold air cuts right through Ivy, bringing her senses back to life and turning her entertaining drunken dizziness and drugged bounce into a sick whirlpool of indignation.

Why the fuck did I divorce my husband? We should have worked it out.

The sound of cars on wet roads *whoosh* through her ears as if she's listening to panned sound effects through head-phones. She clutches her handbag tightly under her arm, when the ground starts to pulsate. She looks at Gabriel as if something is sawing her in half.

"Honey—" Gabriel lights a cigarette. "Death isn't embedded in your side. It's your cell. Vibrating."

Ivy loosens her grip and sighs in relief. She searches her bag for the phone.

"What the fuck time is it? Four a.m.?" Ivy rolls her eyes at Gabriel. He chuckles when she almost loses balance and starts to walk backward. She grabs the phone, then stops in the middle of the sidewalk, holding one arm out to her side as if ready to launch into flight.

"Hello?"

"Oh good, I haven't woken you up. I had a feeling you'd be out and about."

"Kit. What the hell are you doing calling me so late?"

"What's wrong? You're awake, aren't you?"

"What do you want?"

"I want you to come home."

Ivy pulls the phone away from her ear and glares at the keypad as if it has a voice of its own. She looks at Gabriel, who shrugs in question. She puts the phone back to her ear.

"Are you in Seattle?"

"No, I mean *home* home. Australia home."

"Don't be fucking ridiculous, Kit. What on earth would I want to do that for? I'm finally getting my shit together."

"Well, I've got some news about Dad, and, well, it's gotten to the point where I think you should become more involved. I'm discovering some serious shit, Ivy, and I think you should be here. I think we should do this together. Mum has even decided to help. Don't you want to be more involved?"

Ivy coughs in disgust as if Kit's request has regurgitated bile.

"Kit, I don't know what fucking world you're living in,

but it's not mine, okay? I don't give a damn about Dad or about any of the 'serious shit' you're finding out. Let me live my life, and you live yours. Maybe you can try to do that on your own for once too, huh? Or would you like me to hire someone to hold your hand now that I'm not around anymore?"

Ivy can hear Kit take a quick breath as if trying to ignore the hurt. "Ivy, we have another sister. Don't you want to meet her?"

"I've met her. I don't care. I've known about her since I was ten. Big fucking yay."

"You what?"

Silence thickens in Ivy's ear.

"How could you not have—"

"Said anything? Oh, I don't know. Maybe because I don't give a flying fuck. Maybe because some people don't talk about things simply because they don't want some crap in their lives. Maybe because my life is mine, and I can do what I like with it? Got it?"

"But, I thought we … loved each other," Kit gurgles. "I thought we were a team."

"Grow up, Kit. Things change. And love means shit compared to all the other crap in this world. Get used to it."

Kit starts to sob. Ivy feels a pinch of pain expand in her stomach like a bad odour. She should stop. She should apologize. But she can't. The rage keeps swelling and gushing through her mouth in torrents.

"And how the fuck can you talk about love, Kit? You don't even know what love is. You ruined my marriage, you know that? You flaunted your sexy childlike hips in front of Amir—*all the time*! No wonder he came on to you. You led him on. And if you'd loved me you wouldn't have let that happen. You wouldn't have let him even try to touch you." Ivy's knees shake. She feels lightheaded, faint. "Stop calling me. Learn to live without me. We're done."

Ivy hangs up the phone and throws it in her bag. She lifts her head, her mind and body flooded with freedom and guilty triumph, to see Gabriel's hand cupped over his mouth and tears streaming down his cheeks. At this moment, she realizes, she has just pushed away the only person in the world she unconditionally loves.

And she may never be able to get her back.

ailish

She's been standing over the stove for five minutes, and her forehead is already dripping with sweat. She wipes it dry with the back of her hand, licks the chicken-curry-covered wooden spoon clean and rests it on the edge of the pan, when Kit comes stomping down the stairs. *Crying?*

Kit hunches over in the kitchen doorway, clutching at her stomach as if stricken with severe cramps, trying to breathe amid a fit of tears—tears so thick and heavy they are almost silent. Like the slow release of air from a defective balloon.

Ailish turns the hot plate off and dashes to Kit's side, takes her in her arms, and strokes damp hair from her cheek. She walks her to the lounge and sits her on the couch, Kit's shoulders shaking from quick gasps of air.

"Kit. Kit, look at me." Ailish lifts Kit's chin. Her face is flushed and blotchy, shining from salty layers of tears. "Breathe." She takes a jagged breath and releases the air through her open mouth. A small bubble of snot escapes from her right nostril. Ailish hands her a tissue that's tucked under her left bra strap. Kit wipes her nose and shudders, looking into her lap again.

"Sweetheart. What happened? What did Ivy say to you?"

"She's met her already ..."

Ailish tries to understand as best she can through Kit's stammering, weak voice. Kit wails mid-sentence. Ailish cradles her, kisses her nose, and rests her cheek on the top of her head.

Constance contacted Eleanor too? But she hated Eleanor. There must be more Eleanor is hiding from me. I knew it. I just knew it ... Oh no ... What if she knows?

"She screamed at me. The whole time. She hates me," Kit wails.

"As Joseph Campbell says, we must be willing to let go of the life we have planned, so as to accept the life that is waiting for us." Ailish smiles and squeezes her daughter close to her chest. She rocks her back and forth like a child, wishing Kit were just that. If she could, she would pack their belongings and start a new life in a new state, a new city, away from the past.

After a couple of minutes, Ailish levers Kit off her body and holds her by her shoulders. "Sweetheart. Look at me." Kit looks up, a plague of red torment spreading through her whites like ink through veins on an X-ray. "I'll call Eleanor to see if she has any insight into Ivy's outburst. Perhaps she's trying to get over some sort of trauma? And just took it out on you because you were conveniently there? Okay?" *Will Ivy's dramas ever end?* "It's high time Eleanor and I had a chat anyway."

Kit nods and lies down on her side, wiping her cheek dry against a cushion. She switches on the TV and presses Mute. Her crying stops for a moment as she stares at a nothingness Ailish is sure represents the absolute opposite. A few tears roll down the side of Kit's face and into her ear. She uses the tissue Ailish gave her to wipe it. Kit's skin is pale, making her hair look redder than usual. She reminds Ailish of Lolita.

"Will you be okay on your own for a while? Do you want me to call Sein over?"

Kit shakes her head and curls into a foetal position, her unshaven knees sticking over the edge of the couch. Ailish strokes them. The hair is so fine she can barely see or feel it. *She's never shaved her knees.* Ailish smiles at the thought of Kit taking her advice.

"Okay, I'll stay a little while longer," Ailish says, gently moving a strand of hair from the corner of Kit's mouth.

Kit falls asleep, wheezing through a blocked nose. Ailish covers her in a white cotton sheet, like she used to do when she was little. For some reason Kit slept better if she had something covering her, even during a heat wave, her tiny little toes sticking out the edge, the nails varnished with edible strawberry polish. It was the best thing Ailish had ever invented since discovering Kit liked to suck her toes instead of her thumb as a child.

When Kit was a baby, Ailish would lie down beside her after she'd fallen asleep, dreaming that Roger was lying opposite. Would everything have been different now if he'd never walked out during that stupid fight over the Napolitano sauce?

If only Ailish had been straight with Kit from the beginning, starting from Constance's letter and the day they visited Beth and Eydie when she was four, then perhaps they wouldn't be in this mess. Then maybe Eleanor wouldn't have had any reason to keep secrets either.

Have we both really been bringing up our daughters all this time relying on lies to protect them? And from what? Whom? Us? From our memories of a man who broke our hearts? Who disappointed us? And who gave me the right to blame him without letting him voice his side of the story? And what *in the world could you possibly be hiding from, Eleanor?*

In the kitchen, Ailish shoves a few spoonfuls of chicken curry from the pan into her mouth, then puts enough on a plate for Kit, and leaves it in the microwave with a note on the door. She calls Eleanor at home. There's no answer. She calls her office and is put through to the front desk. They say she has just finished surgery and should be in her office soon. But instead of waiting, Ailish grabs her handbag and heads to the hospital straightaway.

She *has* to know how Eleanor knows about Eydie.

eydie

"Ma!" Eydie pulls the drawer out of its casing, throws it across the room, and storms into the lounge. Beth is asleep again, an empty glass clutched in a hanging hand. Eydie kneels down beside her and slaps her mother's face just hard enough for her to wake up. "Where have ya put them? Where have ya put the freakin' letters? Wake up and tell me where ya freakin' put them!"

Beth sits up, blinks, whimpering foolishly, as if Eydie might feel sorry for her. "Put what, darl? I dunno what you're bloody talkin' 'bout."

"The letters from Roger, from Dad. The ones I told ya about at the hairdresser's the other day. The ones I found, Ma! The ones that said to put me into Uni. The ones that had bloody blank cheques in them, for *me*. The cheques ya decided it'd be better to drink and vomit up instead! Don't tell me you can't remember, Ma. Don't bullshit me. Where are they? I want them. Now! I want Dad's address!"

Eydie towers over Beth with her arms on her hips. Beth wipes away some escaping drool from her chin with a shaking hand, jagged nails embedded with grit.

"Darl, I can't ... I can't ... remember."

"This's bullshit." Eydie flings open the alcohol cabinet door. A hinge pops and flies across the room. She clutches the necks of as many bottles as she can, carries them into the kitchen, slams them on the kitchen bench, and then fetches the rest. She unscrews the caps and throws them at Beth's chest. Beth hardly moves, but blinks on each impact, sniffing.

Eydie pours the alcohol into the sink. One by one.

I'm gonna make this fuckin' hurt, ya fuckin' selfish cunt.

Beth cries for her to stop. Her cries screech as she clutches at her hair, grey tears streaming down her cheeks.

"Darl, please, stop! I threw them away. Please!"

"You *what*? What the fuck did ya do that for?" Eydie slams a just-emptied bottle of supermarket gin on the counter. "Well, tell me where the fuck he lives. Tell me. Now!" Beth looks at Eydie in silent horror. Eydie can see her reflection in Beth's eyes and wonders if she can see what she sees—a distorted fishbowl image of her daughter's disappointed yet hopeful face.

Beth shifts her gaze from the last full bottle of alcohol by the sink to Eydie's blazing eyes. Beth still doesn't say a word. Eydie grabs Beth by the shoulders and shakes her. "Tell me where he lives, for Christ's sake!"

Beth takes a quick breath, bringing her tears to a halt. "With his brother. Near Phillip Island. But please, take me with you. It'll be—"

"It'll be what?"

"Safer that way, darl."

"Safer? Safer than all this?"

Eydie pulls a bottle of water out of the fridge, grabs Beth by her upper arm, pulls her forward, and shoves her into her bedroom. She throws Beth on the bed. As she closes Beth's hand around the bottle of water, she says, "This is for your own good, Ma. One day you'll thank me. I promise." Beth glares at her, a silent plea for just one more glass. Eydie walks out of the bedroom, and flicks the latch closed on the outside of Beth's sliding bedroom door. A door with a safety lock.

Among the cheerful sounds of squealing children, in the street outside her house, she can hear the fading sound of Beth's angry fists banging.

Banging.

And they don't sound as threatening as she'd thought.

Because she's finally going to meet family she can trust.

eleanor

Yet another letter has arrived from Roger's brother, Samuel. Eleanor sits at her desk after a six-hour surgery and pulls it out of the patent-leather bag Ailish bought her for her birthday. The style doesn't suit her, she thinks, but it'll do, if only because it's big, black, and bold enough to bang a mugger over the head with.

Four other unopened letters from Samuel hide in this bag. They're wrapped inside her lucky orange scrub cap, the spare scrub cap she likes to use for concealing such unwanted business, hoping the psychological charm of it might make the inconvenience disappear. So far, Samuel has sent one every quarter. The first, a year ago today.

"Ugh." Eleanor grabs a scrunched-up over-used tissue from her pocket and blows her nose. It sounds like a lawn-mower struggling to get started. She takes pride in not caring for discreetness, especially when it comes to natural bodily functions. She opens her desk drawer in search of the sample perfume she received at Myers. She'd only paused momentarily at the Estée Lauder stand, when she thought she'd seen Roger entering the department store.

She dabs the perfume, multiple times, on every pressure point until the inch-long, ten millimetre-wide glass capsule is empty. The stench of formaldehyde has been invading her nasal cavity since early morning. She'd promised to teach her ill resident's new interns how to suture. *When am I ever going to learn how to say no?* She sniffs her wrists. *Great. Now I smell like a cadaver dumped into a jasmine bush.*

She leans back in her chair and pulls her thin, limp grey-blonde hair into a tight ponytail, tight enough to give herself a temporary face lift. She inspects her hands. Her short nails and dry eponychiums stand out against her raw skin.

She glances at her bag and bites the last remaining free edge from her digitus quintus. She spits the nail into the air. *Either read them now, or throw them away and risk not knowing something vital. Such as "he's dead." Gee, that'd solve everything. Not that my therapist would agree.*

She pulls all the letters out of her bag and places them on her desk in chronological order. Grabs her sentimental rusty scalpel from the pen jar.

She stabs at the first letter, denting her desk.

Why did I give him money?

Stab. *He doesn't deserve it.*

Stab. *Not.*

Stab. *One.*

Stab. *Bit.*

An ear-piercing scrape rattles the desk as she drives the scalpel along the surface as if butchering flesh. Her face burns. She realizes she's holding her breath and lets out a heavy sigh.

Eleanor speeds through each letter, anticipating the clincher, but they only contain the mundane content she has been expecting, and wonders why she even bothered getting so worked up about it.

Letter 1: "*... thanks for the funds ... much appreciated ...*"

Letter 2: "*... medical expenses paid. Thanks again ...*"

Letter 3: "*... thanks so much for your help all these months, nursing Roger is getting easier by the day ...*"

Letter 4: "*... all back to normal now ... Is there anything we can do to repay you?*"

"Yes. Learn how to use email," Eleanor grumbles as she rips the first four letters in half and throws them into the wastepaper basket by the wall. "This one better be good."

Letter 5: "*... Can Roger see Ivy? ... I know we had an agreement, but perhaps you can make an exception? He misses you all ...*"

"No way." Eleanor tears the fifth letter into the tiniest shreds possible and throws them into the air. As they waft down around her, like multiplying white blood cells, Ailish barges in, her hair revolting from its usual precision.

"Hi," Ailish pants with narrow eyes. She pushes fly-away strands of hair behind her ears.

"Hi yourself," Eleanor says, blowing a fragment of paper away from her face. "Why were you running? And where have you been lately? I've been trying to contact you for ages."

"Why?"

"What do you mean, why?" Eleanor closes the door behind Ailish with her shoulder. She remains leaning against the door, looking Ailish up and down. She looks exhausted. *That makes two of us.*

"I mean, is there any particular reason why you wanted to contact me?" Ailish puts her hands on her hips, then immediately returns them to her sides, as if conscious of her aggressive stance. She glances around the office and takes a seat at Eleanor's desk. A bead of sweat trickles down her temple.

"Are you okay?" Eleanor asks, feeling Ailish's head for a fever.

Ailish pushes Eleanor's hand away as though fending off a fly. "I don't need you to play doctor with me anymore. I just want … *need* your candour."

Eleanor crosses her arms under her breasts and scoffs. How dare Ailish claim she's been "playing doctor"? She sacrificed her own heart to help her. "What's going on?"

Ailish's jaw clenches as she stares into the stuffy air between her and Eleanor. She licks her lips and folds her hands in her lap.

Eleanor crouches, balancing with one knee on the ground so that their faces are level, and rests her hand on Ailish's thigh. Something must be up. She shouldn't judge this haughtiness. She won't make any assumptions.

"You can tell me anything, Allie. You know that, don't you?"

"I spoke to Eydie this morning," Ailish barks, maintaining eye contact with Eleanor as she stands and backs toward her old small black couch in the corner. The only nonsterile-looking piece of furniture in the room.

Eleanor sits, crosses her legs, shakes her foot. She knew this would come out eventually. She doesn't even know why she kept it a secret. It was pointless. But she believes people feel more in control if they have secrets, independent from the world's demands. So she allowed herself the luxury. After all, she doesn't owe Ailish anything.

Ailish wipes sweat from her top lip and rubs her fingers on her skirt.

"Look." Eleanor sighs. "Constance sent that letter to us both. Okay? I'm sure it was the least she could do after favouring you over me, don't you think? And trying to use you to push me out of her and Roger's lives? So can we forget about it? It doesn't matter anymore. Really. Let the past be the past. We'll keep trudging forward. All right?" Eleanor robotically repeats the exact advice her therapist had given her the day after Ivy announced Kit's endeavour to seek out Roger.

Ailish's face contorts like a confused little girl. "Eleanor, I …"

"Don't. Allie, don't. It's fine. Really. Constance may have been lovely to you. And I'm sure she was capable of it. But she was an outright bitch to me, and I wouldn't be surprised if the whole relationship she had with you was some sort of manipulative scam to get rid of us both. I guess she got what she wanted, huh? I never told you this, but she tried to get custody of Ivy right after Roger left you. Can you believe that?"

"What?"

"Exactly. And why Ivy? Why not Kit or Eydie?"

"Eleanor." Ailish shakes her head and swallows.

"She'd always had a bone to pick with me ever since Roger and I got married. She did it out of spite. She was *not* a nice woman. Believe me."

"Why didn't you just tell me you received the letter?" Ailish breathes so deeply through her nose, her nostrils close. "We could have taken Ivy and Kit to meet her together. You know, when they were little."

Eleanor stops shaking her foot. "Why didn't *you* tell *me* you received the letter?"

Ailish bites her bottom lip and scratches her right eyebrow. "Well, I didn't want to upset you. But you told Ivy, though, didn't you? Didn't you think Kit had the right to know too?"

"Allie." Eleanor clears her throat and rubs the back of her neck. "Wasn't that your responsibil—"

"I'm just hurt that you thought you needed to keep it a secret from me, that's all," Ailish interrupts, clearly trying to avert any blame that might scathe her own ego. "Especially seeing there were evidently no consequences in telling me about it since you knew I'd received the letter anyway."

Eleanor laughs and uncrosses her legs. She leans forward like a mechanic with greasy hands hanging between her knees. "*Me*? Keeping secrets from *you*? Please tell me you're not serious."

Ailish nods curtly. "Yes. Yes, I am serious."

Just tell her you know.

"Oh, for God's sake, Allie. I know your affair with Roger didn't last only one week. All right? I knew that since I walked in on you and Roger in my bed, and it was not the first time I saw—"

"Stop!" Ailish begins to cry, and fiddles with her bra strap while looking at the ceiling.

"There're some tissues in the second drawer," Eleanor says, scratching at an outbreak of eczema on her left palm. Anger broils in the rear of her nasal cavity. But she doesn't want to get angry. She's over this. She got over this a long time ago and hid the fact that she knew about Ailish's affair with Roger to protect *Ailish* from the memory of him. Not for any other reason. So why is she feeling angry now? Has she been protecting Ailish's heart in an attempt to protect her own? Because now that the words have been spoken, the memory smells like dead bowel.

"Thank you." Ailish pulls a tissue out of the box and blows her nose, hardly making a sound, just the slightest of squeaks, like the scuff of a surgeon's sole against the hospital floor.

"Allie. I don't care. Can you understand that? I don't. What happened with us and Roger doesn't matter anymore. I just want my daughter to be happy. And if you're going to let Kit ruin Ivy's chances of getting her life together, I don't know how I'll forgive you for that. You had your chance to allow Kit to meet Roger so many times before we lost track of where he was. You should have taken advantage of the opportunity when you had the chance. And why didn't you?"

"You can't stop Kit from finding her father. She deserves to meet him no matter what. I'm certainly not going to get in the way." Ailish pulls herself together, wiping her eyes dry and redoing her hair. "In fact, I've decided to help her."

"Roger's an arsehole. It's useless. He won't want to meet them. Believe me. Don't you think he would have tried to contact them if he did?" *Roger was the sweetest man I ever met. He was fragile. You suited him, Allie. You suited him a lot better than I did. I devoured his soul like a praying mantis during mating season.*

Ailish rolls the desk chair closer to Eleanor, pointing her finger at her and clenching her teeth. "He was *not* an arsehole." She stands and hovers over Eleanor like an irate boarding school teacher. "We loved each other."

Eleanor stands in defence and cranes her neck forward.

"And do you think we didn't love each other? Is that what you're trying to tell me here? That you have more of a right over him because you loved each other? For crying out loud, Allie, what planet are you living on? We were married. With a child. You and your student crush took away my life. And I have never blamed you for it. Ever. I put all the blame on Roger. Was that a mistake? Should I have put the blame on *you*?" Eleanor tilts her head to the side in question, her heart racing against the clock. "I helped you give birth to my husband's daughter! And now you want …"

Eleanor closes her eyes and takes a deep breath, trying to lower her voice, to control her shaking hands. She puts them in her pockets. The last thing she needs right now is to make a mistake on the operating table because she is upset about something that happened twenty-five years ago.

I made my bed. I chose to lie in it. Cut Allie some slack.

"What is it that you want from me now, Ailish? Why are you here?" Eleanor whispers, supporting herself against the wall by the door. She squeezes her nose.

"I want to know where Roger is," Ailish replies, gripping the handle of her handbag so tight her knuckles turn white. "I want to speak to him before Kit does. I have to protect my daughter. I want to make sure she doesn't get hurt anymore than she already has." Ailish glares at Eleanor as if willing herself to breathe fire. "And the reason for that is my business."

Eleanor swallows. She couldn't possibly tell her where he is. Then Ivy would know where to find him. How horrible for Ivy to see him so weak, when he used to be so strong. It just wouldn't be right.

"You *do* realize that Ivy has just told Kit she doesn't want anything more to do with her? She's devastated, Eleanor. They were peas in a pod growing up. And I'm going to do my best to make her happy again. I'm going to get her what she wants. Surely you can understand that. I'm sure that's all you want for Ivy too. Happiness?"

Ailish looks at the ground, squints at something, and moves toward the door. Eleanor steps in front of her as she begins to bend down.

"I'm sorry to hear that. But you know Ivy's still having a hard time after the divorce."

"Ivy is a grown woman," Ailish snaps.

So is Kit. Eleanor is tempted to ask Ailish what she means by that, but decides against it, hoping to cut the conversation short before it gets out of hand. "I don't know where Roger is. Sorry. Now if you'll excuse me, I have some paperwork to get done." She opens the door for Ailish to leave.

"Fine," Ailish replies without parting her teeth. "But first tell me …" Ailish bends down and picks up a shred of paper, the size of her thumb. Her cheeks turn pink; her nostrils flare. Eleanor can hear the saliva build up around the walls of her mouth. "Would your paperwork have anything to do with this?" Ailish asks, holding the shred of paper close to Eleanor's nose.

It reads: *"Can Roger see Iv…"*

Before Eleanor has the chance to speak, Ailish's hand makes a clean swipe across her cheek. Eleanor holds her own hand against her hot stinging flesh, and wonders why she hadn't had the nerve to make her presence known, and do the same thing, the day she found Ailish fucking her husband up against his office wall. She also wonders why she let the affair continue for three years before plotting the day she would catch them in the act and reveal his infidelity. But what she wonders the most is why she gets such a thrill out of soothing her patients' pain, when she can never soothe her own.

"Allie," Eleanor whispers, still holding her hand to her cheek. "I think you might need to sit down for this."

kit

The sun bleeds an orange glucose shard of light through the blinds. The TV screen is layered with dust, no longer camouflaged by night. For Kit's entire life, the TV has sat in this exact position. In the corner. On a mahogany treasure chest with an intricately designed rusty metal latch. Not once in her twenty-five years has the furniture been moved around. She can't even remember the rug under the coffee table being removed, or steam-cleaned. But somehow everything has remained spotless, soulless, covered by an invisible sheen of emotional filth. A happy homemaker's cocoon inhabited by the manically depressed who succeed in making others believe they are perfectly fine. Kit is not an exception.

Kit watches commercials in mute—graceful images of happy blonde, blue-eyed nuclear families eating Vegemite sandwiches in abnormally green and ridiculously large grassy backyards. Images of overenthusiastic teens throwing Frisbees and rubber balls for golden retrievers that don't need to be given orders, and of blue heelers herding sheep like obedient robots. Of young, outrageously cute crystal-eyed siblings hugging and kissing each other, as if they've never thrown tantrums over toy-snatching. Of parents looking impossibly content, barbequing up a feast for their statistically calculated 2.5 kids, under an unnaturally cloudless sky. All in all, a stereotypical view of Australia, distorted by blank sound, with raging lawn mowers as a backdrop.

The crickets have just begun their nightly symphonic orchestra. The fridge shudders. The water filter bubbles. The clock ticks. The kitchen tap drips … waste-ing-wor-tah. Ailish is in Kit's head, prodding, probing, nagging her to *"Turn the tap off, Kit. You know we've got stage-three water restrictions."*

Kit rolls off the couch to turn off the tap, and notices a note on the microwave door: "If you'd like to be good to our planet, heat this on the stove instead."

Kit smiles. *After all the shit. She still thinks about the environment.*

She opens the microwave door to find a plate of chicken

curry and rice. The floorboards in the entrance hall creak. She stops. Listens. Cocks her head like a dog. She turns around to find Sein sitting at the counter. She gasps and jumps backward.

"Are you off your fucking cracker? You scared the shit outta me," Kit snaps.

Sein smiles, void of joy, picking at a scratch on the surface of the counter with his thumbnail. "Sorry. The fly screen wasn't latched, and I just thought—"

"Don't worry." Kit says. "I'm glad you're here." She sprinkles a little water over the food so it doesn't dry out in the microwave. "Do you want some curry?"

Sein nods, still staring at his scratching thumb.

Kit puts the plate back in the microwave, turns it on, and sits on top of the counter between the stove and sink. She sticks her finger inside Ailish's moisturizer pot and rubs some into her hands and elbows. Sein and Kit look at each other with half-smiles on their faces.

Who's gonna speak first? Will he ask how it went with Mum?

But neither speaks. They just stare, both seeming at absolute ease with each other, yet on edge at the same time.

Kit glances out the kitchen window at the orangeless tree and clean concrete path. Now Roger feels more absent than ever. Before Sein cleared everything away, she felt that perhaps he had always been there with her in spirit, as if he'd left pieces of himself behind for her to nibble on once in a while. But now his pieces are gone. And all that's left of him is his skeleton, the shell that once gave life to the fruit.

Will the pieces grow back next season? Or will Ailish cut the tree down, like she keeps saying, so she has more room to plant her precious vegetables?

The microwave pings. She pulls the plate out and places it on the counter in front of Sein. He looks at it briefly, then continues to pick at the scratch and winks a thank-you. What Kit wants is for Sein to swipe the plate onto the floor. To smash it. Anything is better than this silence.

Slam me down on the counter and fuck me right here, right now.

She wants him to thrust the pain out of her heart, her head, her constant need to escape the possibility of her turning out like her mother even though she knows they're exactly the same.

What is so wrong with being smart? Nothing, really. The only problem is, the smarter you are, the more life seems to hurt. *Is that what I'm trying to run from? My involuntary reaction to analyzing my own pain? Screw this. I'll just have to do this myself.*

"Sein. Move the plate before it ends up on the floor."

"What?" He looks up. Tears well in his eyes.

Kit ignores them. She doesn't want to hear about it. Not now. Right now she needs to feed herself. And she needs Sein's help. She needs him to be someone she knows he's not—an aggressive male nymphomaniac. All Kit wants to do is bang her fist on the bench and yell "Now!" but she doesn't. She couldn't be that cruel.

"Please," Kit whispers, trying to tame her tears.

Sein stands, the stool scrapes on the floor, and he transfers the plate to the sink. Kit wraps her arms around his waist from behind. Her veins pulsate. She shoves her hand down the front of Sein's jeans. He sucks in his stomach. His breath deepens, quickens, as he flings his head back and winces as if she may have squeezed too hard. Without any warning he yanks Kit's hand out of his pants and swings around. Kit steps back. Tears stream down their cheeks.

"What's wrong? What the fuck is the matter?" Kit yells, pulling at her hair.

Sein looks at the floor, shakes his head. A cry like the yelp of an injured animal escapes his closed mouth. Kit just stares, unable to display the anger she feels for him destroying her fantasy. Unable to sympathize with the only person she has ever been able to identify with on an unspoken level.

She steps forward, lifting her arms to give him a hug, but he grabs her wrists. He holds them vehemently in the air, contaminating the space between them with flaming testosterone. Any tighter and his grip would assume the strength of a Chinese burn. Kit's wrists sting, but she doesn't move. She relishes it. A pain that washes pain away.

"Dad told me how Mum died," Sein whimpers, and lets go of Kit's wrists. He hunches over and breaks into a full-blown sob.

Oh my God.

Kit's preoccupation drops from her like a man jumping from a high-rise building. *He needs me.* She rests her head on Sein's chest, keeping her hands by her side, her body heat moulding into his, to form some sort of electromagnetic connection. She envisions their nerve endings soldering together, faintly sparking as they bind.

"Do you want to talk about it?" Kit asks, speaking into Sein's shoulder, and breathing in the familiar scent of his T-shirt. She can feel him shake his head. "Are you sure? You know, we could go get some takeout and lock ourselves in my bedroom. You can tell me."

"Just shut up!" Sein barks, pushing Kit so hard she stumbles into the pantry.

Kit's jaw drops. She thought he'd want that. She thought he needed some comfort. She stares at his contorted face. He wobbles his body in an odd lanky way, as if trying to shake pain out of it.

"Sorry," he whispers. His eyes glaze over. He lifts Kit up onto the counter, wraps her legs around his waist, slides her as close as possible with both hands on her behind, and thrusts his tongue into her mouth. Gentle yet rough too. Kit unbuttons his jeans without looking and pushes them down to his knees with her feet. Before Kit even has a second to anticipate it, Sein lifts her dress, pulls Kit's head back by her hair, and enters her from the side of her knickers. It's over in less than a minute.

Kit's hot. Sticky. Sweaty. Smelly. The best she's felt all week. As Sein fastens his jeans, the front door swings open and bounces off the doorstop. The hinges squeak as it springs shut. Kit jumps off the counter and fixes her hair, looking at her reflection in the microwave door. Sein passes her the plate of curry after taking a mouthful first himself. He whispers, "It's still hot," with a mixed expression of relief and naughty-schoolboy cheekiness. Kit giggles, quickly wiping the shine of her saliva from around his mouth with a tea towel.

They both stand in a respectable position, leaning their butts against the counter, eating standing up, when Ailish walks in. Her hair is out and her cheeks are flushed.

"Hi, Sein. How nice of you to come over. I see Kit's been hospitable," Ailish says, nodding at the plate of curry in Sein's hands.

Sein grins. Kit elbows him in his side, and he buckles over in melodramatic acceptance, pretending to choke on his food. Kit can't believe Ailish hasn't run upstairs yet to make herself "presentable" for Sein. *What's got into her?*

"So how's Eleanor?" Kit asks, with a mouth full of food. "Does she know that Ivy and I are officially the way half sisters should be?"

"And how is that, Kit?" Ailish laughs. "How should half sisters be?"

"Not joined at the hip," Kit says with a smirk.

Ailish drops her handbag on the counter. "I see Sein was able to bring you back to life. Thanks, Sein. You're obviously better at it than I am." Ailish goes cross-eyed, picking an insect out of her hair.

Kit winks at Sein. "Yeah. I guess he is."

"Well, I'm glad. Because I've got some news."

Kit stops spooning curry into her **mouth**. Sein takes the plate from her hands and rubs her **on her** upper back, pressing his lips together in a way one **might call** hopeful.

Ailish sits on a bar stool and crosses **her legs**. "I found out where your father lives."

"What?" Kit cries, looking at Sein, at Ailish, **then** at Sein again in disbelief. "Where does he live?"

"In Phillip Island. With his brother, **Samuel**. But that's not the news."

"Whaddaya mean?"

"Turns out I'm not the only one with secrets. Roger had a stroke." Kit opens her mouth to speak, but Ailish lifts her hand, a signal to shoosh. "He's fine. Recovering. Well. Recovered. Eleanor's been using the savings she'd put aside for Ivy to pay for his medical and rehabilitation expenses."

"You're kidding?"

"Nope. And there's something else that might bring a sparkle to your eye."

Kit raises her eyebrows.

"Ivy knows nothing about it."

brian

Brian opens his eyes. *Did I sleep?* He looks at the lamp crystals on the bedside table. *I'll just get up. I can't sleep.* He lies still for a moment, trying to grasp his whereabouts. How he fell asleep at home and woke up at Ivy's. *Ah. The call. The freak-out. The taxi. The crying. The sex. The sex was good.*

He tries to sit on the edge of the bed without waking Ivy. But fails miserably when his feet touch the carpet, and he accidentally lets out a ripper of a fart. *Damn!* It bubbles behind his balls and sends dread through his chest. He stares at himself in the wardrobe mirror. *Maybe it's just loud because it's quiet in here.* He's afraid to move in case the smell spreads through Ivy's silky cotton sheets. His torso constricts; goose pimples form around his nipples. Ivy giggles and rubs her eyes. *Shit. Can she smell it? I can smell it. Shit.* She nuzzles her face into her pillow and smudges makeup on it.

"Lovely," Ivy croaks. "That's so much better than an alarm clock. Can you stay over during the week too?" She waves her hand in front of her nose.

"Sorry," he whispers.

"'S not as bad as some I've experienced."

"You should go back to sleep. It's only nine o'clock," Brian says, standing and pulling on his boxers. He catches the reflection of his right bum cheek in the mirror. He has a huge hickey on it. *Are those teeth marks?*

"What time did we go to sleep?" Ivy asks, struggling to open her eyes and shadowing them with her hand. She lifts both legs into the air and hooks the duvet underneath her feet.

Brian stands straight, motionless, staring out the window at the grey wet street. He can see a lady fetching the Sunday paper in her pyjamas and gumboots. She rips the plastic off, pulls out the Christmas catalogues, and throws the newspaper in the street bin.

"Not sure, but I came around half four." *And I "came" around five.*

Ivy grunts in agreement, rolls over, and pulls the covers over her head.

Brian stumbles into the kitchen to put on a pot of coffee. But he can't find the percolator. *Does she even have a percolator?* Crumbs crunch under his bare feet and get stuck between his toes. The kitchen bench is bare, and the pantry is full of herbs, self-rising flour, canned minestrone soup, Jacob's instant coffee, and old jars of strawberry jelly and Vegemite. There's one jar of Marmite too, still sealed. *That must be for emergencies.*

The inside of the fridge looks like a hospital ward in the midst of a bomb scare. There's a plate of mouldy blueberry pancakes, a box of Chinese noodles with chopsticks and a fork still in it, and a couple of cans of Malibu and Coke. *No milk.* In the dish rack there is one bowl, one mug, one soup spoon, and one teaspoon.

Packed cardboard boxes, sitting dormant next to the kitchen table against the wall, stare at Brian. They tease him, rubbing the fast-approaching and ambivalent future into his face. *I never asked for this. I should go back in, right now, and tell her we need to slow down. I'm not ready. She'll understand. I'm sure she'll understand. Yeah …*

He returns to the bedroom and pulls the covers from Ivy's face. She smiles with her eyes shut, like a child who's secretly eaten all the Jell-O, or drunk all the chocolate milk. Brian imagines her with a brown milky moustache.

"Babe, do you have a percolator?"

"No. Just use the hot tap, or boil some water in the small pot on the stove. Everything else is packed away," Ivy replies with a croak.

Brian doesn't move. He looks out the window again. Now there's a truck delivering the woman a tree. She's wearing a heavy-looking coat over her pyjamas this time. She pulls money out of her pocket and hands it to the delivery dude. Her husband runs out now to help her drag the tree into the house. He's fully dressed and has his cell phone hooked between his ear and shoulder. The woman trips. She yells something at her husband. He drops the tree to the ground, holds his finger up to his mouth to tell her to shoosh, and continues talking on his cell. She stamps her foot, throws her arms up in the air, and yells something else before running back inside the house and slamming the front door. The dread of another round of domesticity pricks at Brian's pores. *Ugh.*

Ivy opens her eyes and looks at him. "What's up?"

"Ivy. We need to talk," Brian says, stroking her fringe from her forehead.

Ivy sits up and leans against the headboard. She frowns, picking at some dry skin on her bottom lip. Licks it. Brian wants to bite it and make love to her again.

"Um, I know what you're going to say," Ivy says, nodding and pushing her hair behind her ears.

"You do?"

"Yes. And it's totally fine."

"It is?"

"Of course, it is."

"Thank God." Brian sighs. "I was worried I might really hurt you."

"Don't be silly. It won't happen again. Anyway, we'll have moved in together soon, and there won't be any need for me to drag you outta bed at the crack of dawn. So don't fret. I'll be a good girl. I promise." Ivy cocks her head to the side, winks, and pinches Brian on the chin. "You stay here. I'll go make the coffee. I'm awake now anyway."

Brian nods, unable to speak. He did it again. He's letting her do it again. He's doing it again. Being the rebound. He watches her in the mirror as she gracefully inserts her arms into a silk robe and secures it around her waist. She moves closer to the mirror and examines something on her nose. "I'm amazed I don't have more of a hangover," she says, bright and bubbly. "I thought I'd be complete rat-shit today," she adds, then walks out the door with a little skip.

Brian lies down on the bed and stares at the ceiling. *Why can't I fall in love with a woman without any issues for once in my life? Why am I always signing up to be a bouncing board?*

He remembers Ivy before he'd managed to get her to come out on a date. She seemed shy, sometimes introverted. Innocent but experienced. Confident, vulnerable, flirty, reluctant to lead him on. He thought these qualities meant her character had depth. He thought it meant they'd have a lot to talk about, that they would stay up late, drinking wine, confessing their deep dark secrets. But they don't. They hardly talk at all. They just fuck, drink coffee, and smoke. Well, Ivy smokes. And he's beginning to feel that Ivy's character has so little depth because *she* doesn't really know who she is. Dangerous territory.

Last night, when he arrived, Ivy was bawling her eyes out. She asked him to never let her call Kit again, no matter how much she started to miss her. Why? Why would someone want to tie off a connection with someone they love? Before he had the chance to ask why, she was all over him, like ketchup to fries, using sex to avoid talking about it. She blindfolded him and banged him like a bass drum. She was on top. He enjoyed it. He wanted more. So why does he feel so guilty? What if this keeps happening? Will she ever give reasons for her actions, or will he just get lots of sex and no talk? This should be a man's ultimate dream. So why doesn't it feel like one? Why does it feel like a mistake?

Do I already resent her for what she hasn't done? No. The true question is, is she too much like my wife?

kit

Eeny, meeny, miny, moe, catcha nigger … no … catcha tigger by the toe. If it hollers let him go … eeny, meeny, miny, moe … You. Are. It. Kit's finger points firmly down on Sylvia Plath's *Winter Trees*, the book that represents pursuing a career in English literature. In front of her, she has also placed a fish fossil (archaeology) and a twenty-dollar bill (get a crap job, move out). Kit's relieved. *Looks like Mum got her wish. Fine. English lit it is, then.*

"I've made a decision," Kit says to herself in her dresser mirror. "I'm going to become an academic. How does that make you feel?" Kit picks up a pencil and holds it toward her reflection like a microphone. "I feel great. In fact, I don't know why I didn't just study literature in the first place." She points the pencil toward her real mouth and says in a mannish voice, "That's very interesting. So you'll follow in your mother's footsteps, after all. Hmm, but I'm curious, and if you don't mind me asking, what about your father? Would you still like to meet him?" Kit gazes into her eyes, analyzing the melancholy reaction to her own question, and slowly moves the pencil toward the mirror again.

She stares at her reflection. She has faint wrinkles in the outer edges of her eyes. They sort of slant downward—sad, unconfident lines like Ailish's. If they could speak, they'd say, "Please, throw me a rope." She is her mother's daughter down to the last detail. She bets, if she made the effort to check, that their freckles would be mirror images if they stood side by side. A tear trickles down Kit's cheek. "I don't know." Her voice cracks like a struggling radio signal.

"Kit?" Ailish calls, knocking on her bedroom door. "She'll be here soon. Are you going to come down?"

Kit puts the pencil down, wipes her eyes, takes a deep breath, and opens the door to find Ailish standing there in a floral dress and a clashingly floral apron, her wet hands in the air as if she has just pulled them out of soil, and with an unnaturally wide smile.

You look possessed.

"Yes. I'm coming down now." Kit forces a smile into her own cheeks, in half-mockery, and follows Ailish down the stairs. Kit's ready. *Psychologically prepared?* Dressed, yes. Grey-blue knee-length skirt and a plain white T-shirt. Nonthreatening, like Ailish suggested. She's not worried or anxious (well, maybe a little) because she's about to meet her *sister*.

Should I put my hair in a ponytail?

It's perfect, really. Isn't it? Ivy is out of the picture now, and Kit will have someone to replace her with. Well, at least today she'll pretend to act happy about that. The last thing she wants is to scare the poor girl away. Kit's stomach fills with schoolgirl-like butterflies, and she realizes how hard it is to feel twenty-five while still living with her mother. She doesn't feel a day over eighteen. And this has got to change. Very soon. Before her intellectual growth is left to rot in the backyard with the oranges.

Ailish has set up the dining table with a pot of tea and ginger biscuits; cubed watermelon and cantaloupe; and sliced sourdough bread, butter, and jam. *What? No scones?*

"Mum, whydya go to so much trouble? What if it's really uncomfortable? What if we want to get rid of her?" Kit leans her shoulder against the door frame and rotates the silver band around her thumb. It's the only piece of jewellery she can be bothered to wear. In fact, she can't even be bothered to take it off.

"Don't be silly, Kit. The girl is lovely. She sounded lovely."

Ailish rubs her sticky fruit-juice-covered fingers on a tea towel that's hanging over a chair and sighs, staring absently at the table. "It'll be lovely. Don't worry."

"Why don't you ever call her by her name?" And it's just now that Kit realizes she doesn't even know her name.

"Oh? Sorry. Yes, I should, shouldn't I?"

"Well? What's her name?"

Ailish ignores her question and whistles the tune of a bread commercial on her return to the kitchen.

"Why are you so happy?" Kit calls after her.

"Oh, I don't know. It's such a lovely day," Ailish calls back, making a clanking racket in the kitchen sink. "Look out the window. The weather is lovely!"

"Lovely," Kit whispers, pinching the bridge of her nose.

There's a knock on the fly-screen door. It rattles. So does Kit's stomach. The butterflies turn into tangled paper clips. Kit sits at the table as Ailish leaps into the hall. There's some joyous muttering. *Hugs? Kisses?* But Kit refuses to go into the hall to join in. She'll stay here. At the table. Rapidly shaking her right foot. She just needs a few more seconds to prepare. What is she going to say? How is she going to introduce herself? *What if the girl is really shy, and there's a horrible uncomfortable silence, and Mum starts talking about the time when I was two and peed all over her face in order to wake her up one morning? Oh God.*

"Kit! Oh my God, it's you! I knew it. I just *knew* it!" Eydie squeals and flings herself into Kit's arms as if they've been separated for years during a war.

"Oh. Hi. What are you doing here? Is everything okay?" Kit asks, twisting her hair into a knot and letting it drop free again.

Ailish flashes confused looks at both Eydie and Kit. "You two know each other?" Ailish puts her hands on her hips and tilts her head.

"Yeah, Mum, this is my hairdresser, remember?" Kit replies, giving Eydie a quick hug before attempting to shuffle her to the front door. "Eydie, we're expecting a visitor. I'm so sorry, but I'll call you later? You're not in trouble or anything, right? Maybe later, we can go out for …"

Eydie and Ailish start to laugh.

"What? What's so funny?" Kit asks, craning her neck.

"I'm yer visitor, ya dag." Eydie howls, grabbing hold of Kit again and jumping up and down on the spot like a child who won a trip to the fair. Kit feels like an electric mixer. The possibility that Eydie is her sister travels through her like a cold draft.

"What? What do you mean?" Kit asks, loosening Eydie's tight hold. She glances at Ailish, who is at complete ease, swinging the tea towel back and forth by her right thigh with a strange robotic smile plastered on her face.

"I'm yer sister, Kit. Ya can't believe it, can ya? In't this wicked?" Eydie weaves her fingers together and brings her entwined hands to her lips, covering a mutant smile. Kit can see wrinkles form in Eydie's cheeks as the corners of her mouth turn upward bit by bit. She seems eager to pounce for another hug. But Kit feels the colour drain from her face, and she levers herself into a chair. *He sent her letters.* Eydie's giggles taper off, and Ailish's arms fall limp by her sides.

"What's wrong?" Eydie asks, sitting down next to her. I thought you'd be really happy to be my sister. Aren't ya happy? Kit?" Eydie's voice turns from tickled to apprehensive, sliding upward at the end of every question.

Kit's disappointment augments Eydie's voice with the quality of an echo, distant and desperate. The insignificant sound of Ailish's feet scuffing the floorboards increases in muffled volume as if Kit's head is being inserted into a space helmet. If only it was real, and fire would now blast from the soles of her feet and thrust her through the ceiling, away from this mess she started. Away from the figurative slaps she keeps getting.

Just make me disappear. I can't deal with being hurt anymore. Over and over. I can't. Grant me this wish, and I'll never mention Roger's name again. Please.

Kit smiles a frown and rests a hand on Eydie's knee. She doesn't look up. "I'm sorry. I am happy. It's just … why did he send you letters and not me?"

Eydie takes Kit's hand from her knee and gives it a soft squeeze. "I dunno. But if it's any, um, constellation, I never got 'em till it was too late. Ya know that."

Kit grins at Eydie's use of *constellation*, but doesn't correct her.

Ailish takes a seat, scraping the chair on the floor, and

shoves a chunk of watermelon into her mouth with a tooth-pick. Ailish never scrapes chairs. She lifts and gently places them back down. With her mouth full and juice dripping down her chin she asks, "Letters? About what?"

Eydie turns to face Ailish and adopts a polite, respectful tone. "Not much, unfortunately. I just found 'em in me ma's drawer, but they all had checks in 'em, it looks like, because at the top of every letter it has 'check enclosed' written on it. I never saw any of the money, though. Me ma, she … anyway, me ma spent the dough and never told me about any of it."

"Checks." Ailish's cheekbones become taut as she nods in slow motion. She hovers above her seat as if ready to sprint at the sound of a horn.

"Yeah," Eydie pours herself a cup of tea. The teapot lid rattles, filling silence with strain.

Ailish stands up so fast that she knocks her chair backward. Kit and Eydie jump as it smacks the floor. As Ailish picks it up and pushes it back under the table, Kit notices tears.

"Girls, I'm sorry," Ailish stammers, holding a hand to her forehead, half-concealing her eyes. "I just remembered I have something to do in town." Ailish's voice wavers. "Y-you two have a good old chat and catch up, and I'll be back soon." She swallows. It's loud. "Okay?" She unties her apron, throws it on the kitchen counter, grabs her handbag, and runs out the front door. It slams. The calm that follows thickens with Kit's suspicion.

"What just happened? Eydie asks, **staring toward the** front door with a finger hooked through **the teacup handle.**

"I'm not sure." Kit stares at Eydie's **magenta acrylic** fingernails. *How many more secrets has Mum got?* "Maybe she really did just forget to do something." Kit rubs Eydie's shoulder with a smile. "She gets flustered quite easily. Don't worry about it." Kit pushes the plate **of biscuits toward** Eydie.

"Here. Have one."

Kit takes a ginger biscuit herself and bites into it. It crumbles. Small pieces fall under her tongue like misplaced emotions seeking refuge.

ailish

Ailish screeches out of her small suburban street and onto the highway. Her tires burn rubber and create smoke, smogging up her rear windscreen. Her tail end flicks to the right, almost causing her to lose control of the vehicle. *Checks? Checks! You mother-fucking lying bastard. How dare you. What about Kit? If I wasn't so afraid for her well-being, I'd go and report you right this instant, you ruthless piece of …argh!* Ailish bashes her palm on the steering wheel, causing the car to swerve and her hand to throb.

Ailish takes the exit onto Bell Street and makes her way back home the long way around. She needs to drive. To think. To figure out what she's going to do.

On Sydney Road, she gets stuck behind a tram and mindlessly watches as people take their time getting on and off, holding up peak-hour traffic. They're stuck in routine, newspapers hooked under their arms, handbags hugged close to their chests, afraid of muggers, pickpockets, or of simply letting go of their aimless angst. *If only I could live a life of routine and not worry about the past. End this fiasco now. Tell Kit you're finished. That you can't pretend anymore. Just do it. She'll understand. She has to.*

kit

Kit observes Eydie as she browses through the bookshelf in the lounge. Eydie pulls a book out, looks at the back cover, frowns, raises her eyebrows, and puts it back. In the wrong position. She flicks her emo fringe out of her face, over and over, like a twitch, checks her acrylic nails for damage every time they accidentally hit something hard, and clicks her tongue ring against her teeth when she seems to be contemplating what to say next. Habits Kit has never witnessed at the salon. Habits, it seems, that flourish when she feels out of place.

"Kit. I've got some good news." Eydie turns around to face Kit, who is filling her mouth with as much watermelon as possible. She steps forward, pauses, holds her hands in the air as if keeping balance on a skateboard, clicks her tongue ring, then steps forward again to sit next to Kit on the couch.

"What is it?" Kit attempts a smile in the hopes she might make Eydie feel more welcome, even though all Kit wants to do is curl up in bed and cry. She loves Eydie; she always has. But this is all too much. Her sister? Really? Why can't things just go back to the way they were? She should have appreciated how lucky she was. Now so many lives have been changed. And for what? All because of her stupid obsession with a man she knows nothing about.

"Me ma gave me Roger's address. Wanna go meet 'im together?"

Kit laughs. "I've got the address too. Ivy's mum had it all along."

"So why haven't you gone to see 'im?"

"I don't know."

"Oh." Eydie looks out the window as if taking a moment to contemplate what that might mean. "Why?"

"Mum said he recently had a stroke. I dunno. It makes me feel weird. Like he's not how I envisioned him, you know?"

Eydie bows her head and rubs her hands over her knees as if trying to warm them. She pauses and lifts her head, eyes wide with recognition like someone just flicked on her switch. "That's probably why the letters stopped coming."

"Probably." Kit looks at her feet and touches her toes together.

Eydie nods with both her head and torso as if trying to push herself forward in a canoe. She smiles and looks at the photo of Kit and Ailish on the wall above the fireplace. "So he's just a normal everyday guy, hey?"

"Yeah. I suppose." Kit laughs, thinking that there must be more to him than what Ailish is letting on.

Eydie puts her arm around Kit's shoulders and gives her a little nudge. "Let's go and visit 'im anyway. You know, like normal people. For lunch or somethin'. You know, like, a family? What we got to lose?"

Kit shrugs. "What are we going to say to him?"

"I dunno, but why give up on 'im now just 'cause he's not exciting? It's silly. I mean, surely we'll find out some interesting stuff. You said he was in the Army, right? Let's ask 'im 'bout that." Eydie nudges Kit in her side. "Come on. Let's at least meet 'im. Then we can meet our uncle too. And then at least we won't keep thinking about it for the rest of our lives. We can, ya know, move on and stuff."

Kit shakes her head and shoves another piece of watermelon into her mouth. "I think I've already moved on. I don't think I need to meet him anymore."

"Then why ya still looking so sad?"

Kit scoffs.

"You're not upset about 'im not sending ya any letters, are ya?"

It's not Eydie's fault. As much as you want to, don't put the blame on her. Stop being so pettily jealous.

Kit sighs and looks into Eydie's eyes. Hers don't turn down at the edges as much. They're a perfect almond shape. But she has a similar nose to Kit's. They both have a vague Mediterranean bump in the middle. Could that be from Roger? Does she really want to find out?

"Come on, Kit. Life's too fuckin' short. Me ma has a problem with the bottle. Ya know that. He probably sent her money 'cause he knew she wouldn't go out 'n' earn a livin' on her own. Well, at least that's the only freakin' logical 'n' sane reason I can think've. He obviously knew that you and yer ma could look after yerselves."

"You think so?"

"Yeah. I do. So whadda ya say? Come meet 'im with me, will ya? Let's start this family from scratch."

"I suppose it'd be cool to meet Samuel too."

"Yeah! So is it a deal?" Eydie stands and holds out her hand, gesturing for a high five, when Ailish comes storming back into the house, panting and flushed like an overexerted marathon runner.

"There is no way on earth that you are going to meet your father, Kit," she puffs, seeming to be oblivious to Eydie's presence.

Kit stands up.

"What? Why?" Eydie and Kit ask in unison.

"Because he's a … a … he's filth. Full stop," Ailish spits, spraying saliva into the air in front of her. "I'm sorry, but …"

Ailish rubs a hand over her mouth and lowers herself into a chair at the dinner table, trying to catch her breath. She looks at Kit and Eydie briefly before focusing her stare through the window and into the backyard. Her eyes flit toward Kit again before looking at her lap.

"I'm sorry, I'm … I'm just letting my own hurt get in your

way." Ailish stands, straightens her skirt, and then crosses her arms under her breasts. She shakes her head. "I'm sorry. I'm ... just sorry." For a moment she pauses, then stares at Kit and Eydie before turning around and running up the stairs and slamming the bathroom door behind her.

Kit sits back down on the couch. Eydie does the same, clicking her tongue ring and lifting her hands up in question. Kit winks at Eydie and squeezes her hand.

It's time Kit takes control.

Ivy finds Brian's synthetic Christmas tree buried behind a dozen or so brown shoe boxes in his closet. When she moved in, she had expected his shirts to all be ironed and colour-coordinated, but they're not. His closet is completely disorganized. Half his shirts are even falling off the hangers.

They remind Ivy of a gorilla skeleton, the way its scapula protrudes horizontally from its spine, taut and strong enough to support up to three thousand kilograms, but its humerus hangs from the scapula as if fed up with life, weak, and willing to be dragged along wherever its master desires it to go. *Am I a humerus? Am I as pathetic as Kit and too stubborn to admit it? Do I just attach myself to a scapula and let it lead the way? Why do I put myself through this? Do I even want to be here?*

She sneaks a peek inside the shoe boxes and finds an array

of candle-making equipment. Poignant scents of apple and papaya escape as she lifts the lids. She touches a clump of green wax, velvety and smooth like the royal-green cloak she remembers Roger bought her for her dress-up box. She nicks a chunk of wax off with a fingernail and touches it to her tongue. It tastes furry. Like when you accidentally spray perfume in your mouth. *Ugh. Ivy, what are you doing?*

She imagines Brian teaching her how to make candles, and how romantic it would be if they spent the next couple of days making them together for Christmas gifts. *By candlelight.* She smiles at the thought, but immediately washes it away with a frown when she remembers how unkind Brian has been lately.

Ivy has been quite enthusiastic about playing house, but Brian always seems on edge. With every dirty dish that gets left unwashed in the sink, he rolls his eyes. With every item of clothing overflowing in the laundry basket, he rolls his eyes. With every coffee mug that gets left on the bedside table, he rolls his eyes. He sees Ivy putting on makeup when she doesn't have to go out, and he rolls his eyes.

What's wrong with making myself feel good? Maybe he's just stressed at work. But as soon as the thought reaches the nerve endings of her tongue, she realizes she may be making excuses for him. She used to make excuses for Amir. All the time. *But really, I'd be pretty peeved if he had all of his stuff scattered all over my house, right?*

Ivy's belongings are scattered all over the place, creating a hostile environment. Neither of them has even been able to get up in the middle of the night to go to the bathroom without tripping over something and waking up the other.

Last night, when she'd finally put away the last of her kitchen appliances, Brian said, "Now can you start to take a little more care around the house? The place looks like a boar's run riot in here." He's right. The place is a pigsty. And seeing as she hasn't started work at the museum yet, she'll willingly play housewife and clean. *Right after I put the Christmas tree up. We can't not have a Christmas tree, can we? And anyway, I'll probably make a mess putting it up. So it's only logical I do it first. I'm sure Brian will agree.*

Ivy pulls the tree out of its box, and little broken pieces of tinsel fall around her feet. *Fairy dust.* She smiles and hums "Jingle Bells," trying to plunge her psyche into the Christmas spirit. One untainted by heartbreak, such as finding Kit struggling to free herself from Amir's firm hold in their hall last Boxing Day.

She extends the flexible branches and stands the tree up by the window. The corners are filled with snow. Her first white Christmas.

Ivy notices some damp in the skirting boards. *We'll need to get that looked at.*

Oh. Did I just say "we"?

Ivy scoffs, continues to hum while simultaneously biting her conscience's tongue. Perhaps some psychological pain might wake her up and plummet her back into the world she lived in before she moved to Seattle, into a world she would go back to in a heartbeat.

I overreacted. A lot. Amir and I would probably have been fine.

As she lifts a shiny red ball to hook onto a branch, she sees the reflection of her face, distorted and fishbowlesque, as if screaming to be let out. But it's not her own reflection she sees, after all. Startled by the image, she turns her head to find Brian hovering over her with a flicker of Mad Hatter in his eyes. For a moment Ivy feels drugged.

"Hi. I-I didn't hear you come in. How long have you been standing there?" she asks, turning her attention back to the tree. She places a silver ball in a position on the tree so she can observe Brian's full-bodied reflection.

"Not even a second." Brian looks around the house and takes a deep breath. "The place is still a dump. What have you been doing all day?"

"Research. On the Internet. Proposals. For work. I was going to tidy up after I fixed the tree," Ivy replies, standing up from her kneeling position on the floor. She brushes off her knees, and flecks of glitter from the decorations fill the air and gradually waft to the ground.

"Ah, look at that. Pretty, huh? Almost like magic." Ivy smiles. She thinks about giving Brian a kiss hello, but doesn't when she sees the look on his face.

Brian drops his briefcase to the floor with a thud and clenches his jaw.

"What's the matter?" Ivy asks, in a tone so insubstantial it is almost a whisper. "What's happened to you these past couple of weeks?"

Determined not to start a yelling match, she maintains her calm, pretending for a moment that this reaction is the result of fatigue and not because the house is still untidy. Last night's yelling match was enough to last the week. Especially considering it was over something as meaningless as using olive oil to glaze the pasta instead of butter.

Ivy folds her arms below her breasts and looks Brian directly in the eye. She cocks her head. She's not going to let this behaviour intimidate her and must exert a flavour of dominating courage. There's no way she's going to let Brian walk all over her. No. Way. She was a doormat once, and she vowed to never be again.

But she buckles. *Is this really buckling?* And apologizes to keep the peace. *It's almost Christmas, after all.*

"I'm sorry. Maybe this was a mistake. I shouldn't have …" Ivy is about to say that she shouldn't have put the tree up without asking if he wanted one, but Brian interrupts.

"No, you shouldn't have," he snaps. "This whole moving-in-together business was a huge mistake." Brian spreads his hands out in front of him to emphasize how big "huge" actually is.

What?

The room grows smaller around Ivy. The sound of life, the atmosphere, the atoms in the air adopt a shallow hum. A thump in her ears pounds like a draw hoe in clay, as reasons Brian would say such a thing flash through her mind like moments of life before death.

"Pardon?" Ivy asks, drawing her chin to her chest as if

she's having difficulty swallowing. Tears teeter behind her eyes and constrict her throat. It's the same feeling she felt when catching Amir in the act. The need to escape afflicts her like deep vein thrombosis, initiating the possibility of it dislodging and travelling to her lungs. Panic. *And what do I do now?* Ivy folds her arms, waiting for Brian to explain.

Brian looks at the wall, avoiding eye contact. "Remember when you went for the interview at the museum?" Brian asks, not moving an inch from his stance by the front door. He doesn't wait for Ivy to answer. "Well, all I wanted to tell you was that I thought I might be in love with you. I hadn't intended to ask you to move in with me at all." His face goes pale. Expressionless. He puts his hands in his pockets and rolls, once, on the balls of his feet.

"Excuse me?" Ivy screeches, stepping closer to Brian. "And it hadn't occurred to you to tell me that earlier? Before I uprooted my whole fucking life?" Ivy loosens her folded arms, but immediately folds them again. She feels vulnerable letting them dangle by her sides as if suspended in indecision.

"I, uh, thought I could get used to the idea, Ivy," Brian replies, stammering a little. "I had no idea I would feel so—"

"So *what*, Brian?" Ivy asks, a shrill through clenched teeth. She backs him up against the front door, standing so close she could give him mouth-to-mouth.

"I don't know." Brian shakes his head. Ivy can hear his hair crunch against the surface of the door.

"You *must* know," Ivy screams. "Otherwise you wouldn't have found the nerve to say something after all this time. Spill it!"

Brian swallows, shakes his head, his façade of power melting away like a snowman in sun. "Trapped! I feel *trapped*!" Brian retorts, pushing Ivy off him.

Ivy trips backward on a rug and falls on her backside. She's faint. Lightheaded. Lost in a chaos she feels she should have taken control of before it got so out of hand.

"Oh God." Brian kneels down to try to help her up. "Ivy, I'm so sorry, I really didn't—"

Ivy flicks her arm in the air, shoos him away like cigarette smoke. "I can get up on my own."

"I didn't mean to—"

"I know. Forget it." Ivy stands and brushes off her bum. Tears fall down her cheeks, hot with self-disappointment. She's the one to blame for this. She shouldn't have jumped into this so fast and for all the wrong reasons. "So, what now?" she chokes out. "I'm supposed to leave, after I've just moved in?"

Brian walks to the kitchen, hanging his head, and fills the kettle with water. "Tea?"

Ivy glares at him. "Tea? That's what you have to say? Tea."

"It'll be the best for both of us, Ivy. I mean, Jesus, how long have we been dating? One month? It's happening too fast. Don't you think it's happening too fast?"

"Brian." Ivy closes her eyes and pushes down on her eyelids so hard that the blackness starts to resemble the Big

Bang. "Is there someone else?" She sits on the couch and feels between her teeth with her tongue. It begins to rain, and a loud crack of thunder causes her to jolt.

"No. I just need some time, Ivy. I need some space." Brian turns the heating dial up a notch and leans against the kitchen bench, rubbing his brow.

"Space. Huh. Easy excuse, isn't it? Where the fuck is this need for space supposed to leave us now, Brian? Should we just end this for good?" At the bottom of the hurt, the rejection, the dull ache at the base of her chest that wants to take the place of her pulse, Ivy can't help but notice a twinge of relief. She stops crying and wonders if this is an opportunity to get Amir back. Maybe she *should* go back home.

"Ivy. I don't want this to end. I love you. I just want to take it slower." Brian sits next to Ivy on the couch. "Come here," he whispers, and tries to pull her close, but she snatches her arms away.

She wants to say it's over, to stop getting mixed up with men as a way of escaping her problems. She wants to feel like she couldn't spend another moment in this man's house, but the sudden thought of never seeing him again triggers a torrent of tears. *Am I in love with you? Why can't I decide?*

She lowers herself to the floor, surprising herself with a childlike wail, then crosses her legs and wraps her arms around her shins. She hunches over so that her head rests on her left knee, and succumbs to the tears.

"Ivy."

Her heaves echo through the hushed apartment like an abandoned child in an empty football stadium. Brian crouches down beside her, but he doesn't touch her. His warmth permeates through her clothes. *I do love you.* He's the only person she has besides Gabriel. The only person she hasn't pushed away. *Everyone is alone in this world. Everyone.*

Brian's cell buzzes. Ivy's chest tightens, and she jumps for the cell in Brian's briefcase as if an instinctual reflex.

"Ivy, what are you doing? I'm not cheating on you." Brian huffs and runs his fingers through his hair.

Ivy scoffs. "See, that's just proof that you are. I didn't even ask such a thing." Ivy sniffs, unfastening the phone from the pouch attached to the handle. Ivy looks at the screen, then at Brian. Rage creates a pocket of air in her windpipe.

"Oh, really?" Ivy chokes. "Then who the hell is *Janine?*"

"Just a friend. Can you please give me my cell?" Brian holds his hand out, nodding at her as if the gesture will somehow convince her to abide.

But Ivy opens the message. It reads: *Divorce hearing, Mon. Jan 9.*

Ivy looks up. Brian's top lip twitches.

"Divorce hearing? For whom?"

Brian shakes his head in his hands, groans, and levers himself back onto the couch. "Me."

"You're married?" Ivy squeaks, failing at trying to sound hostile.

Brian looks like he's just bitten into a lemon. Ivy hands the phone back to Brian in silence, grabs her handbag off the hat stand, and wipes away her tears with her sleeve. She opens the front door, pausing, opening and closing her mouth two or three times to speak, unable to utter the words bombarding the tip of her tongue. She *won't* say what she wants to say. Such inflammatory outbursts have no meaning in situations like this. Not anymore.

"I-I'll be back tomorrow with Gabe. To get some stuff."

"Wait," Brian says, grabbing hold of the door before it closes. "Call Kit."

Ivy squints and shakes her head in question, wishing he might have begged her not to leave.

"Just call her. She's your sister. She'll understand. Forgive and forget, Ivy. Just forgive and forget."

ailish

Ailish isolates herself in the bathroom. She locks and unlocks the rotund brass latch five times, afraid she misheard the click. It needs to click twice for it to be secure. But the second one is quiet, as quiet as a bubble in soda rising to the surface to pop. Kit says she can't hear it. And that's why the door always swings open when she least expects it.

Ailish leans with her back against the door and lets out a deep sigh laced with a hoarseness she hasn't been able to soothe since she smoked that marijuana. She opens the stiff wood-framed window to its highest point before it tends to slam shut on its own. Ailish has become accustomed to the correct position, but still continues to mark it with black crayon for Kit when it wears off. She has done so since Kit grew tall enough to open the window on her own.

She reaches into the bottom of her makeup bag—which is not filled with commercial cosmetics but with her own moisturizing concoctions stored in old black film canisters with grey caps that snap shut like insults—and pulls out a rolled apricot-coloured facecloth. She opens it to reveal a ready-made joint and a box of Redhead matches. Her emergency stash.

From the rear of the bathroom cabinet behind the sink pipes, she removes a pencil and sketchpad waterproofed by a Safeway bag that is probably more than ten years old. She's never liked to write on lined paper. For some reason she feels it'll influence her writing; it might become too linear if she has to keep her pencil between the lines.

She sits on the tiled floor, secures the joint between pursed lips, and strikes a match. Before lighting the joint she savours the smell of the burning match. She has always thought it smelled like sugar-coated melting rubber. There's something sickly sweet yet grave about the smell, as if it were the soul of Frankenstein finding life again.

She lets the first match burn out until the flame licks her thumbnail. She strikes another match, lights her joint, and begins to write.

Crooked, girls' voices,
literature hums, pounds, theoretical
notes through miniature rooms and rose
soaps. Crash. Advert tunes inside
stethoscope beats, to wind
shield wiper. Little girls cry, big
boys bite their bottom lips; gin
and bear it—the scheduled revelation,
melting ice crackling, sound of pink
jewels hitting tiles—numbed neglect.
Fatherly love can't be found
in cookie jars. Especially when mother
needs grass, to take it
on her back; to see the red raw
rubbed flesh—proof he did it.

ivy

Ivy heats up some ready-made Napolitano pasta sauce from a jar. It smells too rich for her liking, but it'll have to do. The last thing she has a mind for at the moment is grocery shopping. She could order pizza, but even the thought of deciding on a topping would prove too difficult right now.

Gabriel puts some of Ivy's cups and saucers back in her cupboards where they belong. There are a half-dozen broken ones at the bottom of the box. No wonder. Ivy didn't even bother wrapping them in newspaper this time.

Ivy stirs the sauce and observes the way it bubbles. Each bubble that pops leaves a red pockmark on the white stove surface. She watches as the bubbles become fiercer, like molten lava, hell, a place she feels she ought to live. Guilt about how she treated Kit surfaces like ringworm. An itchy, ugly, vicious circle.

"I'm gonna go back," Ivy announces, turning the heat down and wiping up the disease spread all over her stove with a sopping and tattered pink sponge. Gabriel freezes, eyes wide, plate midway between box and cupboard shelf. She prematurely shakes her head at his predictable response.

"But. You just left."

"Not to Brian's. To Australia." Grief stings the rims of Ivy's eyes like new liquid liner. But she refuses to blink it away. *I deserve every pinch of pain.*

"What? Oh, sweetcakes, why? You need to move forward, not backward. Are you sure that's a good idea? I mean, honey, you gotta quit running." Gabriel rests the plates on the kitchen bench as if the news has injected weight into his arms.

Ivy blinks. She won't respond to that. She won't try to explain why it isn't really running; it's confronting. She has to forgive and forget, just like Brian said. Well, perhaps attempting the "forget" part first might be more efficient. And in order to forget, she has to run. It's the only way. It's her first-aid system. And she only has practice implementing the rules of resuscitation.

"Look. Gabe. I've decided I want to see my father. That's

the only reason I want to go back. okay?" *I can't tell you the real reason. You wouldn't understand.*

Ivy turns on the fan above the stove when she realizes the kitchen window is steaming up from the pot of boiling water.

Gabriel nods, raising his eyebrows so high they look like they're preparing for takeoff. He licks his lips. "That's kinda rash, isn't it?"

"Rash? I've only been thinking about it my whole life." Ivy laughs, opening a packet of spaghetti, snapping the 250-gram bunch in half and tossing it into the pot. *If only that pasta were Brian.* Boiling water splashes on her hand. She winces and runs her hand under the tap. *Haven't you burned me enough?*

Gabriel throws the broken plates in the trash and dissembles the cardboard box. He places it on the kitchen table, flattens it out like a bed sheet, and groans.

"I assume you've made up with Kit, then?" Gabriel says, swinging around to face Ivy on one foot and flicking his hair behind his shoulders.

"God, no! Are you kidding me?" *But I should. And I should tell her about the letter from Dad. But she'll kill me. And she'll hate me forever for keeping it from her. Maybe it's not such a good idea to say anything …*

"Wouldn't it be better to make up before you see her face-to-face? That could get a bit awkward, couldn't it? Just arriving on her doorstep after what you said to her?" Gabriel sits down at the kitchen table and watches Ivy wipe away splatters of red off the jade tiles behind the stove. She throws the sponge in the sink without rinsing it out.

"I won't be arriving on *her* doorstep. I'll stay with my mother. Then I'll work stuff out with Kit at Christmas. She'll be in the holiday spirit. It'll be the perfect time."

"Or the worst time," Gabriel mutters under his breath. He grabs a bottle of Limestone Coast Shiraz from the fridge. Another of Ivy's Aussie imports. "Stop being so stubborn and apologize already. I realize you're the victim of constant shit-luck, but that doesn't mean you should make someone else suffer with you." Gabriel tugs off the cork. The hollow pop echoes in Ivy's head like a finger flicking the inside of her cheek.

She pricks her shoulders up. "Look who's talking. I've seen the way you act around your boy. You totally manipulate him."

Gabriel rolls his eyes and tsks. "Honey, don't start. I'm your friend. I want to help you." He tries to grab a pair of wine glasses out of the dish rack with one hand, but doesn't manage it. Ivy grabs them instead. Their hands don't even collide.

"Well, if you want to help me so much, stop telling me what I should be doing and just let me do what I want to do."

They move into the lounge room and sit on the couch. Gabriel pours the wine, biting the tip of his tongue between his front teeth.

"Look. Sweetcakes," Gabriel says, smacking the bottle of

wine on the coffee table. "I know you're angry with Brian. But running away again isn't going to stop your pain. Please, just think about it seriously. You can't keep doing this to yourself. You're going to find yourself running in circles."

"I told you, I'm not running away. And I'd like to get there for Christmas. Can you have a look on the Internet for a flight out tomorrow? I'm going to check if the spaghetti is cooked."

"*Tomorrow*? Are you flipping serious? What about the museum?"

Ivy stands and crosses her arms, "I've got a month."

"A month." Gabriel nods as if trying to understand what that means.

"Yeah. A month. Ron said if I'm back within a month, the job will be waiting for me."

"Oh." Gabriel sighs with relief. "You'll be back in a month?" Gabriel gulps half his wine down. "Thank God. I seriously don't know what I'd do without …"

Ivy screws up her nose and looks at her feet.

"Oh my God, Ivy. You're going to stay longer?" Gabriel bursts into an overdramatic wail and pulls Ivy back down to the couch. He wraps his arms around her so tightly that Ivy envisions herself being strapped into a corset.

"Gabe," Ivy chokes out, gulping for air. "I'll come back. Chill out. I just don't know when yet."

"Phew! You had me worried there." Gabe wipes his brow as if performing in a play.

Ivy gives him a few gentle pats on his upper back. "Can you please find me a ticket with your genius deal-finder skills?" She points to Gabriel's bag with her chin.

"Okay. On it." Gabriel rubs his dry eyes with his knuckles as if they are flooded with tears, and sniffs. He pulls out his iPad from his Beatles' *Abbey Road* handbag and sits back down on the couch as Ivy leaves the room. "Thank God your house didn't get rented. Hey, Ive!"

"Uh, yeah," Ivy calls back, just through the kitchen door.

"Ive?"

"What?"

"Can I stay here while you're away?"

Ivy returns holding a wooden spoon in the air. "Sure. Why?"

"I'm breaking up with my boy." Gabriel smiles as if bracing himself for some bad news.

Ivy, knowing better than to ask for details, just nods and goes back into the kitchen. She drains the spaghetti and serves it—hers in a breakfast bowl and Gabriel's in a proper pasta dish. She calls out for Gabriel to come and get the plates while she changes into something more comfortable.

In her room, she sits on the edge of her bed staring into her open wardrobe. She finished putting everything back in it. Today. And now has to choose what to take out of it again.

She grabs a pair of pink-and-grey polka-dotted tracksuit pants from a drawer and slips them on. The black slinky dress she purchased all those weeks ago catches her eye. She rubs the soft fabric between her fingers as if gently rubbing detergent into an oil stain. She hasn't even tried it on yet. She imagines the way the dress would feel on her skin. *Perhaps I should just try it on now? No. Wait until I feel the way that dress is going to make me look. Save it. For a moment you never want to forget.*

She puts on her white puppy-dog slippers and shuffles into the lounge.

"Gabe? You think you could pack my bag for Australia too?"

Gabriel snorts. Ivy knows he knows what she's thinking. He knows everything Ivy thinks. Her face reads like an open psychiatrist's notepad. Well, that's what Gabriel always tells her.

As she sits down to eat in front of the TV with Gabriel, he gives her a little wake-up slap on the cheek. He's smiling. Like a child who has been told they never have to go to school again. Ivy appreciates his effort. Especially considering his own relationship is going down the tubes.

Is he really happy for me, or is he just trying to make me feel better?

"You know it's summer there, right? Don't go packing me any woollies," Ivy adds, with a mouth full of food. She sucks in dangling pasta, and sauce flicks onto Gabriel's cheek.

"I know! What the …?" Gabriel takes a napkin from the table and dabs at his face as if applying powder. He turns on the TV with a huff. Ivy scoffs.

A documentary about Australian wildlife is on. She tries to picture herself back home. Will her family be happy to see her? Will she be happy to see them? Will they all avoid the dreaded subject of her recent divorce? Whenever did she say she didn't like speaking about him anyway? Just because Eleanor and Ailish decided to take a vow of silence when it came to Roger, doesn't mean that she wants to do the same thing with Amir. Does it?

Emirates …

"Gabe?"

"Wassup?"

"I want you to book me a flight on United Arab Emirates."

Gabriel looks at Ivy and frowns. She has never told him Amir works for Emirates.

"Okay. Why?"

Ivy winks. "I hear the stewards are gorgeous."

kit

"Okay. So here's what we'll do," Kit says, raising her voice for Eydie to hear above the raucous St. Kilda pub crowd, and gulping down a quarter of her fresh icy-cold pint of Carlton Draught. She takes a moment to overcome the brain freeze, contorting her face as if she's overheard a ridiculous rumour. "Mum is organizing Christmas at ours this year, so we should wait until that's over. Once Boxing

Day is done and dusted, we'll call Samuel and organize a day to visit him. And Mum doesn't have to know. I don't want to get her all worked up over this anymore. I mean, if she finds out after the fact, I can deal with it, but I'd just like to avoid any sort of confrontation beforehand. I'm sick of getting people's approval for everything. You all right with that?"

Eydie nods, watching a couple of junkies making a score on the street with a pitiful expression on her face. She rests her folded hands on the bar; her collection of silver bangles clang on the black marble surface as the girl in the street punches the guy in the face and bolts toward the esplanade with a plastic Ziploc bag sticking out of her back jean pocket.

"You sure you don't want a drink?" Kit asks. Eydie nods again, pursing her lips. "Come on. At least get a lemon squash or something." Kit's last word hovers in the air as the background music pauses between tracks.

"Okay." Eydie nods at the bartender, coming back to earth as Sonic Youth's "Kool Thing" starts to play. She looks at her reflection in the mirror behind the bar and scrunches her waxy, messily spiked hair in both hands. She then rubs her nails on her faded black jeans and pushes her top lip up to touch her nose.

"What's wrong?" Kit asks.

"I dunno." Eydie shrugs, stealing conspicuous glances at the young crowd of boozers behind them through the mirror.

Kit imagines Eydie scrutinizing every single person in the room, especially the drunk ones, to sum them up, perhaps comparing them to her mother and creating little scenarios of their lives in her head. Kit does that too, even if for totally different reasons. She's recognized herself in Eydie ever since they met, but more so since they've been spending time together as "sisters." The similarities in character shine through the most when they catch each other staring at strangers. What is it about strangers that make you want to take up photography for that split second of blissful observation? Is that how writers feel? Or is it a moment when you speculate on whether life might have been different *if* ...?

Kit wishes she could offer Eydie some more guidance but doesn't feel qualified, considering she's been brought up with a pretty stable mother, even though the stability has only been evident on the surface. She knows about Ailish's bathroom scribble sessions. And she's known about the marijuana for more than ten years. What teen wouldn't recognize a marijuana plant growing next to a bed of Chamsonette Pink Gazanias?

"I'm so sorry, Eydie," Kit says, shaking her head. "Do you want to go to a café instead? Or take a stroll along the seaside and get some gelati or something? We don't have to stay here. I can drink beer at home."

"It's okay. Don't worry about it," Eydie says, drawing her attention back to Kit. Eydie taps her nails on the bar when the barman serves her the soft drink.

Kit doesn't buy it. After taking another couple of gulps of beer, she pushes it away. "Come on, drink your squash. We're outta here." Kit slaps her hands on the bar top.

Since spending time with Eydie, Kit's been a lot happier, but she sort of feels guilty about it. Does she feel this way because Eydie is less fortunate than she? What if she's subconsciously using Eydie as an Ivy replacement? Or does this situation evoke a sense of purpose? Were they brought together so she could take care of Eydie? To push her in the right direction? To give her courage to do more with her life? Kit would like to think the latter.

Eydie downs her squash through the thick black straw as Kit leaves a ten-dollar bill on the counter.

Out in the street the air smells like beer and beach. They follow the footpath toward the esplanade, wading through environmentalists, colourful hippies, tree huggers, political yahoos, pamphlet distributors, eccentric academics with thinly framed specs, metalheads, gothic rockers and prick-piercing punks, daddy's girls, country girls, wannabe cool girls, alternative musicians, classical musicians, funk musicians, buskers, writers, painters, poets reciting on the footpath with violin cases at their feet, call girls, junkies … and drunks. Eydie clutches Kit's upper arm as they walk.

A guy in a tattered grey tracksuit with a thinning blonde greasy ponytail approaches them asking, under his breath, if they need a hit. Eydie stiffly shakes her head and walks backward, dragging Kit with her. Kit turns Eydie around and speed-walks in the direction of the pier, where the crowd is a little more civilized. Where *kids* actually play. Kit knows the crowd is harmless around here. It's all show. Most are just trying to be cool. But it seems Eydie doesn't get out much to realize that for herself.

"You all right?" Kit asks, stopping for a breather, raising her eyebrows.

"Uh-huh." Eydie nods. "I'm sorry. I'm such wimp."

"No, you're not. Your reaction is normal." Kit winks and gives her a hug. She smells like the latest musk Rexona deodorant.

"I'm so happy I met ya, Kit," Eydie replies, wiping a tear from her cheek and breaking into a self-conscious laugh.

Down at the pier, Eydie buys them both a gelati from a van by the road, when Kit's mobile rings. Eydie takes Kit's ice cream without Kit asking her to.

She watches as Kit rummages through her bag, her face hinting at a contented smile. A lot like the smile Kit remembers having as a young girl when she watched Ivy dig for treasure in her neighbour's yard. *What is she actually thinking? Why has she not uttered one single opinion of her own since the day we met as "sisters"? Why should things have to change? Was the toughness at the salon all an act to hide her insecurities?*

Kit finally finds her mobile phone. Before flicking it open with her thumb, she leans over to her gelati in Eydie's hand and takes a quick mouthful, while Eydie licks melting rainbow drips off her wrist.

"Hello?"

"Hi," replies a reluctant female voice on the other end. Kit's heart beats with exaggeration as if being pumped with fluid. She sucks saliva to the back of her tongue until the roof of her mouth hurts.

"What do *you* want?"

Ivy hesitates. It sounds as if she puts her hand over the receiver and coughs. "I'm coming home."

Fuck. "Good for you. And?"

"Well, I just thought you might like to know. I'd like to meet Dad with you."

"I don't care about Dad anymore," Kit winks at Eydie, who has a concerned frown on her face. "I've stopped looking."

"Why?"

"Not my place to say. Ask Eleanor."

"Oh."

After a long silence Kit can hear some whispering. She decides to hang up without saying goodbye. But just before she does so, Ivy asks who is hosting Christmas.

"We are," Kit replies in a tone so languid she can hear herself slouch.

"Great. Hey, I'm really sorry ab—"

Kit hangs up and tosses her phone into her bag.

"Who was it?" Eydie asks, passing Kit her gelati, now shiny from the heat. Kit flattens her tongue and licks it full circle with attack. "Someone we are unfortunately related to," she mumbles, trying not to cry.

Eydie sighs, tight-lipped, and links her arm with Kit's.

They walk along the esplanade, hooked by their elbows, eating their ice creams in silence. Children squeal, thick white waves crash, car horns toot. Kit's footsteps rattle her knees as if trying to tell her to stop moving, to sit, to look out at the ocean and lap up the "goodness" that surrounds her. People change. She has to move on. But tears threaten to burn through the rear of her nasal cavity like a strong chemical smell. *Don't.*

"She's comin' home, in't she? Ivy, I mean."

Before Kit can summon the control, tears stream down her cheeks, and she walks to the nearest park bench to sit down.

Eydie throws the remainder of her cone into the nearby trash can, rubs her mouth on the back of her right hand, sits and puts an arm around Kit's shoulders. "It'll work out," Eydie says, looking at Kit's jogging knees. "I'm sure she's sorry. We all 'ave ... moments. She probably regrets the whole thing. *'F course* she regrets it. She called ya. That counts for somethin' duznit?"

Kit inserts the last bit of cone into her mouth and crunches it as she speaks. "I don't think she regrets it. I think she just changed her mind about meeting Dad, and I'm the only way she has in. She wouldn't dream of going to Eleanor."

"Ya don't know that, Kit." Eydie's speech slows down as she follows the movements of a middle-aged blonde woman standing on the side of the road in a gold mini and bright-purple boob tube. Eydie's eyes glaze over, and her face goes pale.

"What?" Kit looks at the woman and rubs her sticky fingers on her thighs.

Eydie shakes her head, swallows.

"I just saw Ma."

"Really? Well, let's go and say hello."

Eydie grabs Kit's upper arm with weightlifter strength as she attempts to stand. "No," she snaps through gritted teeth. "She's gone now anyway. Fuck." Eydie hangs her head and balances it in her hands. A tear drops onto her thigh. After a moment of silence she sniffs, swings her head back, and lets out a low guttural growl.

"Eydie." Kit strokes her hair. "What's going on?"

"She just got into some car with some sleazy wanker," Eydie replies, blinking at the sky, trying to stop her tears.

Kit takes Eydie's hand to offer some calm. "What does that mean?"

"She said she'd stopped doing that fucking crap." Eydie looks at Kit and rolls her eyes. They glisten under the streetlamp.

"Doing what?"

"Being a fuckin' whore." Eydie pulls her hand away to wipe her eyes. The tips of her fingers turn grey with mascara, and she wipes them on her jeans.

A what? Kit isn't sure if she says that out loud or whether her lips are just moving up and down.

"Yeah." Eydie nods. "And you know what she told me last night?" Kit shakes her head. "That was how she met Dad."

brian

Sunday morning. Red Sox replay. Background noise. Naked. Cold. Heater taking too long to work. Grabs quilt from couch. Wraps himself in it. Prickly on skin. Especially penis. Itchy scrotum, nostril, big toe. Goes to bedroom. Puts on boxers. The red ones covered in giraffes. Drags toe along carpet. Itch relieved. Wraps himself back in quilt. Returns to kitchen. Scratches bum crack through prickly quilt. Not comfortable. Gets angry at quilt. Throws it at couch. Goes back into bedroom. Puts on tracksuit. Returns to kitchen. Coffee made. Can't remember turning machine on. Farts. Boiled wax gone hard in pot on stove. Too lazy to fix. Smells nice, triggers grief. Brian sobs. *Wimp.*

Brian looks at the Christmas tree Ivy put up the day she walked out. No. The day he threw her out. *You're a complete moron.* He walks over to it and takes a shiny red ball off it. He holds it up, level to his eyes. He looks at himself, at his distorted, lying, son-of-a-bitch face. "You be-*lew* it," he says to his reflection, over emphasizing his facial movements as he speaks. "You *fu*-cker." He throws the ball across the room, and it shatters against the wall. He stares at the spot on the wall where it hit for so long that the rest of the room becomes a blur around it.

The percolator crackles as if telling Brian to get a grip. He turns his head to glare at that too. He squints at it like a bull ready to charge. Then his email pings on his open laptop near the shattered Christmas decoration. He walks over to see what it is and cuts his finger on a piece of glass lodged into the mouse.

"Jesus!"

He bolts to the kitchen sink and runs it under the faucet. Then his cell beeps.

"What the fuck do you all want from me? I'm trying to mope here!" Brian screams toward the ceiling.

Then the doorbell rings.

Brian expels a loud gritty wheeze as he rips a piece of paper towel off the roll by the stove and wraps it around his hand.

"What?" he snaps as he swings his door open, expecting it to be his annoying neighbour who likes to "borrow" a teaspoon of instant coffee on occasion. He doesn't even drink instant coffee. He keeps a jar of it in his cupboard merely for this purpose.

But it's not his neighbour. It's Gabriel. Wearing a T-shirt with "Some respect might be in order" written on it.

"Oh. Gabe." Brian sighs. "Sorry. What are you doing here?" He pokes his head out the door to see if anyone else is with him. "How did you get in the building?"

Gabe looks Brian up and down and pinches his nose as if Brian stinks. Brian sniffs down the front of his sweatshirt by pretending to rub sweat from his top lip with the collar.

"Darling, I could rip your unreliable little balls off and throw them into a wood chipper, but I won't." Gabriel crosses his arms, tilts his head, and flits his eyes toward the paper towel wrapped around Brian's hand.

Brian mutters, removing the paper towel and throwing it on the floor to his left. He chuckles like an idiot. "Thanks?"

"Yeah. Thank me later, schnookums, when you manage to stop Ivy getting on that plane to Australia this afternoon." Gabriel taps his foot. It snaps through the corridor like a cane on a desk.

"What?" Brian suddenly has trouble swallowing.

"Mm-hm. This afternoon. If you want to give her another chance—and I'm pretty sure you do because I ain't seen such a sincere heart in my life as I do in you—I tell you, and I'm not saying that just because I love Ivy and want her to be happy and I know that she sees something in you worth pursuing. I'm saying that because I mean it, and I seriously think you just got overwhelmed and reacted to fear, so, honey …" Gabriel takes a deep breath, smiles, takes Brian's jaw in his right hand, and holds his head up. "Flight EK461, leaves four p.m. It's your last chance, darling."

Gabriel spins around on the ball of his right foot and presses the button to call the elevator. "Oh," Gabriel adds. "I think your building's doorman might have a thing for me." The elevator door opens, and he steps in. And just before the door closes, he pats himself on the butt and says with a wink, "And *this*, my darling, is how I got in."

Brian stands in the open doorway staring at the elevator as he listens to it hum to the ground floor. When the sound stops, he jerks out of his trance and goes back inside, letting the door slam shut with an intense bang. He pours himself a cup of coffee, then takes it into the bathroom and sits on the toilet with his pants still up. He stares at his unshaven face in the mirror.

"Australia," he whispers, as if trying to comprehend the meaning of the word. "That's too far away." He sips his coffee with a wince and swishes it around in his mouth until it turns cold. He swallows half the saliva-contaminated crap down and spits the rest at his reflection. He bursts into laughter. "You're a fucking idiot!"

He stares at himself a little while longer, scrutinizing the rectangular quality of his jaw, watching his stubble grow. By the time he takes another sip of his coffee, the whole thing has gone cold.

It's two o'clock.

"Fuck!"

Brian drops his coffee cup into the sink. It shatters. But he doesn't hang around to clean it up.

Ivy inches another fry between her teeth, looking at the runway through the window. The airport food lounge smells like a cross between a hospital and a playpen. Dettol polluted with endorphins and Rescue Remedy. And restless chatter. Ivy can feel Gabriel staring at her, sucking sloppily on a lollipop, smacking his sticky lips open and closed as if hesitating to speak. Ivy tries to ignore the sound and envision herself on the plane with Amir.

I'm nervous to see him again … Kit will come around …
I think I still love Brian …
We're sisters, for God's sake …
I miss Amir…
Surely Brian still loves me …
Kit can't hate me forever just because I got carried away over the phone, can she?
Maybe Brian will change his mind …
I can't wait to see Amir …

"So what did he say?" Ivy asks, hoping to stunt Gabriel's all-consuming sticky smacking sound. She grabs a handful of fries from the glossy cardboard box and shoves them all into her mouth at once.

"Nothing," Gabriel mumbles with the lollipop still in his mouth. Ivy frowns at his public display of mock childishness. Gabriel stops sucking in response and drops the lollipop into his glass of water. It splashes all over Ivy's fries.

"But I think he'll come. I can feel it in my *Mr. Man*." Gabriel shivers as if a cold breeze blew right through his pants.

"This isn't a joke, Gabe. You should have just told him the truth. I mean, it's not like I'm *not* going to get on that plane. I just wanted to know if we still had a chance. You know, when I come back." *If I come back.* "To start dating again."

"So? At least he'll be here to see you off, right?"

"Yeah, but I didn't want him to come if he didn't know the truth. I wanted him to show he is willing to wait, not because he thinks it's his last chance. He'll just panic and make a rash decision out of fear. He's obviously got issues with that."

I want to try Amir out again, Gabe. I need your advice. But I just can't bring myself to ask you. What will you think of me? I already feel nuts. I don't need you to rub it in. And I know you'll rub it in.

"Sweetcakes, there's no way a guy, *any* guy, is going to risk his pride to simply say goodbye when he thinks he might get another chance to make things right. It needs to be his only chance, or you'll never really know. I had to make it out like he was going to lose you for good."

Ivy shrugs, rubs her nose upward with the palm of her hand, and sniffs. "What's the time?"

"Time to board, according to the screen up there." Gabriel flicks his head in the direction of the departure notice and feigns an elaborate frown.

"Well, I guess you were wrong about Brian." *Now I don't have to feel guilty about "bumping into" my ex.*

"Hey, don't speak too soon. Maybe he's waiting for you to show up at the gate."

"Doubt it." *Please be there. I need to move forward. I need a reason not to crawl back to Amir. I'm so confused. What the hell do I want? A way to negate loneliness? Do I even want either of these men? Oh Christ, Ivy.*

brian

Brian steps foot into the international departures area at Sea-Tac. His eyes dart left and right searching for the Emirates logo and the correct flight number above the check-in desks. His breaths bounce up and down his throat like Ping-Pong balls. He ran from the cab, which was at a standstill in a bottleneck not far from the train line to the airport. He's still in his tracksuit, unshaven, his finger throbbing where the splinter of Christmas decoration stabbed him. Toe's still damn itchy and now inside a sweaty sneaker. Not much he can do about it except flex his toes in an attempt at slight relief.

Did something freaking bite me?

He finds the flight number on the Departures screen. *Gate B10. Boarding.* "Boarding? Which way do I go?" he says out loud to no one in particular, searching for signs left and right. He taps a man in a suit on the shoulder. The man turns around with an unimpressed smile pinned to his face like a flattened piece of chewing gum. The lady he was talking to frowns and jiggles the pounds of plastic beads hanging from her neck.

"Excuse me, do you have any idea how to get to passport control for gate B10 in the least amount of time possible?" Brian asks, realizing the stupidity of his question.

"Geez, it's pretty straightforward, mate," says the guy in a potent Australian twang. "See that sign over there?" He points toward it with raised eyebrows. "Follow the arrow." He nods with a smirk, puckers his brow, shakes his head, and turns back around to face the lady in the beads.

"Right. Thanks." Brian smiles, pouncing in the direction of the sign.

Shit, Ivy. I'm so freaking sorry.

Gabriel and Ivy are waiting outside passport control. Once Ivy passes those doors, there's no turning back. That's it. The land of Oz, here she comes. Pity there's no yellow brick road to follow. She could do with only having one path to choose from. Gabriel and Ivy both dart looks to and fro, searching the crowd for Brian. But there is no sign of him.

"What's he wearing? Can you remember?" Ivy asks, trying not to reveal the budding desperation dwelling in her larynx.

"Er, sweetcakes, he might have changed out of his tracksuit to come here."

"Yeah. Right." A build-up of saliva lines the walls of her mouth. She swallows a threatening panic attack and closes her eyes.

Don't think about it. Don't think about it.

"Final boarding call for Emirates flight EK 461, to Abu Dhabi, with a final destination of Melbourne. Please proceed to gate B10."

"Looks like I should go, Gabe." Ivy reaches for Gabriel to give him a hug. She intends it to be quick but finds herself holding on to Gabriel so tight she can't bring herself to let go.

"I think I'm making a mistake," she blurts without thinking twice.

"Sweetcakes, don't worry," Gabriel purrs, prying Ivy's arms off him and waving away his own imminent tears. "Even if you are, you're just a flight away from coming back. Nothing is forever, and you can rectify whatever mistake it is you think you're making by getting on a plane and flying home. *This* home. Here in Seattle, with me. Where you belong." Gabriel hugs Ivy again and rubs her back as if trying to burp a baby.

That's not the mistake I mean, Gabe.

They stare at each other at arm's length, clearly trying to hold back tears. But Gabriel breaks the composure by becoming a blubbering mess.

"Oh, sweetcakes!" he cries, jogging on the spot like a two-year-old having a tantrum. "Please stay safe. You better come back, or I'll come down there to physically drag you back, you hear?" Gabriel says almost incomprehensibly through his tears. Real tears. He squeezes Ivy's cheeks together until her lips pout.

Ivy nods more times than she can count, tears streaming down her face. She sucks in salty guilt via an inward heave, picks up her hand luggage from between her feet, and takes one last glance through the crowd before moving toward the sliding metal doors. Doors that are about to determine her future. Brian or Amir. Companionship or security. Love or lust. Or habit?

With one last sloppy kiss on Gabriel's cheek, she turns to face the doors and marches toward them, her steps vibrating through her thighs. The certainty of what she's about to do floods her stomach with a desirable longing for change. She pauses as the doors slide open after detecting her presence.

A child screams.

Her thought of turning around one last time to check for Brian is deterred.

brian

Brian bolts through itinerants waiting for their boarding calls. He can see the gate in the distance. Crowds of people, families, lovers, saying goodbye to each other. *I can't see her. She's got to be there. She's got to be waiting. Why would Gabe even bother getting me to come if she isn't going to be waiting? Fuck, Ivy, I love you. I'm sorry. Please be there. Please.*

He notices Gabriel's wild yellow-and-purple shirt. *Yes!* He searches nearby for Ivy. But he can't see her. *She can't be gone. No, no, no!*

She's walking toward the gate. "Ivy!" he calls, flinging both arms in the air as he runs. She stops walking. Pauses at the open doors.

She heard me! Oh, thank God!

Brian picks up speed. Dodging prams, baggage, and toddlers. Just as he approaches Gabriel, Brian taps his hand on his shoulder as if tagging a baseball base, and bends over panting.

A child screams.

When he looks up, Ivy has disappeared.

Gabriel turns around in shock. His eyes are red and puffy.

"Brian," he gasps, bringing his hands to his mouth, tears streaming down his pink cheeks. "You just missed her."

Brian bends over again, trying to catch his breath and hold back the scream he wants to set free. He falls to his knees, pulling at his collar. "I know," Brian pants. "That's it, isn't it? I've lost her. Have I lost her?"

Gabriel bends down and helps Brian back to his feet. He brushes off his knees.

"You look like a rotten mess, darling. You need to shave."

"Seriously, Gabe? You're worried about how I look?"

"Yeah. I am. Because we're going out for a drink. Just you and me. And you know why we have to go for a drink, Brian?"

"Why?" Brian asks, defeat gurgling through his heavy breaths.

"Because we're going to plot to bring her back. You and me. Together. We'll get our gal back. That's a promise."

ivy

By the time the cabin crew begin their routine takeoff checks, she is buckled in her seat. They close overhead lockers, and make sure people's footrests are down and seat backs are up. The vague hum of the idle motor reminds her of so many things: her first archaeological dig in Cyprus, her research grant in Indonesia, her girly holiday with Kit on the Gold Coast in Queensland, tagging along to a medical conference with Eleanor when she was only ten. But most of all it reminds her of her honeymoon with Amir in Spain.

After being in a relationship for ten years, from high school and through university, they still had the lust. But the question is, can she now control herself? If she truly feels something for Brian, then she should be able to control herself. Well, that's the logic she has come up with, anyway, and it's how she intends to find out whether Brian really is what she needs. She must test this theory out to see if she is over Amir, or whether she just thought she was because she fell for Brian. And did she fall for Brian because he was persistent and gave her the attention she needed to feel human again?

Ivy purposely leaves her footrest down, just in case Amir passes by. Then he'll be forced to speak to her. She *knows* he's on the plane. She checked, called the airline. Sneaky. She wasn't going to go to all the trouble of getting on an Emirates flight and not get what she came for.

Ivy leans back in her seat and puts her feet on the foot-rest. The old man sitting next to her grunts and stares at them. "Don't worry," Ivy says with a wink. "I'll put the footrest away as soon as I get told to." The old man raises his eyebrows and grunts again. He swallows a few times in a row as if it's a nervous twitch, and she watches as his huge wrinkly Adam's apple move up and down. He removes the in-flight magazine from the pouch in front of him. He's wearing a wedding band. Looks a little tight.

Has your wife gotten used to that grunt of yours? Are you happily married?

The reason Ivy believes the marriage between her and Amir didn't work was because Ivy's success threatened him. He had a temper and always tried to gain the upper hand. Amir's flirtatiousness, and possible promiscuity, threatened her and caused her to doubt every single look or slightly teasing gesture she witnessed when they socialized. This, in turn, was the foundation of her nagging, prodding, whining nature toward every single domestic incident until civilized conversation became so scarce that she couldn't even remember the last time they'd had a "chat."

All this pent-up resentment had surfaced because of something Amir attempted to do, but didn't actually do. And he *didn't* do it because Kit dealt with it like an adult. Something Ivy selectively forgets to justify the divorce. Kit, despite not liking Amir very much, convinced him to apol-ogize to Ivy, to admit his mistake, claiming that Ivy would understand and forgive him if he was honest. It didn't have to end in divorce. But Ivy didn't see his honesty as a blessing. Jealousy overpowered her rationale, and within one day of "the incident," she filed.

"Excuse me, ma'am. Could you please stow away your footrest for takeoff?" a stewardess asks with a complexion much like Amir's. She bends down to gesture toward Ivy's feet as if selling an item on TV.

Damn. "Sure. Excuse me," Ivy replies, as the stewardess stands upright. "Is, er …"

Ask if he's on the plane!

But you know he's on the plane …

Ask if he's in economy class …

No, don't be silly. Just walk through the plane later and look for him.

But what if when you walk through he's in the lavatory or something? You can't go walking up and down like an idiot the whole flight.

Ivy spots the back of his head just in time. He's speaking to one of the cabin crew members by the kitchen. "How long till we take off?"

"About fifteen minutes, ma'am," the stewardess replies with a curt nod.

Ivy elevates herself in her seat with a cushion and the blanket wrapped in plastic to see above the row of heads in front of her. Amir turns his head and looks in her direction. She ducks to her left, and her forehead brushes against the old man's shoulder. He grunts. Again.

Why are you ducking? You want him to see you, you idiot!

She sits up straight again, but Amir has turned his back to the aisle and is walking in the opposite direction.

Shit.

The engine rumbles, and the plane begins to reverse away from the chute. But Ivy's desperate to get out of her seat and follow him.

What's wrong with you, you numb nut? This flight lasts for hours.

A force of panic convinces her to yell out his name, as if his being out of sight will mean being off the plane.

"Amir!" Ivy calls, holding an arm in the air. Everyone goes silent, and heads turn. Amir swivels around on one foot, frowning as if trying to discern who she is. The corners of his mouth twitch a little before forming a huge teeth-bearing smile. He picks up speed and reaches her seat.

"Ivy," he says in his half-British, half-Arabic accent, eyes twinkling in the artificial light. Ivy's heart pumps in her ears. Her hands become clammy, and her tongue sticks to the roof of her mouth.

I've missed you.

Seeing his face again sends a flutter of hormones through her limbs—a feeling that had only just begun to surface with Brian. Will she let his smooth Arabian skin and gentle brown eyes tempt her back into a relationship she knows doesn't work, but *does* on so many irrational, chemical levels? All she wants to do right now is grab Amir's face and plant a sloppy kiss on his thick luscious lips. But she doesn't. She is not starring in a romance novel, and she's not about to make a spectacle of herself.

"I'm going home for Christmas," Ivy says, searching his eyes for the love they once shared, hardly able to wipe the grin off her face. "Would you like to come?"

Oh my God. Did you seriously just ask that?

The grumpy old man between them looks left and right as they speak, following the conversation religiously. This time, however, he doesn't grunt. He lets out a short closed-mouth scoff through his nose and offers Ivy a subtle wink and an elbow in her side.

"I'd be honoured," Amir replies. "As friends, I assume?"

Maybe. Can friends have sex?

"Of course." Ivy nods, reaching to touch the top of his hand. "As friends."

ailish

Ailish enters Melbourne Central, an artificially cooled department store, and sighs with relief. It's got to be at least forty degrees Celsius outside, yet she still refuses to turn the air conditioner on in the car in fear of wasting fuel and contributing to the ever-approaching apocalypse. Sweat drips between her breasts and crotch as she speed-walks to the public toilet to wipe herself down. Upon exiting, she notices the blaring Christmas carols, screaming children, and the amalgamated scent of candles and incense and pet shop piss. The fuzzy vision of consumerism envelopes her like a low-hung cloud, the milieu making her feel a bit woozy.

It is a time to be merry, Ailish. Smile. Enjoy the holidays.

She spots Eleanor standing outside Readings, where she told her to wait, and flashes a forced grin. Not because she doesn't want to see Eleanor, but because she can't seem to muster a natural expression amid the chaos playing devil's advocate in her mind. She should be thankful, relieved. Kit has finally met Eydie, and she knows Roger's whereabouts. If Kit were to change her mind and decide to visit him after all, Ailish could get to him first. The cat's legs are out of the bag. She doesn't need its body too. What could possibly go wrong now? There's technically nothing to worry about.

But it's not worry that is burdening her. It's guilt. Guilt is the catalyst for the stiffness she is constantly trying to shrug off from the inside out. She knows she's never going to feel normal again until Kit actually meets Roger.

The secret is safe with Harold. Of course it is. And surely Samuel wouldn't know. He is probably as naïve about Roger's past as everyone else is. There's no way Kit will ever be affected by this now.

Eleanor waves, and glances at a passerby, scratching the side of her nose.

We forgave each other. We're fine.

Ailish takes a deep breath as she approaches. They kiss each other's cheeks, holding their gaze a little longer than might seem natural, and linger in a silence that borders on the uncomfortable.

"Turns out no surgery today, then?" Ailish asks, focusing on a small scar under Eleanor's left eye. As much as she despises the use of idle chitchat to begin a conversation, she can't grasp any other solution fast enough to ease her discomfort. Ailish rests her hand on Eleanor's shoulder. Eleanor rests her hand on top of Ailish's and gives it an affectionate squeeze.

"Nope. Baby's not quite strong enough for it yet. We're going to wait a few more days."

"Oh." Ailish nods and flicks her tongue from her front teeth with a sigh. "So who are we buying for first?"

"Well, we might as well take a look around and get something for Kit while we're here. Didn't you say there was some particular book she wanted?" Eleanor picks pills off her overworn tank top and blows them from her fingers. They land on Ailish's shoulder. Eleanor doesn't notice.

"No, but there is a book I'd like her to have." Ailish stops Eleanor from entering the shop by tugging on her top. "Elle, we *are* fine with everything, aren't we?" Ailish searches Eleanor's eyes for the young, compassionate, self-less individual she met twenty-five years ago, a woman she seems to have lost touch with since the girls grew up.

Eleanor makes soothing noises in the back of her throat and takes Ailish in her arms. Her hug is just what Ailish needs. But it feels forced.

"Of course we are. The past is the past. We're alive, healthy, and so are our children." Eleanor releases the embrace and shakes Ailish by her shoulders. "And it's Christmas. Let's enjoy it."

Ailish, on the brink of becoming teary, swallows the urge

to break down. It is not the time or the place. In fact, it never is.

They browse the bookstore separately. Eleanor heads toward the autobiography section and Ailish toward fiction. She scans the shelves like a sniffer dog until she finds exactly what she's looking for. Marilynne Robinson's *Housekeeping*. She picks it up. Strokes it. Waits for its potent aura to travel through her fingers, her arms, toward her head. But the giddiness she usually feels doesn't surface; the book's unique and mystical quality seems tarnished, flawed, false like plastic flowers. She can see its beauty, but she can't smell it.

She opens the book and stares at the blank white inside cover.

She closes her eyes.

Flicks through the crisp white pages. They fan her face.

It's not the copy hidden in her desk drawer. The slice of the Roger she used to know.

Yes. Why didn't I think of that before?

"Did you find it?" Eleanor approaches with a couple of books, inch-thick, hooked under her arm. Ailish blinks a few times, as if being woken up from an accidental doze. Eleanor frowns and rubs Ailish on her back. "Are you all right?"

"I found it, but I actually don't think it appropriate after all." Ailish puts the book back on the shelf next to *Gilead* and *Home*.

"Let's go and have a look elsewhere, and you can think

about what you want in the meantime." Eleanor lays her books down on a shelf displaying a vast array of colourful plastic folders. "I'll come back for these later." She winks. "I need to buy something for Ivy, but I haven't the faintest idea what she's into anymore. I wouldn't be surprised if her tastes have changed since living in Seattle. What do you reckon?"

"Why don't you just send her some money and have her buy something herself?" Ailish follows Eleanor through the food court, past the German sausage shop. Aromas of weisswurst, sauerkraut, and gourmet mustard fill her nose with a sudden need to splurge on junk. The last time she ate fast food was a year ago when she had a hankering for fish fingers and purchased three frozen packets from the supermarket, then ate them in secret, locked in the bathroom. Afterward she lit a joint and scribbled incomprehensible shite on her sketchpad.

"Oh, you don't know?" Eleanor jiggles her shoulders side to side. "She's coming home."

"Oh. For good?"

"Well, no, for Christmas. Far as I know. Unless she has other plans I don't know about. Wouldn't surprise me. She doesn't tell the full truth about anything these days. I don't know what's got into her since the divorce. It's as if her whole life has had to become this huge secret in order for her to be independent. It doesn't make sense. I don't see what there is to be ashamed of."

"Doesn't that worry you?" Ailish clutches her handbag to

her chest. An instinctual habit she's adopted in large crowds since the surgery.

"It did. Well, it *does*. But she's made it pretty clear to me that she doesn't need my advice. Well, *want* it, anyway. What I fear the most is that she holds back from seeking my help to maintain her ego. That can't be healthy, can it?" Eleanor pauses in front of a salad bar to check out the array of fruit. She screws up her nose and flicks her hand in dismissal. "It doesn't help that she lives on the other side of the world either."

"Didn't you ask why she was coming back?" Ailish asks, praying Eleanor knows.

"Of course I did. But she just said she misses her family and friends and would like to spend Christmas with us."

"Hmm." Ailish wonders how society has caused the human race to fear honesty so much. And she is no exception. *That's a good essay topic. I might use that next term.*

They walk into Portman's. Eleanor scans the racks of clothes, then heads toward the summer dresses that are on sale.

"What do you mean, 'hmm'?" Eleanor sifts through the dresses, feeling the fabric, checking the zippers and buttons for loose threads.

"Well, doesn't it surprise you that she suddenly wants to come home?" *You're kidding me. Now I have another secret I have to keep? No. You will* not *keep it. Just tell her what Kit said.*

"Not really." Eleanor snorts. "She mentioned nothing

about nothing. I seriously hope she and Kit kiss and make up before Christmas day. Otherwise it'll be a snide-remark parade." Eleanor smirks, glances at Ailish. "You know what they're like. I'm telling you now—we'll be constantly trying to talk, talk, talk to prevent that silence triggering some sort of confrontational verbal diarrhoea. I mean, at least for our sanity, is there any way you can convince Kit to forgive her?"

Ailish bites her bottom lip and pulls out a dress she thinks will suit Eleanor—a lilac cheesecloth V-neck frock—in the hope that it might cushion what she's about to say. Eleanor pouts, nods, and hangs it over her arms before moving to the next rack. "Elle, I'm afraid Kit's forgiveness is going to be the least of your problems."

"Why?" Eleanor looks up from the dresses with a frown.

"Ivy called Kit the other day and told her she's decided to meet Roger." Ailish scans Eleanor's face in preparation to soothe her.

"What?" Eleanor shrieks, stumbling and accidentally unhooking a couple of dresses from their hangers and letting them fall to the floor.

Ailish picks them up and puts them back, making sure the sizes on the dress tags match the sizes marked on the hangers. "I thought I'd better let you know so you can prepare for the consequences."

Eleanor flings the dress she's holding over the rack, buries her face in her hands, and walks out of the store. "Oh, shit, fuck, shit, fuck!" She takes a deep breath, holding one hand to her forehead and the other on her hip.

Ailish chuckles. "Now you know how I've been feeling all this time with Kit."

"What am I supposed to do now?" Eleanor asks, looking up with flushed cheeks and glazed eyes.

"Just *tell* her. If there's anything I've learned from this whole experience, it is that there's nothing wrong with hiding something you fear might be disappointing to someone you love. It's absolutely understandable and logical in its own right. She'll forgive you. And to be honest, the visit will probably be so exciting, Ivy won't want to leave." Ailish's stomach turns at her flippant sarcasm. The thought of Roger being a bore is almost as hurtful as the recent weeks put together. Roger used to be fuller of life and enthusiasm than anyone she has ever known. She can only imagine what the stroke has done to him.

Eleanor massages her brow.

"Ivy loses interest fairly quickly anyway," Ailish continues. "We both know that. Let her meet him. Let her become disinterested, and then it'll all be over with and we can get on with life, with everything, and go back to normal."

"Fuck!" Eleanor yells, clenching her jaw.

"Eleanor," Ailish whispers through closed teeth. "We're in public."

"Sorry, it's just that I knew the moment Ivy called to ask me where Roger was for Kit that everything would fall apart. Ivy is going to flip out. I told her I'd keep the money for whenever she was ready to use it."

"Well, just don't tell her then. You told Samuel to keep it a secret. Right?"

Eleanor nods.

"There's no reason she has to know. And it's not all that bad a secret, Elle. Just think of it as an anonymous donation. There's nothing wrong with that. You donate to the Royal Children's all the time."

"You think so?"

"Of course. Why not?"

"Okay. An anonymous donation," Eleanor says with a sigh. "I can live with that. I can."

Ailish rubs Eleanor on her upper back and winces internally at the secret she is desperate to exhale.

I will *tell her. After Christmas.*

Ailish takes a deep breath, stands up, and holds out her hand. "Come on. Let's finish buying those presents."

On Ailish's way home, with a backseat full of gifts wrapped in recycled wrapping paper, she drops by her office at the university to grab the book. Just as she locates it and slips it into her bag, Harold pokes his head through the door.

"'The best way to appreciate your job is to imagine yourself without one,' Ailish. It's Christmas, you should be imagining yourself without one," Harold says, shaking his head and entering her office.

Ailish turns around with a little spring in her spin and smiles with a flirtatious click of her tongue. "Why is it, Harry, that you only ever quote Oscar Wilde to me?" she asks, putting her hands behind her back and leaning forward to give him a quick peck on the mouth. "You're not trying to hint at anything, are you?" she adds, lifting herself to her toes.

"Ailish Healy!" Harold exclaims in a playful tone, folding his arms against his chest. "How could you possibly even *suggest* such a thing? I am, without a doubt, as straight as a lamppost, dear." He winks. "I should be asking you such a question, should I not?"

"What do you mean?" Ailish puts her arms around his waist and gazes upward with her chin resting on his chest.

"I should be asking if perhaps *you* like to swing in the opposite direction." He wobbles his head and raises his eyebrows. He takes her hand and spins her around to waltz. Ailish curtsies and follows his lead.

"I beg your pardon?" Ailish asks, slipping smoothly into the dance. *One, two, three. One, two, three.* Harold hums "Air on a G String" before easing into his reply.

"You've been willingly fooling around with me, on and off for ten years now, Allie dear, and you have never once followed through on any of my humble offers of commitment," he whispers, kissing Ailish on the forehead. She rests the right side of her face on his chest in silence and closes her eyes.

It's time to let go.

"Nor have you introduced me to your family. I'm very thankful, I think you must know, of finally having the pleasure of meeting your lovely daughter through her doing an internship here. Do you really think I'd have a problem with meeting the remarkable product of Roger and your beautiful self?"

Ailish shakes her head without lifting it from Harold's chest. His shirt smells vaguely of mothballs, but it's comforting. She'd forgotten how much so. Harold maintains his lead, moving Ailish into each elegant step as if they are as light as carbon paper drifting to the ground from a high-rise building.

"He was one of the smartest fellows I'd ever known. And I have definitely come to accept that, to you, no one can replace him. *But.*"

Ailish lifts her head, ready to interrupt, but Harold gently pushes it back down again.

"I certainly do *not* want to accept that you might not ever be willing to let me into your heart. As Harry. I know I will never replace Roger. But do you ever think you may learn to love *me*? For who *I* am?" Harold stops dancing and lifts Ailish's head. "You know I love you. I have ever since the day I met you as an innocent, struggling student."

"Harry. I *do* love you for who you are. I just ..." Ailish stares into Harold's kind slanting eyes, full of heed and yearning.

"You know as well as I do that I am not the kind to judge." Harold touches a finger to Ailish's lips. He whispers, "You are a good mother, Allie dear."

Ailish swallows. Rests her head on Harold's chest again. A tear melts into his shirt. "I am?"

"Push what you saw from your mind. It's been such a long time."

But I'm burdened with guilt. The longer I keep this inside, the more I'll end up pushing Kit away trying to hide it.

"So," Harold says, holding Ailish by her shoulders at arm's length. "You said you had a little surprise for me?"

"Oh, yes. I almost forgot. How would you"—Ailish pauses and adopts an exultant smile, tilting her head to the side in lure—"like to join us for lunch on Christmas day?"

eleanor

She sips her cup of coffee at the kitchen table, with *The Age* newspaper spread open in front of her, checking the clock every few minutes. It's five a.m., and Ivy is due to walk through the door any second now.

Eleanor had intended to pick her up from the airport, but Ivy sent her a message saying she had found a ride and would see her at home. A ride with whom, she has no idea, nor does she give a rat's arse, but she sure hopes Ivy doesn't invite them in. She can't find the enthusiasm to get dressed and presentable for anyone, let alone a complete stranger after completing a forty-eight-hour shift at the hospital, and a major eight-hour surgery to boot. But perhaps she'll slip on a sports bra just in case. No need to scare the poor stranger out of their wits with her droopy post-middle-aged breasts and daunting dark nipples crying, "Hey, look at Mama," through the thin cotton fabric of her nightdress.

After putting her undergarment on, Eleanor returns to

the kitchen table and opens the newspaper to the puzzle pages to distract herself from her guilt-ridden anxiety. The stress of whether to tell Ivy she's spent all her money on a man she is supposed to hate is beginning to grate on her psyche.

One across. Crushed fare given to each tender convert. Twelve letters. What? I can't do cryptics to save my bloody life.

"What do you think this one is, Allie?" she says out loud, as if Ailish were, in fact, sitting by her side.

She looks at the clock again: 5:10. Does she tell Ivy the truth or not? And is it really a big deal when all she was doing was trying to protect a man from another disappointment? And after Ivy's divorce, she couldn't bear telling her he would no longer be the man he was. Ivy needs a strong, confident, and motivated father figure in her life. Not another weak and vulnerable influence to push her further down a dead-end road. So she made sure Ivy would never find out, by bribing his brother. Knowing very well he didn't have the funds to rehabilitate Roger in a private hospital, it was an offer he couldn't refuse.

My actions were justifiable.

"Right. You're impossible," she says to the crossword as she sifts for the entertainment section.

What movies are on tonight? How 'bout it? A place where we won't have to talk. That will at least get me through the first night. Eleanor clicks her tongue. "Relatively stress-free."

 ivy

Ivy and Amir roll into Eleanor's driveway in his company Smart. Amir has recently been promoted to cabin crew supervisor, and he seems proud of it. Probably more proud than he would have been if they were still together. A sign that he has most definitely moved on. *Right?*

He switches off the ignition and turns to face her. The combination of crisp car interior and Allure Homme aftershave tickles Ivy's nose. Ivy smiles and sighs, ogling Amir in his chic black-and-beige uniform, wondering whether it would be inappropriate to kiss him on the cheek for being so polite to drive her home. Amir clears his throat, pulls up the hand brake, and slips the gear stick into Neutral.

"Thanks for the ride." Ivy focuses on his coarse five-o'clock shadow, remembering the amount of times she'd wake up in the morning with "pash rash" around her lips.

Oh, please just kiss me like you used to.

"It was a pleasure." Amir clears his throat again after hesitating to say more. Silence pounds at the windows. His expression becomes pained as he looks toward Eleanor's front door. Ivy swallows, wondering whether it is her cue to get out, but Amir interrupts. He gestures toward the house with his chin.

"That brings back nice memories. I miss the times I spent with you and your family."

Ivy gets a flash of Amir holding Kit's arm against the wall

and closes her eyes to try to block it out. She doesn't want to feel bitter about this now. She wants to forgive him. Isn't that what Brian advised her to do? Forgive and forget? Yes, he was talking about Kit, but she should also apply it to other people in her life. Like Amir, for being promiscuous and gorgeous, and her mum, for being distant and disciplined.

And Dad, for leaving me.

"Yeah," Ivy sighs. "Me too."

The faintness of dawn through the windshield sparkles in Amir's eyes when he brings his hand to Ivy's cheek. He strokes the side of his index finger along her jaw. His skin is smooth and warm. She closes her eyes as his touch resonates through her whole body, as if fuelling her like sun and water to flora.

I want you back. I want you to take away my hollow heart. Please.

They both open their mouths to speak at the same time and nervously laugh at the coincidence.

"You first," Ivy says.

Amir looks out the window again and shakes his head as if disappointed in something. "I never meant to hurt you," he whispers. "It's been hard. Without you. Really hard." He breathes in loudly through his nose as if about to break down, but regains control with his last two dynamic words.

Ivy nods at her knees. "I'm the one who should apologize, Amir." She folds her hands in her lap, not knowing whether she should touch him or not. "I never stopped to consider that I should have given you another chance. And I should have been more encouraging toward you and your career instead of being so self-centred and obsessed about mine. You know, I—"

Between her last word and a blink, Amir's lips touch hers. The kiss paralyzes the tiniest microorganism within her. It's *the* kiss that eclipses the hug. The only thing that has ever plucked her from this living hell.

eleanor

The doorbell rings. Eleanor looks up from the newspaper with a tiny gulp. She pinches and smacks her cheeks to give them a bit of colour and puts her hair in a ponytail with the thin black hair tie she keeps permanently on her right wrist.

Don't want to be looking like a drained old hag.

She gets up. Checks that her nightdress isn't tucked inside her knickers.

Now that would really scare away the guest. Maybe I should tuck it in my knickers on purpose.

She opens the door. Brings her hands to her mouth with a gasp.

"Amir!" she cries, reaching for Ivy to give her a welcoming hug without taking her eyes off her ex-son-in-law. "What are you doing here?" Eleanor envisions her glands swelling from the shock. She gives Ivy a look. And Ivy replies with a perceptible, yet invisible, shrug through the mere expression on her face.

"Ivy and I bumped into each other on the plane. It's nice to see you again, Eleanor," Amir says, holding out his hand to shake.

Bumped into each other? Oh, Ivy, you sneaky little bugger.

Eleanor looks at his hand and shakes her head.

"Come on, Amir," she says, arms stretched out in front of her. "Give me a hug. We're not doing business here. You're family! Well." Eleanor stops short. "I still think of you as family, anyway," she adds with a wink.

With one arm around Ivy and the other around Amir, she shuffles the couple inside. "Go on. I've just put a fresh pot of coffee on. Where's your luggage?" she asks, sticking her head out the front door once she has given them a little push toward the kitchen.

"They bloody lost it," Ivy replies, laughing sarcastically. She drops her hand luggage to the floor by the kitchen table.

"What? You're kidding?"

Ivy shakes her head.

"Well, did they say when they would locate it?"

"Nope. They said they'd call."

"Oh. Well, I'm sure Kit will lend you some …" Eleanor trails off into silence.

Ivy twists her mouth with repentance. "Don't worry. I'll deal with it," Ivy says with a flick of her hand.

"Ivy," Eleanor whispers. She leans against the fridge door

after pulling the carton of skimmed milk out of it. She glances at Amir, who has already made himself comfortable with the headlining features in *The Age*. "Why would you say such horrible things to her? You two have always been so close. I just don't get it." Eleanor purses her lips in the hope that she hasn't stepped over the line. The last thing she wants is to argue within a minute of her daughter's arrival.

"Mum, I'll fix it, okay? I was drunk. I wasn't thinking straight."

"I hope you fix it. Otherwise you'll have to spend Christmas in the nude." Eleanor laughs, trying to make light of the situation. "Would you like something to eat?" she adds, a little louder for Amir to hear.

"No thanks." Ivy stretches her arms toward the ceiling, revealing a tattoo around her belly button she didn't have before she skipped the country, and blows air into her cheeks. "Bloated from plane food." She peers at Amir through the wide archway and winks at him. He winks back.

What's going on here?

Eleanor opens the fridge again, wishing she could just rip off her bra and knickers and free-ball the whole day. "How about some watermelon? It's great this time of year." She looks up to see Ivy and Amir both shake their heads. She closes the fridge. "You must be feeling quite hot after being in such cold weather. Are you hot? Would you like me to turn the air con on? How about some chilled water?" She opens the fridge again and pulls out a large jug of prechilled tap water with slices of lemon in it.

"Mum. Relax. It's just me and Amir," Ivy says, flicking a teaspoon in her palm. It thumps like a weak heart in a distant stethoscope.

Amir chuckles while loosening his tie. "I see you're still obsessed about pleasing your guests, Eleanor."

Eleanor rubs her brow with a smirk.

I'm a mother. One day you'll understand.

"Forget the watermelon," Amir says. "Come. Sit. We have something to tell you." Amir pats the empty seat next to him. He's covered neck to toe and not shedding a single drop of sweat.

Ivy puckers her brow, shakes her head, and mouths something to Amir that Eleanor can't make out. Ivy notices Eleanor watching and exhales a muted sigh.

"Well, it's too late now *not* to say anything." Ivy groans, squinting at Amir the way Eleanor is accustomed to. Ivy shakes her head and begins to laugh—a guttural, comic, repetitive, "oh fuck, brace yourself" laugh as she lowers herself into a chair.

"Mum, look, before we say anything, I just want you to know that I'm as surprised as you are. But it just happened. We saw each other again, and that spark we've always had, it just … you know, and we feel …"

"Ready to give it another shot," Amir concludes. He takes Ivy's hand across the table and massages between her thumb and forefinger. The pressure point that encourages tranquillity.

"Another shot?" Eleanor asks, hoping she didn't hear

correctly. How dare Ivy put this poor man through a divorce and then "bump into him" on the plane?

You're supposed to be the older sister, Ivy.

"Yes," Ivy replies. "We're getting married again."

brian

"So, tell me again what you're going to say when you turn up on her doorstep." Gabriel looks into Brian's eyes so hard he feels like they're going to pop out and bounce across the café floor.

Gabriel licks the straw from his thick strawberry shake, up and down, then sucks all the contents out of it before poking it back into his tall pink glass. Why they decided to meet at Ditsy Daisy's, where Brian is sure to get depressed about how he ditched Ivy, he does not know. But it has definitely boosted his drive to get her back, and to never let her go again. Ever. Again.

"Er ..."

"No! Not *er*! You do not hesitate. Do you hear me? You do not hesitate." Brian is sure that if Gabriel were not in a public place right now, he would certainly be yelling like a banshee. "Breathe. Start again. Without hesitating," Gabriel spits through gritted teeth. He punches Brian on the shoulder from across the table, which seems totally uncharacteristic of him. *What's with this machismo?* If Brian didn't know any better, he'd think *Gabriel* was the one trying to get Ivy back. *Is he in love with her? No. Don't be stupid. He's gay and you know it. Oh. Is he coming on to me?* Brian shakes his head. *Stop it. You're not in preschool.*

Brian takes a deep breath and exhales in spurts as if training for Lamaze. "Ivy, I should never have let you go. You are the best thing that has ever happened to me in my entire life. I can't imagine it without you. Please forgive me. Please come back to Seattle," Brian recites like a recorded public service message.

What's so damn special about this? I need to think of something better.

"Good. Now try repeating it with a little gusto, and it'll be perfect." Gabriel snaps his fingers.

Brian repeats it, raising his eyebrows where Gabriel deemed it appropriate. He can tweak it while he's on the plane. He'll find something to say to Ivy that will really hit the spot. Something to do with archaeology. Now all he has to do is find out what it is about archaeology that she loves the most. But how? They never really talked about it. Well, they hardly talked. Period. That will certainly change.

He glances toward the waitress who replaced Ivy. She's tubby. But cute. Another blonde. Brian rests his elbows on the table and his head in his palms. *Tubby. Cute. Blonde. My brother. I'll ask him to ask the deputy director. Yes, you're a genius.*

"You're a genius!" Brian smacks Gabriel over the head with a flat hand.

"Oi!" Gabriel cries, waving his arms in front of him like

he's doing a desperate doggy paddle. "Please. Touching is not necessary. Thanking me with words will suffice, darling."

Brian looks out the window of the café and watches the snow flutter onto the street and melt on impact.

I wonder when the first-ever candle was found …

eydie

"What the fuck is wrong with me spending Christmas with Kit, Ma? No doubt you'll be so off your fuckin' tits you won't know what day it is anyway." Eydie glares at Beth's twitching lip, grinding her back teeth. Her jaw aches, but she can't stop herself from applying more and more pressure until the pain near resembles a wench dislodging a molar. Beth spits in Eydie's face. It's thick and it stinks like vomit, gin … cock.

"Ugh, you fuckin' whore!" Eydie screams, wiping the phlegm off with one hand and attempting to punch Beth with the other. But Beth stumbles backward into the yellowed lamp shade and inadvertently dodges Eydie's fist. The lamp shade tips and crashes down. The light bulb smashes. Electric sparks fly into the air and threaten to set the shade alight.

"Dontchya treat me like that, ya little bitch, or I'll throw ya arse out on the street," Beth snarls, regaining balance. Beth stands so close to Eydie's face that she can smell the regurgitation of her own contempt. Eydie shoves her backward, wishing they had a pool she could accidentally push her into. Beth falls onto the couch. Her legs spasm on the armrest like fish out of water. Eydie towers above her, trapping Beth's legs against the couch between her knees. She bends over, breathes disgust into Beth's face, feeling confidence turn into multiplying sin.

"Why? Ya think I should *respect* ya or somethin'?" Eydie growls, digging her right index finger into Beth's temple. "Why should I respect a fuckin' drunk who sells her body for booze? Huh? I still can't figure out why a smart man like Roger would have even considered getting into bed with ya sorry fuckin' arse!"

Eydie pushes the couch toward the alcohol cabinet, with a force she didn't know she had until it crashes against it. An open bottle of vodka, which was sitting on the top, falls onto the couch, missing Beth's head by an inch. Its contents glug onto the vinyl upholstery and gush into Beth's tatty hair. Beth tries to sit up, but Eydie pushes her back down.

"And ya know what? I'm done trying to figure out why, Ma. And I don't give a shit anymore. The only thing I give a shit about is that I'd have better fuckin' chances of gettin' somewhere in this life without you in it. You're the one who's holdin' me back, Ma. *You.*"

Eydie pokes Beth between her breasts, which have separated and sagged to the sides of her torso. Beth's yellow bloodshot eyes well up with tears. Becoming the vulnerable puppy Eydie persistently gives in to. But she won't give in this time. It's time to stop feeling sorry for her. "So go ahead. Throw me the fuck out on the fuckin' street. Because all I do is live my piss-weak life makin' sure you're not gonna fuckin' die on me. And I'm sick of the guilt. I'm sick of wanting you to die. I can't do it anymore. I want to fuckin' get outta this fuckin' hellhole and *live*!"

Eydie removes her pointed finger and paces the room. Beth sits up. The crackle of the upholstery mingles with Beth's cough. She tilts her head to the side and wrings vodka out of her hair. The sound of it dripping onto the carpet is thick and heavy, muffled by the fury pounding in Eydie's ears. She turns around to look through the miserable excuse of a kitchen window. The view stinks. The green whiff of cut grass is now tainted with toxic shame. And all she can see is a dividing fence, not even a meter away, and the neighbour's freshly mowed front lawn. A reminder of what they don't have.

Eydie considers packing a bag and staying at Kit's for a few nights to calm down. But it's not the right time. She'll intrude. Kit needs to be alone with Ivy. *They've got to fix things.* And Eydie couldn't bear to be the one to prevent it. She wants to be able to love both her sisters, the two sisters she's been blessed with at her greatest time of need. She imagines they'll one day become a team and be there for each other no matter what. No jealousy. Just unconditional love. The kind of love that's supposed to be rewarding, not riddled with suffering and guilt and regret and denial. The kind of stuff you see on PG-rated TV.

Eydie takes a deep breath and turns around to find Beth trying to clean the couch with used tissues. Shiny grey tears stream down her cheeks, her wheeze erratic, as if she has food lodged in her throat. A chunk of green snot lingers below one nostril. She sniffs, and it disappears up her nose. She gags, coughs into a soggy tissue.

Eydie whispers, "Ma? I'll do that. Go 'ave a bath," feeling a pang of remorse creep from her stomach to the back of her throat. But Beth doesn't speak. She looks up for a moment and forces a shaky smile.

"Ma, I'm sorry." A tear escapes from the corner of Eydie's eye, but she quickly wipes it away with the top of her hand before it runs down her cheek.

"Nah, love," Beth replies, shaking her head, lifting cushions off the couch. "You're right to be ashamed of me." Beth lowers herself to the floor, clutching a vodka-soaked cushion to her chest. She bursts into a dull heave and gulps on the inhale.

Eydie crouches down beside her, takes Beth's face in her hands. "Ma, I can't help ya anymore. And I can't live with ya anymore. Ya gotta get some help. And if not for yerself, I'm beggin' ya, please do it for me. 'Cause I love ya, Ma. I really *do* love ya."

Beth's tears stop with a hiccup as she lifts her head to look into Eydie's eyes. Beth strokes, clutches at Eydie's bicep. "Love, go spend Chrissie with Kit tomorrah. I got no right stoppin' ya from 'avin' a bit a fun." With one last squeeze of Eydie's arm, Beth stands up and shuffles to the bathroom.

"I'm sorry," Eydie whispers again, just as Beth slides the bathroom door open to enter.

Beth swivels her head around and says, "I've always loved ya, sweetheart," with a wet wink. Eydie nods with pursed lips as Beth slides the bathroom door closed behind her. The toilet flushes, the shower starts running, and so does the tap in the sink.

Then Eydie hears a thump. As if Beth has slipped in the shower.

Eydie pauses to listen, to see if she can hear her get up again. But all she hears is running water.

She puts her ear to the door. Nothing. She looks down.

And blood pools around her toes.

While Eleanor sets the table in the dining room for Christmas lunch, Kit and Ailish fill Eleanor's state-of-the-art double kitchen sink with bags of ice to chill the wine, champagne, and beer. Kit's relieved the plans have changed. She couldn't bear the thought of having Christmas lunch at her own house and not having the freedom to leave if things were to get uncomfortable between her and Ivy.

Ivy has snubbed her all morning, but Kit refuses to break *this* ice. It's not her responsibility. She's not the one who abused the shit out of her sister over the phone—a sister who has always been able to read between the lines.

And now I bet she's too proud to apologize.

Amir pulls the ham out of the oven as Ivy mixes the mayonnaise into the potato salad. Whistling. Giggling discreetly, nodding her head to her own music.

Jingle Bells, Amir Smells, Ivy laid an egg. Roger took a point-two-two and shot them in the head.

Kit focuses on her sister's back as Ivy moves closer to Amir and nuzzles her face into his neck. Ivy licks his ear with the tip of her pointy tongue, giggles again, and brings her hand to her mouth to stifle the sound. Amir lifts his shoulder to his ear to rub away her saliva. He playfully pushes her aside with his hip. She pushes back, initiating pendulum hip movement. For a moment they seem like innocent children experimenting with a crush. But then Amir puts his hand down the front of Ivy's shorts. They go quiet as she opens her legs an inch.

Ugh. Where are you, Sein and Eydie?

Ailish nudges Kit with her elbow while drying her hands on a crisp white tea towel. Perhaps a hint to confront Ivy about the phone call. Kit shakes her head just enough for Ailish to tell the difference between a response and flicking hair from her eyes. Ailish shrugs, disguising it by rotating her shoulder to loosen up. She reaches for packets of chocolates and biscuits from the pantry to the left of the sink. She hands a couple to Kit and gestures for her to serve them on the plain white china plates stacked before her on the counter.

"Now? We haven't eaten yet." Kit feels her cheek twitch.

"Just to have them ready so I don't have to think about it later." Ailish smirks. "I intend to get ... what is it you call it? 'Shit-faced'?"

Kit scoffs and rips open a packet of pistachios. "Right. No choof tonight, then?"

A waft of jasmine flows through the room, accompanied by the rustle of Eleanor's mauve satin pants. Ailish sneaks a glance at Eleanor and lightly pinches Kit's upper arm. "Shh."

Eleanor approaches from behind and whispers something in Ailish's ear. Ailish nods, raises her eyebrows in response, then smirks with a shrug.

"What is it?" Kit whispers when Eleanor walks out again with the bowl of potato salad from Ivy.

Ailish opens her mouth to respond, but is interrupted by the doorbell and smooth waves of a man's deep voice introducing himself to Eleanor at the front door. Ailish wipes her hands, unties her apron, and flings it into the sink filled with chilling bottles without looking. She scurries out of the kitchen while securing a hairpin with all eight of her fingers.

Kit can hear some "jolly" mumbling. And then silence. And thick footsteps.

Ailish appears in the archway of the kitchen holding Harold's hand.

Dr. Whittaker? Holding Mum's hand?

"Everyone, this is Harry."

Harry?

"A very close friend of mine." Ailish squeezes his arm and looks up at him. Adoration spreads over her face like rouge. "Harry, you've met my daughter, Kit." Ailish looks at the floor and squashes something with the ball of her right foot.

Harold releases his hand from Ailish's grip, takes one step forward, and holds it out for Kit to shake as steady as a Madame Tussaud's wax sculpture. "A pleasure to see you again, Kit. You look absolutely smashing in that dress." Kit shakes his hand. His skin feels as if it's been dusted with talcum powder. After three defined shakes, his eyes grow wide before stepping back into his position with a nod.

Kit, although her arm hairs are standing on end at the surprise, wants to laugh and give the man a big hug for finally breaking through her mother's overcooked chastity.

"And this is Ivy. Kit's sister. And Amir, Ivy's, er … husband. And you met Eleanor at the door." Ailish swivels her head left and right trying to locate her.

Eleanor calls out, "Present," from another room, as if her attendance is being ticked off in class.

"Also Kit's boyfriend, Sein, and his father, Fareeq, should arrive in a min—"

"And Eydie," Kit interrupts. "Don't forget Eydie." She glances at Ivy, who turns her head in the opposite direction and stands on her tiptoes to reach a packet of serviettes from the top cupboard. *Serves her bloody right.*

"Yes. And Eydie. The other sister. We're one big happy family!" Ailish laughs with too much enthusiasm. The false laughter and throat-clearing that ensues is interrupted by another knock at the door.

Oh, thank God!

"Ah. Here they are." Ailish introduces Sein and Fareeq to Harold and seats everyone at the dining table. Kit blows Sein a kiss as she brings in the remaining dishes of food. He blows one back, going pink in the face. Fareeq offers a silent chuckle and nods a friendly hello, his quiet, kind face a symbol of survival. He had watched his wife get stabbed to death by a burglar caught off guard in their own home. No wonder he didn't want to burden Sein with such a memory.

No more complaining. Just ride with the tide.

"Right, let's dig in," Eleanor says, fanning her face with her hands. "Sorry, Ailish, I'm closing the windows and turning on the monster. I can't bear it."

"It's your house." Ailish shrugs with a smile and grabs the knife to start slicing the ham.

"Wait." Kit stands. "Eydie's not here yet."

All voices ebb. Everyone stares at Kit as if expecting her to combust.

"I'm going to call her. She was meant to be here over two hours ago."

Eleanor and Ailish nod and say "okay" in unison as if their thoughts are connected to the same rotary circuit.

Kit moves into the entrance hall, where the beige-grey landline is secured to the wall by the ornamental display of chronologically arranged family photos that resemble magazine cut-outs. She can hear her family shaking their napkins open and resting their cutlery on the edges of their plates. She puts the phone to her ear, muffling the distant mutters from the right side of her head.

When she returns, abrupt laughter comes to a halt when they all see the look on Kit's face.

"Kit. You've gone completely pale. What's wrong?" Ailish stands as if to offer an obligatory gesture of respect. Sein frowns and shakes his head in question.

"Eydie can't make it." Kit licks her lips and swallows a build-up of saliva. "She's … in the hospital, she …"

"Oh no, is she okay?" Amir's face is contorted like squashed Play-Doh.

What the hell do you care?

"She's fine, she … Beth … her mum … she's in a coma."

Ivy finishes clearing the table while the rest migrate to the lounge for sweets. Only the rustle of summer clothes and collision of dirty plates fill the air with a hint of Christmas spirit.

How could Kit ruin the day like that?

Hardly anyone said a word during lunch. Only Eleanor and Ivy were hospitable enough to break the silence now and again. She runs hot water into the ice-filled sink and puts the bottles of booze in the fridge to make room for the dishes.

No one has even met Eydie's mother; what's the big deal? Why on earth did Kit cry through the whole meal? She hardly knew the woman. Pathetic. Who gives a toss about the drunken whore? And Eydie's no better. A high school dropout with a future in sniffing peroxide. Bloody lovely.

Ivy gazes out the window, listening to the ice crackle. The sound resembles a quiet cackle.

I'm such a bitch.

She turns the tap off, puts a few dry plates away, and notices that Eleanor has held on to her Peter Rabbit cups and saucers. She remembers making mud pies with those in the backyard. Eleanor scolded her for taking them outside. But Roger hid a couple in the garage for Ivy to use when Eleanor wasn't looking. He told Eleanor that he'd accidentally broken them when doing the dishes.

I'm so sorry, Kit. You do know I love you, right?

Ivy dries her hands and joins everyone in the lounge. She enters in the middle of Harold quoting something, his eyes wide with enthusiasm and pride.

"Oscar Wilde once said, 'But what is the difference between literature and journalism? Journalism is unreadable and literature is not read. That is all.'" He laughs like a bubbling cauldron. Ailish smacks him on the arm like a teenager with a crush, and everyone chuckles in what seems a delay in getting the joke. Kit smiles with a little scoff, as if she's afraid to show she enjoyed it.

Who would've thought. Kit a literature buff. She sure did a good job of hiding it all these years.

Everyone turns toward Ivy in the doorway. Amir shuffles a little closer to Kit on the couch to make room for her to sit with them. Ivy grimaces behind a fake smile.

"Kit. Can I speak with you for a sec?" Ivy flicks her head in the direction of the hall.

Kit looks up just as she grabs a Lamington without a saucer and drops coconut shavings all over her lap.

She takes a quick bite, chews it briefly, swallows, then rests it on a serviette on the coffee table. Ailish glares at her. Kit shrugs and stands, smacking her lips. She walks straight past Ivy without making eye contact. Ivy follows, slightly skipping to catch up.

Ivy's old bedroom is scattered with half-filled boxes and old clothes spread out on her king-size bed.

"What's going on here?" Kit asks, as if she's got a numb mouth. She picks up a folded T-shirt with Roxette on the front of it. She smirks. Perhaps it triggered a memory. But her smile fades with haste before throwing it back down, as if it disgusts her, without having the decency to refold it.

Ivy sits on edge of the bed, ignoring Kit's impertinence, and pats next to her right thigh for Kit to sit too. Kit shakes her head, crosses her arms, squints, and looks out the window. She cranes her neck at something. Ivy doesn't look.

Stop pretending not to care.

"Kit. I want to apologize." Ivy picks her thumbnail and focuses on the patch of freckles under Kit's left eye. She used to always cover them up with makeup.

Kit shrugs, still squinting out the window. She puckers her brow.

"So, what's up?" Kit asks. "You gonna go back to Seattle?" Kit finally sits next to Ivy and looks into her lap.

Ivy shakes her head, hesitant to make some sort of physical contact with Kit. "I'm not sure. I'm thinking of continuing my PhD in Sydney. I was gonna ask you. Do you want to come with me? Start fresh?" Ivy notices a hint of scorn in the way the corner of Kit's mouth twitches. "We could share a house."

"You're kidding, right?"

"Nope."

"What—is this your way of apologizing to me?"

"You could say that."

Kit tilts and scratches her head behind her ear. "Nah. Sein and I are going to look for a place to rent together. Thanks though." Kit nods, offering a weak smile. A tear trickles down her cheek, and she leans her head on Ivy's shoulder.

"You're such a bitch," Kit sobs, half-laughing.

Ivy puts her arm around Kit and squeezes her to her breast. "I know. I'm sorry," she whispers. "I was dealing with some stuff, and was totally off my rocker with blow and margaritas. I'm *really* sorry. You know I would never have said that stuff if I was sober."

Kit nods into Ivy's breast, rubbing moisture into her black Bonds T-shirt. "I hope you're being careful with all that stuff. I know you never agreed with the doctor's advice. But still, you should be careful."

"I'm not sensitive to chemicals, Kit. I just get angry about some stuff when I'm drunk. But don't worry. I can control it."

Kit stands. "Just like you controlled it on the phone with me."

"Kit. Don't."

"Okay, okay." Kit licks her lips. "Whatever." She spins around on the ball of one foot like a rotating statue, sniffing in her tears as if a pointless form of expression. "Hey, have you still got that big chunk of citrine we found in the neighbours' garden when we were little?"

"Yeah, I think so." Ivy sighs with relief.

Done and dusted. Knew she'd come 'round.

"Must be in the closet somewhere."

"Can I have it?" Kits claps her hands together with a grin. A child on the hunt for Easter eggs in the backyard.

"Sure. Why not? Should be on the top shelf behind the duvet in some random shoe box."

Just as Kit pulls one of the shoe boxes out, Ivy remembers the letter.

Fuck!

Kit grabs a shoe box, hoping to find the chunk of citrine. The first piece of treasure Kit and Ivy ever found together. A gem that symbolizes joy and happiness and is said to be the signature of wisdom and peace, to help one's connection with Spirit. But Kit does not want it for these qualities. She wants it because it is said to enhance creativity and memory, and to motivate writers. She wants to write. She has decided. It's final. She doesn't know what yet, but she is adamant to have something published one day, just like her mother. She's realized that she doesn't need her father to know what she wants anymore. She has everything she needs already. Here. At home. With her *family*.

She opens the shoe box, and Ivy jumps up, red in the face.

"No!" Ivy tries to grab it from her. "It's not in that one. Let me have a look for you." But Kit doesn't let go, and after a brief tug-of-war, the box flies across the room when Ivy yanks it out of her hands. Clay beads, fossils, small white pebbles, old tubes of pastel lipsticks, and eye shadow scatter all over her Persian rug. And an envelope. With Roger's name above the return address.

Ivy gasps and bends down to retrieve it, but Kit snatches it first, slips the letter out, stands on her tiptoes, and holds it above her head. For a moment she thinks it's some sort of ominous love letter, and chuckles at Ivy's exasperation.

"Fuck!" Ivy screams, clutching at her head. She falls backward onto her bed with a groan.

Kit unfolds the letter. Smirking. Curious. But then it hits her. The stone in the stomach, rotating, catching and tearing off sensitive tissue in its wrath. She shakes her head, jaw agape.

"You ... you fucking bitch," Kit whispers, reading the letter over and over. Her entire body buzzes with anger. "How long have you had this?" She sneers as if the sentence were one word, teetering on the edge of a livid scream.

"Kit, I was going to tell you. I promise. I've just never been ready to see him until now. I …"

"Who the fuck said *you* had to see him?" Kit glares at Ivy, who has now rolled onto her stomach and hid her head under a pillow.

Kit's pulse beats in her ears.

"For years," Kit growls, "you've known I wanted to meet him. And you keep this from me? I … I can't believe this." Kit reads the letter again and again, and her need to meet Roger returns as strong as an addict's craving for a hit.

Ivy moans and kicks the headboard.

Kit looks at the stamp on the envelope.

She'd received it more than ten years ago.

brian

Brian is standing outside Ivy's house. On Christmas Day. *Am I insane?* He paces. Outside the front gate. Rehearsing his speech over and over in his head. He looks up. He can see someone peering at him through a window. He shades his eyes from the sun with his left hand to see who it is. It's not Ivy. *Maybe it's her mother? God, what am I doing?*

He leans against a tree at the side of the road. Sweating like a pig. Picks at the bark, flings it at a cat.

Why didn't anyone tell me the sun in Australia is so intense?
He composes himself. Uses his T-shirt to dab his face.

He knocks on the door, wipes his sweaty hands on his back pockets. Notices he's holding his breath and lets out a croaky sigh. A good-looking dark-skinned dude answers with an accent he can't place.

"Hello. Can I help you?"

Brian holds out his hand for him to shake. "Hi. I'm a friend of Ivy's from Seattle. Is she home?"

"Seattle?" The man nods. His eyes light up. "Come in, come in. I'm Amir. You must be Gabriel. Ivy is going to be so happy to see you. She didn't tell—"

"Gabriel?" Brian laughs and shakes his head. "No, no. My name's Brian."

"Oh. Well, welcome, Brian. I think she's having a D&M with her sister in her bedroom, but I'll tell her to come down."

D&M? What is that? A drug?

"Can you wait here for just a second? I'm sure she'd like to introduce you to the family herself."

Brian nods a thank-you and rubs his hands on his back pockets again. He looks around at the vast array of family photos on the walls. There's one of Ivy on her first day of primary school, high school, and university. All captioned with exact dates in solid-black felt-tip pen. There's also one of her panning for gold in Sovereign Hill, in which everyone seems to be dressed up in era attire. There's graduation. There's one of her at some archaeological site, holding a Greek-looking urn under her arm. And one … *in a bridal gown?* Brian's gaze slips to the groom.

His hearts sinks.

Ivy walks in with Amir. Her face flushed. She looks like she's been crying. As she shakes her head in what seems to be shame, tears roll down her cheeks. She wipes them away with the tops of her wrists.

"Brian, I … I'm so sorry. I guess I … I should've told you."

kit

Kit sits on Ivy's floor, staring at the letter.

Ten years. Ten years.

"Fuck it," she says, and stomps into the lounge room, where Eleanor is yelling at Ivy. Her footsteps complement Eleanor's rage. Everyone, including Harold and Fareeq, are staring into their laps.

"Where *is* your head? That poor man," Eleanor howls, pushing the plate of Lamingtons across the coffee table as she stands, just enough for it to reach the edge but not fall off. "How could you do such a thing? He comes all the way to Australia to see you. And you just ask him to leave? Without even asking him if he's hungry? Wants a drink? A glass of water, at least? Ivy, where is your head? Your *heart?* She pounds her fists on her chest. "How did you become like this? I'm ashamed. *Ashamed* of you."

"Mum," Ivy growls through gritted teeth, "Amir is here.

What do you want me to do? Ask if he'd like to join us in a threesome?"

"Ivy!" Eleanor barks, bringing her hands to her head. She sits in an armchair, trying to take deep, steady breaths.

Amir grabs Ivy's arm, mutters something, and attempts to pull her out of the room. But Eleanor lifts her head and slaps her hands on the armrests. "Don't *either* of you go anywhere. I'm not finished."

Ailish, Harold, Sein, and Fareeq stand and start collecting their belongings to leave. Ailish gestures for Kit to grab her bag. But Kit shakes her head.

Don't chicken out now, Kit.

She walks into the centre of the lounge and holds up her hands.

"Wait, I have something to say." Kit clears her throat. "I've had enough of all the shit everyone keeps stashing away in this family," she snaps, then swallows, lowers her voice a touch when she sees the astonishment on everyone's faces. "So, I think it should all just come out in the open ..."

Kit clears her throat again, crosses her arms as if it might shield the consequences. "Ivy, you can't go to Sydney to complete your PhD."

The air conditioner stops humming automatically. The art-deco clock ticks, louder than ever. Someone says "shit" under their breath.

"Whaddaya on about, Kit?" Ivy spits, wiping tears from her eyes.

Eleanor glances at Ailish and says, "You didn't."

Ailish nods, but avoids eye contact and leans into Harold's side. He rubs her shoulder and mutters something incomprehensible.

"Kit. Please," Eleanor pleads, almost in a whisper, and begins to massage her temples and glare at the floor.

Kit wishes she hadn't done this now.

How could I allow myself to stoop to their level? You stupid idiot.

But the daggers have been removed. And she can't just let their limbs bleed out. No matter how much it's going to hurt. You have to be cruel to be kind. The only cliché in existence that Kit feels comfortable using.

"Eleanor has spent your entire education fund," Kit blurts out as fast as she can. The hard rock she felt earlier is now hot jelly, melting into her legs. Eleanor's face blanches.

"What?" Ivy squeals. She glares at Eleanor. "Mum? Is she serious?"

Eleanor nods, still massaging her temples, now with her eyes closed.

"On what, Mum?" Ivy snarls. "Did you go and get your boobs done?"

Eleanor snaps out of her stance and looks Ivy straight in the eyes. "Of course not! What kind of woman do you take me for?"

"Then, what?"

Eleanor squints at Kit and then Ailish, lowers herself into an armchair. "Oh God, just tell her, for crying out loud. The cat's out of the bag."

Kit opens her mouth. Nothing but an airy stutter comes out, shame choking her like a puff of thick tarred smoke.

"I gave the money to your father, Ivy," Eleanor says, as if simply telling her where she put the mustard. "He had a stroke. He was broke. I helped." She flicks her hand as though shooing away a fly. "End of story."

Sein laughs and Fareeq elbows him in the side, twitching his head as if to say they had better leave. They head for the front door. Kit mouths, "Sorry," and "I love you," with a hesitant pause in between as he passes by. He brushes the back of his hand against her thigh.

"Thanks for having us," Fareeq says, "but I think it's time we headed off." He nods a thank-you to Eleanor and Ailish, without directing his gaze anywhere in particular, then tugs on Sein's elbow as the family nods back, forcing smiles of gratitude, as they leave the room and move toward the door.

The sound of front door opening and closing envelopes the room.

And Ivy slaps Eleanor in the face.

ailish

She escorts Harold to the front door.

"Perhaps this is the time to tell her, hmm? Take her aside. Discreetly. There's no need for the rest of the family to know," Harold whispers, giving her a soft farewell peck on her top lip.

Ailish sniffs. "I can't."

"You can. You'll feel better. You've had a heavy heart for way too long." Harold hugs Ailish like she is the only woman on earth worth it. She rests her head on his chest, taking comfort in the steady beat of his love.

A steady beat. If only it could lull me to sleep.

He leaves with a tap on his nose.

In the lounge room, everyone sits in silence. Kit, at the dining room table, rests her head on her folded arms and closes her eyes. Amir thrusts his tongue down Ivy's reluctant throat before disappearing out the back door. It slams. Eleanor's face has become so red that she looks like she's broken out in a rash.

"Elle." Ailish apologetically touches Eleanor's shoulder, but she flicks it off with a tsk.

"How could you keep this from me?" Ivy asks Eleanor with a phony sniff. "I had plans for that money."

Eleanor scoffs. "Plans? What plans? You've done a pretty good job of destroying every single plan you've had for yourself, Ivy. I wouldn't bother concerning yourself with that much."

Ivy opens her mouth to speak but Eleanor interrupts.

"You know what, *darl*ing? I think it's about time I teach you a little life lesson—"

"Life lesson? You stole money from your own daughter. Perhaps you might like to rethink who it is exactly that needs one!"

"I stole money? It was mine in the first place! For God's

sake. If there's anyone in this room who has done wrong, Ivy, it's you. How do you *deal* with it all? How do you keep all that shit inside you? Don't you just want to squeeze all the … the … rot out of you?" Eleanor screams, clutching at her scalp. "What did I do? I didn't bring you up like this. How did you become so selfish?"

Ivy looks out the window and starts to cry, blubbering like a child coming down from a sugar high. Eleanor groans and takes a deep breath.

"If any of you," Eleanor says in a hoarse whisper, "has anything else to reveal about this family, I suggest you spit it out. Right now." She glares at Ivy. Ivy shakes her head. She glances at Kit; she shakes her head too. Then she stares at Ailish.

Ailish opens her mouth but nothing emerges besides mute deceit.

Eleanor raises her hand. "Don't tell me, Allie. I don't think I can bear it," Eleanor replies in a gentle, disheartened tone.

Ailish bites her bottom lip and shakes her head. "It's nothing. It's nothing. I don't have anything to say."

"I hope not. Because I've had enough. Enough of all this … of all *this*!" Eleanor claws her fingers and waves her hands around in circles, clenching her jaw and snapping her head side to side as if she were being electrocuted.

Eleanor takes another deep breath and composes herself, as if figuratively pinning a large full stop in the middle of the room.

"This mess started with Roger." She sighs. "And it's going to end with Roger. Tomorrow."

ivy

At the Hilton, Ivy taps her fingers on the front desk while the young blonde receptionist locates which room Brian is staying in.

"Room 242. Bit late for a visit, isn't it?" she says with a nasal twang that borders on chipmunk pitch.

"That's none of your business," Ivy snaps, and turns on her heel.

She steps into the elevator and presses 2. The number lights up. Red. As if telling her she'd better stop.

Just do it. You owe him this much.

The elevator door pings open, and she scans the brass door numbers to identify which direction to turn. She turns right, and when she reaches his room, the door swings open before she has a chance to knock.

Brian blinks and steps backward. "Oh." He looks at his bare feet.

Ivy smiles wryly. "May I come in?"

"Sure." Brian steps aside for her to enter and gently closes the door.

Ivy stands in the middle of the room and spins around full circle. "Nice." She nods.

"Yes." Brian runs his tongue over his front teeth. They both open their mouths to speak at once.

"You first," Ivy says, slapping her hands on her thighs.

"No. You. Please." Brian sits backward in the seat at the dresser, legs spread, arms crossed on the backrest. Ivy sits on the bed and briefly bounces on it. She smoothes the bedspread at the sides of her thighs and clicks her tongue. "I'd like to apologize."

"Go on then," Brian mumbles, looking at the floor.

"But first, I have to say, you really shouldn't have just jumped on a plane. You should have *called*."

Brian scoffs and rests his head on his forearm. "No, Ivy, *you* should have told me about your ex-husband."

Ivy bites her bottom lip. "You should have told me about your wife."

The sound of a room service trolley passing by soothes the absence of speech. Ivy kicks off her sandals and crosses her legs under her bum. The bedspread rustles, and she is reminded how good Brian is in the sack.

"Getting remarried?" Brian lifts his head and looks Ivy in the eye, his stare emitting pure indifference. He purses his lips.

Ivy lies on the bed, looks at the ceiling, wishing she could just vanish from this planet and start fresh on a new one.

"No. I'm not."

Brian stands and drags his feet to the bathroom. "Plans?" he asks, his voice adopting an echoic quality that resembles an accusation. "Staying here or heading back to Emerald?"

"Neither." Ivy sits up and notices a pile of used tissues on the floor on the other side of the bed.

Brian returns from the bathroom, drying his hands on a dirty white towel. He throws it on the dresser. Straight-faced.

"Well." Brian raises his eyebrows and adjusts the band of his trousers. "Thanks for coming to, uh, *apologize*, but I think it's best you leave." Brian opens the door and stares straight into Ivy's eyes.

Ivy slips her feet back into her sandals, swallows, then hooks her arm through the handle of her bag.

That's it? This can't be it. He's playing me. For sure.

She approaches Brian with a slight wiggle in her walk and summons a sexy smile. She moves in close, takes hold of his shirt collar with both hands, and breathes into his neck. She whispers, "One last fuck for the road?"

Brian pushes her off. She stumbles backward, hitting her shoulder blades against the plaster wall. The hollow thump mimics exactly how she feels inside. Exactly how she's felt her entire life.

"Ivy. No," Brian snaps, and then hangs his head in his hands. He rubs his face. Looks at the floor. Sways side to side and puts his hands in his pockets.

"Actually," Brian says, looking up and meeting Ivy's glazed eyes, "you make me fucking sick."

kit

Kit stands outside Samuel's suburban sea village house with Ailish, Eleanor, and Ivy. Dry overgrown grass tickles Kit's calves. She lifts a leg to scratch and notices tiny red welts on her shin as if she's been attacked by fleas. A psychosomatic reaction to events yet to unfold?

On the inside, she feels at ease. Ready for anything. Ready to grab on to the first piece of driftwood that passes her by. But on the outside, there are other voices. Voices she doesn't know if she can trust anymore. Voices that come from bodies and souls who like to choose the biggest and best waves, preferably ones with GPS.

The four women follow the narrow cracked concrete pathway to the front door. The handle is rusty, the dark-brown paint is peeling, and claw marks are strewed all over it as if a dog's been scratching to be let in.

Eleanor knocks on the door. She clears her throat three times and scratches her chin twice. A frail man with very short grey hair and a slight hunch opens the door. It creaks. Kit holds her breath.

Oh my God, is that him?

eleanor

With a tight-lipped smile, she holds out her hand for Samuel to shake and tilts her head to the side. He chuckles and shakes her hand with vigour. The loose flab of her upper arm wobbles like a skin flag.

Maybe I should *consider plastic surgery.*

"So wonderful to see ya again, Eleanor. You're still as

stunning as evah," Samuel says with a croak, and then launches into what seems like a smoker's cough. His breath is as potent as a rotten lung.

Eleanor blushes, but purses her lips as though trying not to appear flattered.

"Thank you, Sam. May we come in?"

Ivy feels like she falling into the cracks of the decrepit wooden deck. Eleanor moves to her left so Samuel can see the three of them behind her. He nods as if expectations have been met.

Why did I agree to this?

"Is it them?" A man's gruff, firm, yet kind voice travels through the corridor and out to the patio.

"Yep!" Samuel calls behind him. "Make yourself presentable, will ya?"

"Righteo." Creaking couch springs follow a stunted groan, as if it took great effort to stand up.

Ivy glances at Kit to see if she appears as uncomfortable as she feels. Kit's body goes stiff, she clasps her hands behind her back, and she looks at her feet, wriggling her nose, eyes closed, as if about to sneeze.

Ailish smiles as if inhaling woe.

If only you'd been in my shoes, Kit, you wouldn't have looked for the bastard. Look what you've bloody got me into. I shouldn't be here!

Samuel gestures with a low murmur for everyone to come in. He has a long, thin scar below his left eye. The sight of it triggers a flash of him pushing her around her backyard on a toy black bulldozer. The wheel got caught in a pothole and tumbled over. When Sam was dressing her grazed knee, Roger galloped over with a Mr. Whippy cone, told Sam to scoot, and sat there on the lawn feeding her the ice cream. She remembers licking drips off Roger's hairy wrist.

The thought makes her feel sick and weak.

Samuel looks the four women up and down as they step inside one by one. "Ya all look much prettier in person than ya do in the snaps Eleanor sent," he says, shifting his full weight to one foot at a time as if delegating pain. He takes a few heavy breaths before leaning against the wall inside the front door.

Ailish grabs Eleanor's arm as they step inside. "Photographs? You sent him photographs?"

Eleanor nods about ten times in the course of five seconds and raises her eyebrows. "I had to do something."

Ailish gives Eleanor's arm a light squeeze. "That was very kind."

Eleanor rubs Ailish's upper back with a tender smile, glancing at the floor. But Ivy catches Ailish rolling her eyes and mouthing, "Oh God."

What the hell is that all about?

"Ladies, I'll fetch Roger for ya. Wait here. He gets a bit, er, weird. About his *space*. He been a bit shy since ... well, ya know. The left side of his mouth is still a bit slow. Doesn't like staring. Just sayin'."

Is this guy for real?

Ivy frowns as she watches Sam hobble down the corridor, wondering if the first sight of Roger is going to make her want to puke.

kit

Anxiety is setting in. The lull she felt earlier has liquefied like a dissolvable pill. This whole thing is beginning to feel futile. And will she even want to see him again after this? What if she feels absolutely nothing after setting eyes on him? Or even worse—what if he feels nothing? What if seeing her again just solidifies the reason he never contacted her directly? What if she meant nothing to him, and only included her in Ivy's letter out of obligation? Is she the bastard child? Not worthy, born out of wedlock, the baby he could have easily left in a basket on a stranger's doorstep? But none of it makes sense. Why then did he send letters to Eydie?

What is so wrong with me?

Kit notices Ivy's face turn white—fear surfacing for oxygen, fuel, via her over cleansed pores. It reminds Kit of the way she felt when she discovered Roger's surname on Ailish's office door. Like her entire life evolved under pretence. But that feeling soon passed. Especially once she saw how it had affected her mother too. If only Ivy could look beyond her own pain, then it might eventually ease.

"There's no need to be so afraid. He's only human," Kit whispers into Ivy's ear, thinking it may have sounded more malicious than reassuring. But there's no time to explain that she actually cares.

She loves her.

But it doesn't mean she has to like who she has become.

Kit's hair tickles Ivy's cheek when she leans over to whisper consoling bullshit into her ear. Her immediate instinct is to push Kit's head away, but then she realizes what she just said.

He's only human. Huh. Right.

Kit contorts her mouth to the left, shrugs her shoulders, and clicks her tongue in her cheek. Ivy pulls back to look Kit in the eye. There is an air of confidence about her she's never noticed before. It's as if she's stopped fighting her own personality. Ivy's tempted to respond with kindness, but as her common reflexes would have it, it doesn't happen.

"Listen to yourself," Ivy says. "Who do you think you are? The Dalai fucking Lama?"

Eleanor and Ailish turn their heads and frown.

"*Mum.* Oh my God." Ivy grabs Eleanor's arm and yanks her closer. "What were you trying to achieve here by making me see Dad now?"

Eleanor jerks her arm from Ivy's grasp as if preparing to throw a shot put. She squints, clenches her jaw, and shakes her finger as if scolding a misbehaving kindergartener. "You are thirty years old, and you're still running. It's time you learned how to stop."

kit

"What?" Ivy growls, putting her hands on her hips. She looks fifteen again, her face warped and twisted like the time Eleanor caught her trying to convince Kit to smoke.

Kit bites her thumbnail and glances at her mother. She's ironing out the front of her tailored floral skirt with splayed fingers. Roger could walk down the hall to greet them at any second, and they want to bicker? Are they crazy? Is that what they want Roger's first impression of them to be?

"I'm not holding your hand anymore," Eleanor yaps. "Learn to live through the shit on your own. Now *shoosh*, for Christ's sake, and introduce yourself to your father like a decent, compassionate human being." Eleanor spins around and wobbles her arms as if trying to shake her anger away.

Kit can't help but smile. What Eleanor said resembles a lot of what Ivy said to Kit the night she verbally abused her on the phone. Kit faces the skirting boards to shield the satisfaction she can feel spreading across her face.

Finally. A taste of your own medicine.

ailish

She listens to the low murmur of male voices swim through the long musty-smelling corridor. She notices shifting shadows on the walls and beams of sunlight appearing and disappearing against the glass of a large painting above a small antique desk. Her stomach churns. *This is it.*

eleanor

Twenty-five years ago Roger was as pristine as a surgical instrument. Every morning he would gather his papers, his books, and his students' assignments and march off to work with one of the most satisfied facial expressions she can remember in her lifetime. It wasn't a smile; it was an attitude that shone through his eyes like he knew the meaning of life and no one else had a clue. He would wear the same brown-and-white tie and cream-coloured shirt every day. He owned five of the same. He even washed and ironed them himself. She often wondered whether any of his students asked him if it was the same unwashed shirt he wore. She closes her eyes and tries to imagine what he might look like now.

Eleanor chuckles at the thought.

But then, along came Ailish. A stunningly petite freckled redhead with the vocabulary of a well-educated eighty-year-old to sweep her man off his feet. Eleanor couldn't compare. So she just stopped trying. And focused on saving lives that mattered. Some that had hardly even begun.

Ailish squeezes Eleanor's hand with a tiny gasp.

Eleanor opens her eyes.

And there stands Roger at the end of the corridor, in exactly the same shirt and tie.

He smiles, nods, and gestures for them to come through.

"Ladies ... it's been years."

kit

Kit is the last to follow Roger into the lounge room. Everyone takes a seat on different pieces of furniture. Eleanor and Roger on the two-seater fawn couch. Ailish in the armchair. Ivy on a kitchen chair, given to her by Samuel. Samuel sits on a kitchen chair too. But there's nowhere for Kit to sit. Everyone stares at her. She scans the room looking for somewhere out of obvious view.

"I'll fetch you a kitchen chair, dear," Roger says, hardly moving a muscle in his face. He tuts at Samuel on his way out and glances at Kit again before disappearing behind the door.

Samuel mouths, "Sorry," with a wink, and pours everyone a glass of water from a yellow-stained jug in the shape of a swan. Ailish stares at the jug with a half-smile on her face. Kit can see the jug's reflection in her mother's eyes and wonders if it might have some sort of sentimental value.

Roger returns with a plate of thickly sliced oranges and his elbow hooked into the back of a rickety wooden chair. He places the oranges on the table and the chair next to him, by the couch. He pats it for Kit to take a seat. Kit looks at the chair, not quite comprehending the fact that he is placing her right next to him.

Roger watches Kit with a strange grin as she quickly slides into the seat, flattening her skirt below her bottom.

They're all still staring at her.

Roger too.

She focuses on Samuel's hands as he pours, willing her knees not to tremble, wishing the staring. Would. Stop.

The purr of silence and pouring water whirl around her. Her cheeks flush. Her eyes flit toward Roger, who winks at the exact moment she allows herself to focus on his face. He has acne scars, just like in the dream she had. And something about his eyes is familiar. A solemnity that runs beneath their surface.

Samuel finishes pouring the water and hands everyone a glass. When he gives Roger his, he passes it to Kit. She looks at his sun-spotted hand, surprised at how steady it is after the stroke. Surprised at how calm she feels.

Ivy is staring at the floor. Eyes wide with indistinct anger. Sam, Ailish and Eleanor start to "chat." Words. Words that disguise distrust. But one thing Kit has learned these past few weeks is that words do not heal; they're merely a Band-Aid. And all of a sudden she doesn't feel much need for them here.

This silence is real.

It's her raw connection cable.

Roger clears his throat. Kit takes the glass with a thin-lipped smile. One of thanks, of understanding, she hopes it seems. Her stomach relaxes even more as she looks into her father's eyes. They are gentle and kind. And wounded. He reminds her of Eydie. Broken. Wise. Kindred spirits clutching to split driftwood. A piece of which she hopes to clutch to one day.

"Thanks," Kit whispers and takes a sip.

Roger pats her knee and holds his hand there for a second longer than one would naturally.

Kit looks at the faded ginger mohair rug under the coffee table. It's hairy and hippy-wild and misplaced among the antique furniture and decor. Just like Roger.

Just like Mum once was.

Roger hesitantly takes a slice of orange, bites into it, faces Kit, and smiles with the rind covering his teeth. Spit escapes the left corner of his mouth, but he doesn't seem to care. His mute laugh moves his shoulders up and down. The wrinkles at the outer edges of his eyes and mouth are as deep as the lifetime of laughter Kit imagines he's had without her.

Or sorrow.

Kit giggles and sputters some water down her chin.

Roger tears the rind off the fruit, puts it in his pocket. As he quietly chews and swallows the orange, he strokes Kit's cheek.

Ailish glances toward them, her eyes as hard and shiny as glass balls. But Roger's hand is so soft and warm that Kit doesn't take much notice of Ailish, and can't help but hold it flat against her cheek and close her eyes, to lose herself, for a just one moment, in his fatherly touch. A touch so natural, yet so uncertain—forbidden.

Roger pulls his hand away, and Kit flicks open her eyes.

Ailish is in tears, standing above them, pointing a sharp finger at Roger.

"Y-you abused her!" Ailish barks.

And the room falls silent.

ailish:

21 years ago

Ailish and Beth sit on opposite ends of the couch, staring at the muted television, the football, waiting for Roger to return from the bathroom. The ice in Beth's vodka crackles. The fan hums and rattles. Eydie sucks on Beth's breast, gurgling. Sometimes, it seems, she's choking on her own breath.

Poor child, Ailish thinks. *I hope Roger finds a way to bring her up on his own.*

Crash!

Ailish and Beth glance at each other, jump to their feet, and speed-walk to the bathroom.

"Kit?" Ailish calls. The door is closed. Roger is whispering. Kit is crying. Beth knocks, balancing Eydie on her bony hip. "Rodge? Hon?"

"Are you fucking kidding me, Beth? Open the damn door!" Ailish yells.

Beth hiccups, nods, jiggles the handle with ill effort. But it doesn't open.

"Oh, for Christ's sake," Ailish hisses, then grabs a firm hold of the handle and pushes her hip heavily into the door. It swings open and ricochets off the wall. There are rose soaps scattered all over the floor.

Roger looks up at Ailish and Beth in shock, and quickly moves his hands away from Kit's crotch.

Her knickers are wrapped around her knees.

kit

"Mum. What?" Kit can't have heard that correctly. No way.

Ailish's face is bright red. Ivy's bottom lip is on the verge of trembling. Samuel lights a cigarette, straightfaced, coughs and splutters on his first drag. Eleanor frowns, reaching for Ailish's hand to move her away from Roger's chair.

"Pardon?" Roger shakes his head, shifts in his seat. He glances at Kit and reaches for her hand, in what seems an attempt of reassurance.

"Don't you ..." Ailish lunges toward Roger, but Eleanor grabs her by the band of her skirt and pulls her backward.

The heel of her sandal hooks the rug and she stumbles, but gains her balance again.

"Mum! Stop." Kit stands and holds Ailish by the shoulders, looking at her fiercely as though trying to get through to a stubborn child. "He can't have abused me. We've never even *met*. Remember?"

roger:

21 years ago

Roger looks down at Kit's four-year-old hand tugging at his pant leg. Delicate. Petite. Beautiful.

"Excuse me. Can you show me where to pee-pee?" Kit chirps.

Ailish nods with a forgiving wink from the couch beside Beth. Beth smiles. Sips at her vodka tonic while Eydie sucks at her left breast, vomits a little, and then begins to wail.

Roger takes Kit by the hand and walks her toward the bathroom, leaving Ailish and Beth to sort themselves out.

Surely it will be fine. Maybe they'll talk. End up becoming friends.

Kit drags her free hand along the corridor wall humming "Three Blind Mice." She smiles up at Roger and starts to skip alongside him. He reaches the bathroom door, opens it, and gestures for Kit to go in.

"Here you are, your sweet highness," Roger says with a wink.

Just as he's about to close the door to give her some privacy, Kit speaks. Her tiny voice gets lost in the bathroom's acoustics.

"Sorry, dear? What did you say?"

Kit's eyes widen in pre-empted panic. "My mummy always helps."

Roger clears his throat. Peers down the corridor. Closes the bathroom door behind him.

He kneels down next to Kit and rubs her baby-smooth upper arms. He can feel goose pimples grow below his scarred fingertips. Years and years of paper cuts. His passion leaving a permanent imprint.

You are such a precious little thing. One day I'm going to teach you how to write. You will be my little genius. I promise.

Roger smiles wide. He's sure his crooked teeth are showing and that one day, when Kit's old enough, she's going to tease him about them in innocent jest.

"Okay. Tell me what I need to do."

Kit giggles, wrinkles her nose, looks at him like he's a complete idiot.

"Lift me up, silly."

"Oh! I see. But don't we need to pull down your knickers first?"

Kit grasps the hem of her skirt, twists it awkwardly until it's tight around her legs.

She looks at the window, where a basket of rose-shaped soaps sit, and nods.

roger

Roger swallows a lump in his throat and lifts himself out of his seat, being careful to carry all the weight in his arms and legs. Just like Eleanor advised.

Ailish hangs her head, the colour in her face returning to normal. Tears stream down her cheeks in silence, her shoulders shake, and she lets her arms swing limp at her sides.

He glances at Ivy, who hasn't yet made eye contact with him. He doubts she ever will. Eleanor is still looking at Ailish. Her frown embodies true concern.

Roger tentatively takes Ailish's hands.

She lets him.

They hang heavy in his like large wet leaves.

He admires how much they have maintained their slenderness and moisture, their evidence. He remembers these hands the very first day they left an assignment on his desk. They oozed confidence, wit. Liberation. The epitome of love and generosity.

Of understanding.

But her hands always said things her mouth never did.

Just like his.

epilogue

Eydie flicks through *Elle* magazine by Beth's bedside, turning the pages every five beeps, seeking comfort from the mechanic rhythm, the suck and whoosh breathing life back into her mother's selfish body.

Twenty-four hours. She hasn't slept a wink. And the only thing she's eaten is the glue from her nails.

She takes a sip of coffee, her eighth one today, and feels her stomach constrict.

Beth grunts.

Eydie looks at Beth's taped fingers. They twitch.

Without looking at her mother's face, she puts her magazine down and stares at Beth's ghost-white hand.

Her fingers stretch and then relax.

"Baby," Beth croaks.

Eydie sniffs, rubs her nose, looks at the floor. She takes Beth's cold hand in hers, and gives it a gentle, consoling squeeze.

acknowledgements

First of all, thanks go to my partner, Spilios Tzemos, and my parents, Erika Bach and Demetri Vlass, for their continuous support and encouragement while I write and write ... and write. I love you all dearly. So much more than you could possibly know.

To Dawn Ius for being like a sister to me (but not the sisters in this book!). Not only a sister, but the most wonderful friend any human could possibly ask for. Without you Dawn, I would lose my motivation to write. Thank you for being my ... everything.

To Nicole Ducleroir for titling this book. Killer title, Nicole. So perfect. Thank you so much.

To Paula Berinstein for helping me brainstorm the plot. You are a fabulous idea person!

Matthew MacNish for reading and loving the latest draft, and for pointing out that it very rarely snows, or gets icy, in Seattle (last minute change indeed).

To Susanne Lakin for her vigilant proofreading skills. To Glynis Smy and J.C Martin for reading an early draft and helping me snag some major plot holes.

To Neil Marr for telling me that my original ending was ridiculous and for leading me in the direction of a much much better "conclusion". I've always disliked endings tied together with a pretty pink bow. Heaven knows why I attempted to do such a thing (Phew! Good thinking, 99.). RIP Neil Marr, you will be in the hearts of many for years to come.

And of course, a very special thanks to Amie McCracken for her enormous help in producing *The Bell Collection* edition.

Enjoyed this book?
Go to *vineleavespress.com/books*
to find more from *The Bell Collection*.

To sign up to Jessica's newsletter
and/or connect with her on social media
go to *jessicabellauthor.com/contact.*

Are you a writer?
You might be interested in Jessica's
Writing in a Nutshell series.